Other Books by Xequina

The Mermaid Girl
Dispatches from Lesbian America (as editor)

Santora, The Good Daughter
Xipactli Publishing, 2001

The Only
Female Cross-Dresser
in Memphis

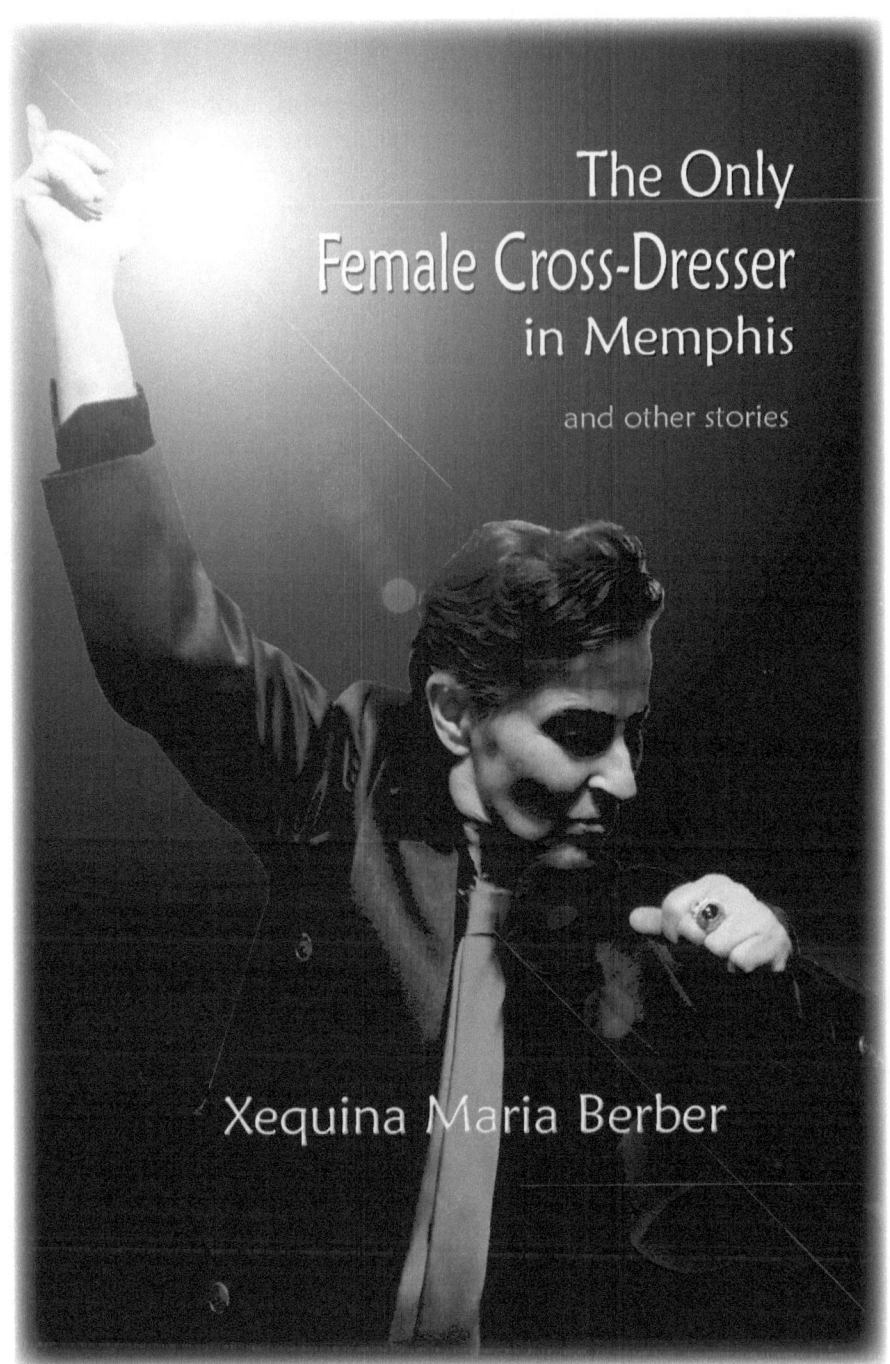

The Only
Female Cross-Dresser
in Memphis

and other stories

Xequina Maria Berber

GusGus Press
Bedazzled Ink Publishing Company • Fairfield, California

paperback 978-1-945805-56-1

Cover Photo Design
by
Xequina
makeup and photo
by Cynthia Wilson

Cover Layout
by

Frontispiece: Johnny Magnolia as St. Sebastian, Patron Saint of Gays, 2021,
painting by Xequina
Johnny Magnolia, 2008, photo by C.R. Smith
Three Butches (Bird, Jazmín, & Tori), painting by Xequina
Portrait of Johnny Magnolia, 2010, painting by Xequina
Johnny Magnolia Must Die, 2021, painting by Xequina
Portrait of Xequina as an old dyke, 2021, photo by C.R. Smith
Johnny Magnolia Today, photo by Sandy Morris, 2012

GusGus Press
a division of
Bedazzled Ink Publishing, LLC
Fairfield, California
http://www.bedazzledink.com

This collection is dedicated to our proud, wonderful, and zany lavender community, without which there couldn't have been a book. (Thanks for all the drama!)

Fiction

Tales of a Southern Butch (Based on the Life of Johnny Magnolia)

Lesbians in Magic, Fantasy & the Supernatural

Memoir

Essay

Saint Sebastian

Foreword

There's legends—and then, there's *big lies* and outrageous *defamation* of innocent character.

For example, if you read the legend about me in this here book, you better keep in mind that it's dyke folklore—which is nothing more than gossip about a particular lesbian's life, in this case *mine*. For the most part, I don't mind. "The only thing worse than being talked about, is *not* being talked about," said our very own gay boy, the magnificent Oscar Wilde. But X, the author of this book, got taken in by *my* ex, Lil Queen, and all her spiteful, vengeful slander. But this here's the truth: thanks to that little bi-atch, my rising star as a gospel singer got all shot to hell, what with her making a scene at one of the biggest revivals in the Deep Shit South. She disrupted the holy proceedings, got on stage and snatched the mic away from me, announcing that I was a no-'count religious hypocrite, womanizing, hound dog dyke-drunk, then goes and accuses the wrong woman—the bishop's wife, no less—of being my lover (we only kissed, I swear it), and to add injury to insults, LQ turned around and punched me right in the nose—which was big enough as it was.

LQ was merely escorted off the premises, but my performance was cancelled. I left in the limo I arrived in—yes, with another woman, so what? (She had money. Lots of it.) And that's when, pissed as hell, LQ started spreading those stories about me and the Devil. But even "the most rapturous voice to lilt into gospel music since Elvis" (that's what *Rolling Stone* said about mine!) aint worth a damned nickel now that the rumors about me and lezzies and Satan have gone all viral. Did you know that even Christians are into the cancel culture thing? I'm a pariah even to my most devoted Christian former fans—all those self-righteous, hypocritical, holier-than-thou, homophobic, hateful children of the Devil's dogs.

But never mind all that. What X has done here, is taken those self-same tawdry "facts" and changed them around some, focusing on the good, the bad and the damned ugly, to make a beautiful legend about me that will go down in the infamous annals of lesbian herstory. What's more, after hours of interviews—which I granted only so I could gaze upon her lovely countenance—she's told a passel of other stories from my life (ahem—the section entitled *Tales of a Southern Butch*), spruced them up, and made them nice and shiny for lesbian consumption, because I know the general public aint one bit interested in *our* stories.

You should read them, not just because a good portion of them are about me, the illustrious, one and only, Johnny Magnolia, but because they're damn good stories. I couldn't have written them better myself. And to top it all off, she put me on the cover! (I think she likes me.)

Oh yeah, I'm supposed to say something about the other stories. I hope I'm not flattering myself to say that I believe she used me as inspiration for some of them. I thought I recognized myself here and there. Hey, they aren't bad either.

Anyway, back to the point. If you read *The Legend of Johnny Magnolia*, don't go around saying that you "know for a fact" I'm dead based on LQ's mean lies (ooh sorry, plot spoiler.) If you do, that'll make you an effing liar. Got it?

Johnny Magnolia
Santa Rita Jail
Dublin, California (yeah, I got in trouble here too)

Introduction

I am a storyteller, and this is my first collection of stories about lesbians. The short story wasn't always my medium; it had always been the full-length novel. After I came out (very late), I got to a point where there were so many stories to tell, I had to start writing short stories.

The advice I'd read more than once was "if you want to be a writer, quit your job. Find a way to make *writing* your job." So I did. When my savings ran out, I worked as a temp as little as possible, and lived in an impoverished garret I called The Crow's Nest, in Emeryville; at that time the least expensive town in the Bay Area.

The Crow's Nest was aptly named, not just for the twisting staircase I climbed to reach my two rooms in an old Victorian, but for my storyteller-muse, Crowspeaker, who a psychic friend told me lives in my throat. The throat chakra is where our creativity comes from. When it's blocked, one has difficulty expressing oneself. Only now I understand that my throat chakra has been blocked in a specific way most of my life.

I spent most of ten years in the Crow's Nest trying to write the Great American Novel. Over time I came to understand that it was actually the Great White, Patriarchal Novel, and it wasn't my true voice. So I struck out on my own and began writing stories for women. It was the beginning of authenticity in my writing.

The rest of becoming unblocked would happen after coming out. Although I've been storytelling and writing since third grade, being released from the closet also liberated a flood of inventiveness, making this the most creative period of my life. It makes sense; being in the closet had a lot to do with not knowing myself, and without knowing who I was, how could my writing be fully honest?

So even though my whole life I've hung out with people who were gay (my *family*), and I was interested in queer subjects (*my* subjects), I still had a lot of catching up to do. I now watch queer film and read the literature with identification and pride of ownership. There were old mysteries and romances, even lesbian science fiction. I went back farther, and read classics like *Rubyfruit Jungle, Well of Loneliness, Patience and Sarah, Thérèse and Isabelle, The Demeter Flower*. Adrienne Rich, Sarah Waters, Jeannette Winterson, Judy Grahn, and May Sarton. I read gay male literature as well.

I also read what I could find of pulp novels, like the Beebo Brinker series by Ann Bannon. I was disturbed by the internalized homophobia of the characters. I learned such books could only be published and sent through the mail if the lesbians were punished in some way, like ending up in a mental institution.

Mainstream film wants the lesbian to die in the end, especially by suicide (*The Children's Hour*, 1961—acceptance of her wrongness in this world); be killed by the male love interest, (*The Fox*, 1967); or best of all, sacrifice herself (*Chloe*, 2009), thus keeping the world the safe for heterosexuality. If fiction is philosophy, it would appear the lesbian themes have been infected by the mirror in which a larger society reflected misunderstanding, perversion, and fear. This imbedded hatred is what kept me out of touch with my true sexual identify for so long.

We have to tell our own story. Homophobia, both societal and internalized, is part of that story; but we have many other options besides isolation and death. So when I turned my creativity toward lesbiana, I wanted my characters to be proud of who and what they were; to see nothing wrong with being a woman who loves women. Part of the conflict in some of my stories is the interaction between homophobic characters with those who have refused to drink from the poisoned well of the status quo.

My first creative efforts were to rewrite the lyrics to popular songs that my partner Rome Smith and I performed together for the community, or that she performed solo as her drag king persona, Johnny Magnolia. I covered such topics as the lesbian honeymoon, polygamy, lesbian vampires, and the lavender glass ceiling.

From this I moved on to comics—an old obsession. I featured Johnny and her best friend, Bro Fox (Leesha Faulkner, niece to author William Faulkner), reimagined as high school friends, and their antics while supporting each other in their adolescent self-discovery as young butch women. I also painted portraits of Johnny Magnolia, like the frontispiece for this book, as St. Sebastian, one of the patron saints of gays (the other is Santa Librata).

When I turned my attention to short stories, I wanted to write about characters for whom lesbianism came naturally; women with dignity, who were self-accepting, proud to be out. My model was my partner Rome, having known and accepted her queerness since she was four, who had many tales to tell. With her permission, I wrote stories from her life as Johnny Magnolia. In this way, I developed my lesbian story chops and vicariously lived the lesbian life I missed out on. These stories are in the section titled, *Tales of a Southern Butch.* They are non-fiction, although parts have been fictionalized and the proper names changed to protect the guilty, the ridiculous, and the obsessed.

After seeing a documentary on the life and mysterious death of Robert Johnson, father of the Delta Blues, I asked myself, *"what would this story be if Johnson was a lesbian?"* From thence came "The Legend of Johnny Magnolia," using details from her own legendary Southern Gothic life.

After reading *Ex-Lover Weird Shit: a Collection of Short Fiction, Poetry and Cartoons by Lesbians and Gay Men* edited by Debra Riggin Waugh (which incidentally features the cartoon *I Loved Satan's Daughter* by my girlfriend), I thought "I can do one of these," and wrote "Seeing Her Again," about a woman who can't get over her beautiful, faithless ex. "Delta of Love" came about from a line I read in *Lesbian Connections* magazine, about two high school girls everyone thought were friends, who had been lovers all that time.

In the section *Lesbians in Magic, Fantasy and the Supernatural,* I took my inspiration from traditional American and English folktales in "Queen of the Cats" and "Tammy Lynn" by asking myself "what would these stories be, if they were told by a woman/lesbian?" "Prayers for La Llorona" and "Horsewoman" were inspired by legendary figures from my Mexican culture: the tortured ghost La Llorona, and the monstrous female Xtaybay, who usually preys on men. In "Ode to Jimmy Jean" I return to Southern Gothic to tell a story inspired by Bobby Gentry's song, "Ode to Billy Joe," with a female Billy Joe MacAllister. "The Pooka," a true story that vibrated with the supernatural as it happened to me, features a literal jumping of a fence that foretold my coming out.

"Jealousy, a Dark Comedy" is a record of how I found my way through a debilitating jealousy that has infected most of my relationships. Under the definition of comedy, Google states that not all examples of comedy as a literary device are funny; and an old definition of comedy is any narrative with a happy ending (*Oxford Universal Dictionary on Historical Principles*). As my essay's title indicates, this is a scorpionic comedy, but it does have a happy resolution. And lastly, this collection concludes with a rant on how I learned to avoid lesbian drama in my relationships.

Though I identify as femme, I tend to write from a butch point of view. What does this say about me? Maybe it's the result of having written my first stories from a butch point of view. Maybe if I had come out as a child I would have been butch, but butchness was systematically and ragefully shamed out of me with such statements as, *"You hold your fork like a man." "You walk like a man,"* etc. I've also been told gender isn't a choice; you're either one or the other.

But gender isn't so simple. Just look at our own community. *"Every time I see you, you're a different gender,"* a friend once told me. I think everyone is bisexual, and gender is fluid, or would be if society wasn't so uptight and diversity hating. I believe we all have distinct and different selves that are expressed at different times, including dreams.

It is my hope that you will have as much fun reading these stories as I had writing them. I hope that you will take pride in these stories as part of your culture as a queer person. Maybe you will even be inspired to tell your own stories.

FICTION

Delta of Love or, Hiding in Plain Sight

I SAW DINA and Donnie as I was leaving the downtown library. It was early October, the weather still warm. They were looking at me, so I waved. I'd known them for years, we were in the ninth grade now, but we'd never talked much. Dina had straight black hair and was still a tomboy. She wore boys' clothes, T-shirts, and vests, and now black, lace-up work boots. It looked like they were talking about me, because they both grinned at me. I wondered if it was because I had developed a lot, and I was wearing skirts and dresses more. Embarrassed, I held my books and folders closer to my chest. But just as I started to head away, Dina called me over.

"Hey, Dulce, come here. What are you up to?"

"Going home. I've been working on that assignment for social studies all afternoon," I said, rolling my eyes. "How about you?" To be a good conversationalist, always ask people a question back, my sister Carmen had told me.

"Want to go to Gooey Looey's?" Donnie asked. His voice cracked and he turned red. He'd gotten taller over the summer and dressed nerdy with button-down shirts and bow-ties.

"Yeah, you must be hungry by now," Dina said.

"Well—" I glanced down at my books to think about it, and Dina said, "Oh—I'll carry those for you," and took them right out of my arms. Next thing I knew, we were on our way to the hamburger place, me in the middle. They were doing all the talking, which was good because I felt shy. Donnie would make a joke, and I'd giggle, then Dina would make one back, and I'd laugh. It seemed like they were competing to see who could make me laugh more. But I was confused; I could swear Dina called me over because Donnie asked her to, but he was Dina's boyfriend, had been since sixth grade.

They ordered hamburgers and fries. I just got the Gooey Salad and an iced tea so I wouldn't spoil my appetite for dinner at home. They wouldn't let me pay, saying I was their "guest." They were making me feel really special.

Dina sat next to me in the booth, her arm and thigh pressed up against mine. I moved over to give her more room. She put her arm on the banquette behind me. We talked about what we did for summer and school and stuff we were doing, Donnie and Dina still making wisecracks and ranking on each other. Dina was right up against me again, and there wasn't much more room on the banquette, so I just stayed there.

I had my own group of friends of course, but I started hanging around with Dina and Donnie too, especially on the weekends. Mom liked that we always went out as a group—safety in numbers, referring of course to not being tempted to have sex.

Carmen couldn't believe the new friends I'd "dragged home," and told me oddball friends would make me unpopular at school.

"Especially that Dina," she said. "People probably think she's a lesbian. Good thing she has a boyfriend, even if he's another weirdo."

Lesbian: a relatively new word for me. There was a negative mystery about homosexuality at school; kids whispered about it, and you felt sick with fear. Julian was a guy in my class who kids said was "queer" because he was effeminate, talked in a high, soft voice, and waved his hands around like a girl. But he was really funny and kind, and he would do anything for you. I liked him. People like him were called fairies, and were made fun of, sometimes to their faces. Sometimes Donnie got picked on like that too, just because he dressed too tidily, with bow ties and his collars raised.

But hanging out with Dina and Donnie made me stop caring about popularity. That was only to attract boys anyway. Who cared? Unlike my boy-crazy sister, I had my eye on Stanford or Cronkite. I was focused on school work and the school newspaper club. I was going to be a journalist.

I'd never had friends like Dina or Donnie before. They were cool and interesting-weird, and I adored them. They opened my world up beyond school and my usual social groups. Donnie was a math whiz and could do amazing things with computers. He was always finding cool websites online, and liked strange movies we would all watch and talk about. Dina liked to read fat books, was a poet, and a really good artist. She started drawing comic strips about the three of us, and we loved seeing and hearing her latest installment. I also liked the way she had a mind of her own. Like, she was the only girl in Machine Shop because she wanted to learn about fixing things.

She had a job as a busgirl. One Friday she picked up a shift, so Donnie and I went to a basketball game at school, even though we mostly talked through it. I was worried about my parents finding out I'd gone alone with him—I still wasn't allowed to date—but I should have been worried about Dina. She called me out about it on Monday at lunchtime, in the cafeteria.

"Get this straight, Dulce," she said loudly into my face. "Donnie is *my* boyfriend."

"You mean because we went to the game?"

"Yes, unless there's another time you're not telling me about."

"No."

I was really embarrassed. I glanced over at the table where Dina had been sitting. Donnie was gaping like a big loony bird. My sister Carmen had told me never to fight over a guy. *Just ignore him and be yourself.* As head cheerleader, she knew how to handle boys.

"Dina, it looks really bad to fight over a guy." Donnie wasn't really the issue; I didn't want Dina mad at me. I loved our triangle of friendship and didn't want to mess it up.

"Stay away from him then."

"But I'm friends with both of you!"

"So you admit you like him," she challenged.

"I like you both," I said stubbornly.

"Whatever. Just stay away from him," she said before stomping away.

Of course, everyone in the lunchroom was staring at me, even the teachers. My face felt like it was bursting. I went outside and sat with other friends, but of course they wanted me to tell them why I was crying.

"Oh, Dulce, you're so much prettier than Dina, no contest," Riba said.

"Yeah, Donnie will choose you over Dina any day," Serena said.

But I didn't *want* him to choose me over Dina. It had never been my intention to "get" Donnie, or flirt with him, or have anything other than friendship. Dina was right; I shouldn't be going out with him if she wasn't there. I looked across the yard at them sitting together, Dina showing him something in her Cat Woman notebook. Suddenly I felt sad. I had lots of friends, but Donnie was Dina's boyfriend *and* best friend. Dina didn't have any other girlfriends. If Donnie and I became an item, she would lose both of us. And we would lose *her*. I dried my eyes.

"I'm not trying to get Donnie. The three of us are *friends*. I hate it when girls compete with each other over a guy, it's such a cliché," I announced. "Women should support each other."

Yet I hadn't been very supportive of Dina. I'd never done anything alone with her, like going shopping, or making a cake like with my other friends. I guess because those things didn't seem like something she'd want to do. But how did I know, since I'd never asked?

It seemed like she was avoiding me all week, although it could have been because she was always with Donnie or one of the other guys she always hung out with. So after school on Friday I saw her with some of them in the schoolyard. I broke off from my friends and went over. She gave me the once over and smiled.

"Hey, Dulce. How are you?" she said, like she'd never been mad at me.

"Fine, thank you." I glanced at the guys. They had gone silent. "Um . . . you were right. I apologize for going to the game with Donnie without you. I won't do it again."

She gave a little shrug. "It's okay." I felt encouraged, even if those guys were all listening.

"Want to do something tomorrow?" My voice sounded small and squeaky to me. I cleared my throat. "Just you and me? You could sleep over. Um, I mean, if you're not busy. I should have asked you sooner, sorry, I just thought about it—" I was babbling. I couldn't believe how hard this was.

Dina looked stunned.

"What? You want me to spend the night with you?" Her face was turning red. The guy next to her elbowed her. I ignored him and all those grinning dorks. She ran a hand over her hair. A dimple appeared on her cheek. It showed up when she thought something was funny, but keeping a straight face.

"No—I mean, I don't have any plans," she said. "Uh, sure, I'd love to come over."

I told her to come early for dinner. "Don't forget your toothbrush and nightgown," I said, and then felt like a twit. Of course she wouldn't forget something so basic.

As I walked away, I heard the guys slapping her on the back and joshing her.

"Oooh, Dina, gonna have a sleep over with your *girl*-friend!"

One crooned in a high voice, "Don't forget your nightie!" Making fun of me.

"Yeah, do you even *have* one?"

They all burst out laughing. Guys were so immature.

Carmen thought I was brilliant.

"Making friends with the opposition. Way to go, little sis."

She could think what she wanted. I was just glad Dina had forgiven me, and we could all go on being friends.

She showed up wearing a plain yellow blouse with her jeans, a brown cloth bomber jacket, and even a pair of loafer-type shoes instead of the leather combat boots she always wore. She had a big paper bag with the top rolled up.

"Is that your stuff? Let's put it in my room."

My sister came out in curlers and a ratty old robe. The one night of the year she has dinner at home, and it had to be that night. She stopped short when she saw Dina.

"Oh, are you spending the night?" As if she didn't know. She said it resentfully, like Dina wasn't really welcome. Dina just nodded. She was acting self-conscious. At dinner she was very formal, answering my parents' questions, but otherwise not saying much. I wondered if she'd been on over-nights before.

"The meatloaf is really good," Dina told my mother.

Carmen, who kept looking at Dina and rolling her eyes, put her fingers down her throat like she wanted to throw up. I didn't know whether it was about the meatloaf or Dina. I gave her a dirty look, hoping Dina wasn't noticing her. After dinner she thanked my parents for dinner. Carmen went upstairs, thank goodness.

"We'll clean up," Dina told my mother, taking the dishes out of her hands. "You go sit down."

"Well, thank you, girls. We'll head out then."

"Where are you going?" I asked.

"To a planning event for *semana santa* at the church. We should be home before ten. You can have Donnie over, but no other boys," my mother told us.

"No, it's just us tonight," I said.

"What's *semana santa*?" Dina asked as we cleared the table. "Isn't *semana* a week?" She was taking Spanish.

"Yes. It means Holy Week. It's a big deal at St. Liz. That's the church we go to."

Dina worked very quickly and efficiently like the bus girl she was. In a jiffy, the dishes were in the dishwasher and kitchen was clean. We watched a goofy zombie movie for a while, then went up to my room.

"Let's put on our nightgowns," I said.

Dina got pajamas out of her bag and took off her blouse. She had a tank top on underneath, and under that it looked like she was wearing a sports bra. We talked about the movie while I took off my clothes and put on a pink nightie.

"Oh yeah, and what about that guy who ran the crematorium, singing those German songs?" I asked, picking up my brush. I glanced at Dina. She was sitting on the bed, still dressed, eyes wide and staring at me like she didn't know what to do. After gym class, could she still be modest? I turned my back to give her privacy while I looked through my tapes for ABBA.

"Let's dance," I said, turning on the tape player. She had changed into boy's pajamas.

Dina sort of danced, but also did things like boxing moves, and making faces while jumping around, and just generally acting silly to the music, making me laugh. It was really fun. I couldn't believe I'd never invited her overnight before.

After that I said, "Hey, let's try on makeup. I got some new stuff, tell me what you think."

I got out all my makeup, eyeshadows, mascara, one that made your lashes look like patent leather, and a bunch of lipstick, some hand-me-downs from Carmen, or from my mother, which were lame, but I hadn't wanted to hurt her feelings. Dina just watched as I put it on. I wondered if she'd never seen anyone put on make-up before. She had always lived with her father; it was probably why she was still a tomboy. Finally she picked up the purple eye shadow.

"Can I put this on?"

"Sure."

She rubbed it over her eyes, then got the blue and put it on under her eyes, and finally put on mascara and got it all over her lids and rubbed it in, then took an eyebrow pencil and made lines under her eyes.

"Hey, do I look like Al Pacino in *Scarface*?" She was Italian, and proud of her heritage.

"No, you look like a drug addict."

"Cool," Dina said, grinning at herself in the mirror. Then she got one of my mother's red lipsticks and put it on in one stroke all the way around so it went in the corners and over the lip line in most places. "How about now, do I look like a zombie?"

The door opened then and Carmen came in. "Dulce, can I borrow your pink angora?"

"Sure," I said. I got it out of my dresser. She was staring at Dina.

"Cute, Dina. You look like a dead drag queen."

Dina's face fell.

"Get out!" I said, throwing the sweater at her and slamming the door. We could hear her snickering through the door. "What's a drag queen?" I asked Dina.

She didn't answer. She was using tissues off my dresser to rub off the make-up. Now the vibes were all weird. I gave Dina some cold cream.

"Here, this will make it easier."

When most of it was off, she stared at herself in the mirror. Some mascara was still rubbed into her eyelashes.

"*Now* you look like Al Pacino," I said. "Leave it on, it looks good like that." She smiled a little. I put on some plum lipstick. "How does this color look with the eyeshadow?"

"Fine," Dina said, glancing at me. Then: "It's a gay man who dresses up as a woman."

"What is?"

"A drag queen. What your sister said."

"Oh, that." I was afraid Dina was going into one of her moods, which I hated. She'd get quiet, and could get snappish. I could just kill my sister. "You mean a transvestite?" proud that I knew the word.

"No, a transvestite is a straight man, a heterosexual who dresses like a woman sometimes. A drag queen is a gay man who dresses like a woman and usually wears wild makeup and wigs . . . sick, huh?"

"No. Why should only girls get to dress up? I wish I had some wigs, we could put those on too. Why do they do it, is it like performance art?"

Dina shrugged. "I don't know, sort of I guess. They do it because it's fun. Because they're expressing their feminine side. I think it started because this society doesn't make room for men to express their femininity." She was watching me in the mirror. "I think your sister was making a reference to fag bashing."

I put down the lipstick. "Oh god, really?"

Carmen had said a *dead* drag queen. Did she mean what Dina said, or was she just trying to be funny? But it *wasn't* funny. I thought about poor Julian, how he came to school once with a black eye and a bad bruise on the side of his face. He wouldn't talk about it, but I had a feeling it was connected to the bullying.

I knew by now that people called Dina a "dyke," and I remembered some stupid guy talking about a girl getting pushed over a cliff just because she was a lesbian. It hadn't been a big cliff, but I realized that was actually a bashing too.

"That's really scary," I said. "I hope that's not what she meant, but I can ask her."

"What do *you* think about gays?"

I turned to face her, crossing my arms over my chest.

"I don't care what they do. It's nobody's business who someone wants to sleeps with, or what they wear." Dina was blinking really fast with a surprised look on her face, and I realized I was shouting. "Sorry. Why do people care, anyway?" Dina still looked disconcerted, which was rare for her. Usually I wasn't so opinionated. I turned back to the mirror. "Just ignore Carmen. Who cares what she thinks? Just because she's going to be prom queen, doesn't make her the queen of everything."

I wiped off the purple lipstick and put on a bright pink; gross. I toned it down with white. Then I kissed the mirror, leaving an impression. That gave me an idea.

"Hey, want to practice kissing?"

"*What?*" Dina's expression darkened. "Are you—?"

"Don't get upset. I do it all the time with my other friends."

Dina blinked. "You *do?*"

"Sure. So we know how when we're with guys, you know? All the girls do it."

"They *do?*"

I laughed at the incredulous expression on her face.

"Yes, it's better than the back of your hand. Want to try? If you don't like it, we can stop. But I thought maybe you could teach me some stuff." I'd never seen Dina and Donnie kiss, but they must have in private. Dina was quiet while she thought about it.

"You're not going to talk about it with your other friends, are you?"

"No. Why would I do that?"

Dina kept staring at me as if she was trying to feature it. Finally she said, "Um, okay, sure. Let me brush my teeth first."

I thought that was more of Dina being on her best behavior, since none of my other girlfriends bothered to do that. She got her toothbrush out of that paper bag. I went with her to brush my teeth too, and protect her from my idiot sister just in case.

When we went back to my room, Dina locked the door. She was a little shy at first and seemed to be trembling, so I took the lead. I just leaned forward and kissed her. I could tell her teeth were clamped shut, and she immediately wiped my lipstick off.

"How was that?" I asked.

"Fine."

"Hm. Well, no offense, but you should relax your mouth. You kiss really hard." I wanted to ask if she kissed Donnie like that, but thought it was better not to. "Here, let me show you." I put my hands around her face. "Relax your jaw . . ."

We kissed again, and after a while she got used to kissing another girl. My other friends were all concerned about technique, but after a while, Dina started making it more fun. She put her arms around me and started being very experimental. She made up kissing games, like she'd say, "let's kiss like they do in the movies," or "let's do really sloppy kisses."

I had a double we shared when we finally went to bed. I didn't feel like going to sleep and kept talking to Dina in the dark, but Dina seemed very stiff again. She was also on the far edge of the bed. But the next morning when I woke up, she was behind me, spooning. For the most part, it had been a pretty successful sleep-over.

Best of all, the three of us continued hanging out. Sometimes Donnie would be there on sleep-over night, and we'd eat popcorn and watch a movie. After he left, Dina and I sometimes took a bath together. She had a beautiful body; you didn't know how slender she was because she always wore boys' clothes in a big size. She thought she had a big ass, but I thought her butt was cute. Sometimes I'd sit in front of her between her legs, and she'd wash my hair, and make designs with my hair full of shampoo, like straight up in a point, "You're a space queen," or two big horns, "Now you're Snow White's mother," or a pompadour like Mary Wilson, her favorite Black singer.

Dina bought lipstick for us to try out: neon colors; flavored ones; one called Vampire Red, another called Pussy Pink she was really jazzed about.

When I tried it on, she said, "It's not that color at all."

"What isn't?"

"Vaginas."

"How do *you* know?"

"From the porn I've seen," she said. "That's some guy's fantasy of what he wants women to look like down there."

One night when it was just the two of us, and everyone was going to be out for hours, she put on a porn video she'd brought over. I'd never seen one, and was shocked. It was *Behind the Green Door*, which had been a big sensation a few years before. I figured it was something her father had.

Later, Dina asked me, "Want to try tongue-kissing?"

"What?"

"You know, French kiss. Like they did in the movie."

"I haven't done that before."

"Neither have I." I wondered about her and Donnie, and then realized he probably didn't know how, and she wanted to show him. Anyway, that's why we had those sessions, to learn to kiss. She could teach him now.

"Stick out your tongue," she said.

We touched the tips of our tongues. It felt strange, but I liked it too. I remembered touching tongues with another kid when I was little. Dina put her arm around my shoulder and pulled me close to her, with her other arm around my waist, then put her tongue in my mouth. Then she pushed me down on the bed, which I really liked, especially after that movie.

Another night Dina said, "We should try doing other stuff. So you'll know how to handle guys when they try to go farther."

"All right."

This time as she kissed me, she started "feeling me up," slowly at first. I giggled when she pinched my nipple, and when she reached up and put her hands on both my breasts, I fell over on my bed laughing. Dina climbed on top of me and put her thigh between mine, and it felt really good, so then I tried to feel *her* up, but she grabbed my hands and held them over my head. I pitched her over with my hips and climbed on top of her, and she grabbed me around my arms and held me tight so I couldn't do anything, us both giggling.

"Pretend I'm a guy doing this," she said. "Tell me to stop."

"No, no!" I yelled. "Let me go!"

"Break away from me!" she yelled back. "Fight me!" So I struggled hard and got away from her. I was strong too.

We were laughing and screaming, and there was a loud knocking at my bedroom door and the handle was turning. We sat up quickly. I opened the door. It was only Carmen.

"What are you doing here?" I asked. "I thought you went out." She ignored my question.

"What's going on?" She looked around suspiciously, as if we had a boy in there. Dina was sitting on the edge of the bed, hands folded in her lap, face red.

"None of your business." I slammed the door and locked it again. I jumped back on the bed with Dina.

"Where did you learn all this stuff?" I asked.

"Oh, you know, it just comes naturally if some guy tries to mess with me. I mean, I don't want to get pregnant. That's how it starts."

So I guessed she was talking about Donnie, even though it was really hard to imagine him being one of those horny guys my girlfriends were always talking about. But she also hung out with a lot of other guys, so maybe she was talking about them. I liked thinking about her defending herself so strongly. And she *was* strong. She lifted weights.

The only thing was, I hardly ever tried to stop her like I would have with a guy, unless she reminded me to. Then I would fight her the way she fought.

"Don't be afraid to hit them if you have to. Go for his eyes, or his throat. Grab something and hit him with it if you have to. Women should do whatever they have to, to protect themselves."

Then she would jump me and yell at me to fight her off, and if I didn't, she'd dry hump me, or hold me from behind and pretend we were dogs having sex, and of course we'd be breathing hard and laughing and yelling the whole time. When my parents asked what all the commotion was, and I told them Dina was teaching me self-defense. After that first time, Carmen never said anything, but she always looked at me knowingly, like that was supposed to shame me or something.

Dina and I experimented with other stuff too. The most daring was when we talked about 69-ing. We had done a lot of other fooling around, so I let her do it to me. It drove me crazy, and we had to stop so I could turn on the radio loud, so no one could hear me. For some reason, she didn't want me to try it on her. She was really shy about it, or maybe she was saving it for Donnie, I don't know, I never asked. But I loved all that fooling around. I was finding out what it was like to get hot and sexual, and be experienced, yet not get a reputation. I felt really sophisticated.

Dina and I were a lot closer now, almost crowding Donnie out, and sometimes he would look at us like he was trying to figure us out. Then I would back off, or try to include him more. But he never got jealous of me the way Dina still did sometimes. If Donnie helped me with my math, or we had been talking together too long, even if she was in the same room reading a book or drawing, she'd pick a fight at school, always in public. After that first time I didn't get so upset, especially because it kind of seemed like Dina was putting on a show. It confused me; I thought maybe she was trying to show Donnie how much she loved him.

As for Donnie, sometimes he'd ask me out when Dina was doing something else, but I always said no.

Finally I asked, "You know Dina's going to get mad if we go without her. Why do you keep asking me?"

He shrugged. "Dina is the one who told me to go with you."

I couldn't believe it. Why would she do that? Was she testing us? Looking for a reason to get mad at me? Then I find out *she* put him up to it. And another thing: why was it always *me* she got mad at? Why not Donnie?

It took me a while to figure it out. Donnie was in a programming internship by then, had come out, and had a twenty-year-old boyfriend.

Dina had a part-time job in a bicycle shop, had also come out, and was a militant feminist. I was in a private, all-girls school where the student body was worldly and even jaded, and at least half of them lesbian. Including me.

We were all each other's "beards." Dina had picked those fights to make it look like she was jealous. That way no one would ever suspect we were baby dykes, and guess what we were really up to on those steamy, adolescent girl evenings.

Seeing Her Again

1

BIRD. ALONE IN her attached apartment. Reading Russian novels and tracking the characters in a notebook; learning to bake bread; trying her hand at lovelorn poetry. Mooning over Candy, her first and only love. Over now for two years, she still woke up weeping from dreams of her.

The loss of that love had made Bird a virtual recluse. She felt like a fool before the whole community, all who knew what was going on, and how Bird was being played. Because it turned out not to have been love at all; not on Candy's side. Bird had fallen into the trap of being used—*again*, only this time by one whom she had profoundly trusted and so dearly loved.

Her first couple of years out of the closet—long before Candy, being used hadn't mattered much. Everyone had the youthful energy and tolerance for high dyke romance drama. Relationships ran their course in a week or less. Bird was twenty, loaded with hormones; everyone wanted to sleep with her. Sex was fun! She got a reputation for being a stud. She had thought she had a natural talent for lovemaking.

Then it began coming back to her, piece by piece, memories about how she gained those skills: her alcoholic, drug-addicted parents using her first as a sexual aide ("Come on Bird, hop on."), then as their little rent girl to horrid, creepy men ("What's the matter? You know him, he's our neighbor. You said he was a nice man.") Then their moral outrage when she told them she was a lesbian and they had kicked her out of the house ("You're sick. You can't be our daughter until you get help").

The horror of those memories shut down her sexuality. Friends either couldn't believe what she was telling them, or couldn't listen to it. Drinking and dope made her more confused and ashamed. Disgusted and frightened, she found a progressive Christian church and learned to meditate and pray, but she needed more. Someone steered her to the rape hotline. The answering counselor was able to hold everything she told her. Bird found such relief unburdening herself that she put the hotline number on speed-dial.

After several false starts, she found a therapist who turned out to be wonderful. Under her guidance, Bird focused on her recovery, attended support groups, and journaled daily. At a certain point she took a job at the hotline, helping other victims. Although she dated some during those years, she'd lived in a sexless limbo.

She met Candy just before turning thirty. Gun shy, Bird moved cautiously. They became friends, opening up to each other, telling each other about their lives, their thoughts, gradually warming to attraction. After a few months, Bird found herself falling in love and becoming willing to try physical intimacy again. She was overjoyed to find sex was no longer triggering. There was no remembered terror, revulsion, or shutting down. Bird was able to be fully present, to appreciate every moment massaging Candy's creamy skin, losing herself in that mass of tawny hair, in her glorious goddess breasts, in the earth scent of her intimate parts.

Bird's slow, exploratory approach to intimacy had a freeing effect on Candy as well. A survivor of an abusive religious upbringing, she was able to abandon herself to sensation where she never had before. They couldn't seem to get enough of each other. Riding the wave of ecstatic, new-love energy, they spent all their spare time together. Bird took Candy to all the lesbian events, proud to show her off. She felt lucky to have found the love of her life, her soul mate. They seemed to know each other's moods, each other's very thoughts. They rarely argued. Bird was grateful every day to have someone so amazing in her life.

After several months their relationship stopped being so public. Candy started taking night classes, then got a job as a legal assistant and became swamped with work. They didn't go out anymore, but Candy would call Bird at odd times, last minute, or late at night.

"Hi, are you still up? Can I come over?"

"Of course, anytime, baby," Bird would say, hoping she sounded more alert than she really was. She'd get up, shower, and was dressed, and packing Candy's favorite dildo; their array of sex toys—purchased together—set out by the time she arrived. Candy was usually dressed to the nines with alcohol on her breath; Bird could tell she'd been out partying; probably some work event.

It doesn't matter. At the end of the day, it's me *she's with,* Bird told herself.

It was a pattern: Candy would be amorous, they'd have wild sex, then Candy was up and out again.

"I'm so sorry, Bird, but I have to study, and I have a legal brief to prepare for work tomorrow. I don't know how I'm going to get it all done."

Bird didn't think about it. She could be as flexible and as accommodating as Candy needed. But in the community, people started asking questions.

"Did you and Candy break up?" this from Delia, someone who offered relationship workshops at the hotline.

"No, of course not. She's just really busy right now, working full time and going to law school, and then there's my weird hours here. But things are great between us."

Delia had looked doubtful, which really pissed Bird off. Why did everyone keep asking, and look so incredulous when she insisted they were still together? But Bird told herself she didn't have to convince anyone about their special connection.

You'd be jealous if you knew how deeply committed we are to each other. Candy takes time out of her incredibly packed schedule to be with me, and it's always amazing. I wish we could talk the way we used to, or even just cuddle for a while. That's what I really miss. But it's okay, it won't be like this forever.

She *had* asked herself many times why Candy was interested in her: average looks, working-class, a two-year degree for which she had worked hard and been so naively proud; while Candy was classy, brilliant, had attended a seven-sister school, and was the most beautiful woman in the world as far as Bird was concerned. But she'd seen stranger combinations in the dyke community: a Ph.D. of philosophy with a partner who had barely completed high school, a librarian with a construction worker, so really it wasn't so unusual.

Jazmín, her best friend, told her Candy had been hanging out with some big butch, but secure in Candy's love, Bird brushed it aside.

"It's probably just a friend." She was proud of not being possessive.

And sure enough, when she asked, Candy confirmed Sandy was an old friend who had recently moved to town.

"We've been friends since we were kids. We're catching up, and I'm showing her the town, how to get around, you know."

Then Candy stopped calling for those late-night trysts. She stopped taking Bird's calls; was vague and infrequent when answering texts. After not being able to reach her for weeks, Candy finally answered the phone, and informed her that she was, after all, dating Sandy, and that she was only one of several women she'd been casually dating for some time.

"You know, Bird, *most* people would figure out their relationship was over if they hadn't heard from someone in months. Don't take this personally, but you're not ambitious enough." Bird was therewith dumped.

Bird left home, wandering in a daze until she found herself in Jazmín's neighborhood. She collapsed in Jazmín's front room. Jazmín brought tissues, made a bitter tea she said was for shock, and burned a leaf of yerba santa over her.

"For clarity and spiritual healing," she said. She sat down and stroked Bird's back as she sobbed on the end of the couch.

"I can't believe it. She never gave me a clue."

"Bro', what did you think it meant when she didn't have time for you anymore?"

"That isn't true. She *made* time to see me!"

"No, she didn't. She made time for *sex*."

Bird was stunned by this distinction.

"But ... she loved me. She said so," Bird stated, but conviction was already leaking from her voice. It had been well over a year since Candy had said that.

"Bird, if I loved someone, I wouldn't blab to everyone what an amazing 'lay' she was, like at the women's concert last summer. I felt like slapping her."

"*Lay?* She called me that?" Bird stared at nothing. "I asked her to that concert. She told me she couldn't go."

"Yeah, she was there all right, kissing on some rich old dyke. *Cabrona.* I never would have told you, but you're in serious need of a reality check."

It was the sex that had Bird believing things were still wonderful between them. She couldn't believe that two people could have that intensity of connection and feeling, and not be in love.

Can I not tell the difference between being loved, and being used?

Candy had *known* about the early abuse, it was the most painful intimacy Bird had shared. She had known how numbing, shaming, and annihilating the experiences had been for her; had held her as she wept and raged over it. If Candy had fallen out of love with Bird, painful though it might be, Bird could have accepted that. What she couldn't understand was Candy knowingly using her—for months.

Did she ever really love me at all?

Her humiliation before the community was almost as bad as the break up itself. How it must have looked, her yapping about everything being hunky-dory and how much in love they were, while Candy had been going out with other lovers. Bird not only felt like the fool with the booby prize, she felt like a sitting duck for all the users in the world.

Having exhausted her roommates with her stories and grief, she moved from the communal household where she'd lived for years, into her own place. It was a dump in the poor side of town, but she could afford it: an L-shaped flat with old appliances. L for love. L for lost. L for left.

Now, unable to hear the anguished stories of abuse, Bird quit the hotline to work at a vegetable distributorship. She chose the hard, fast-paced, night-time shift, not only for the extra pay, but to distract herself. She was always available for overtime; longer shifts ensured she would pass out when she got home.

The worst times were when nothing could make her sleep in the light of day. Hollow-eyed and wired, Bird cleared the backyard of weeds, pruned the trees, and planted a garden. She scraped, sanded, and painted her tiny back porch.

From that she moved on to painting her narrow home: periwinkle blue with yellow trim. After refinishing the floors, she named it St. Drogo's Rest, after the patron saint of coffee and ugly people. It was appropriate as coffee was her one vice, and Candy's indifferent rejection had ultimately convinced Bird of her own repulsiveness.

Crying was like a drug, a behavior she found weak and shameful. Yet sometimes there was nothing to do but break down, and she surrendered herself to it, lying on the floor and howling until the dog in the adjacent house, owners at work, howled too. Coyote partners, echoing their lonely sympathy.

But it was also a creative time for her. She checked CDs out of the library and revived her high school Spanish, which she practiced with Jazmín. She developed a bread recipe using yeasty porter ale. She walked the neighboring dog, a border collie, trained, and taught him tricks. She wrote poetry about the beauty of what her lost love had been, about her "crypt of sorrow," sometimes embarrassing even herself when she re-read them.

At work, everyone liked her. One or two of the women had crushes on her, but Bird never encouraged them. All the light in her heart had gone out. Her employers noticed her resistance to dyke drama, her professionalism, and hard work, and promoted her to supervisor. She toughened up, slimmed down, and developed muscles and a "six-pack." Sometimes in boxers, she flexed her muscles in front of the full-length mirror, wishing Candy could see her. Everything she did, read, and thought, led her back to Candy. She was unable to let her go.

Bird had burrowed into her grief and solitude, making an underground temple of them. And on the walls, written with invisible ink, was the wish that Candy would remember what they'd once meant to each other, and come back.

2

"COME ON," JAZMÍN said. "The party will be fun. It's a Western theme, with road-kill barbeque."

"Gross," Bird said, rolling her eyes. Jazmín was always trying to get her to go places. "Are you serious?"

"Of course not. That just means bring whatever to throw on the grill. What happened to your sense of humor?"

I haven't laughed since the day Candy left.

"Helene wants someone to start off the dancing. I told her you would do it."

Bird shuddered. "I don't know . . . I haven't danced in two years."

We used to do all the line dances.

"There has to be an easy one you must remember," Jazmín said. "How about that one you taught me, *Elvira*?"

"Why don't *you* start the dancing?"

"No, I'm embarrassed, and I'm not that good. Please? I'm making your favorite strawberry salsa with lots of cilantro," Jazmín cajoled.

"Is *she* going to be there?"

Jazmín frowned. "How should I know? For crying out loud Bird, I thought you were over that old ho'."

"I just don't want to see her, is all. And don't call her that," automatically defending her ex. *Well, I wouldn't like it if Jazmín called anyone a "ho'." It's disrespectful of women.*

Jazmín snorted. "Sorry. I thought you were over the Virgin Mary-who-can-do-no-wrong."

She wasn't that either, Bird thought.

Jazmín narrowed her eyes. "Ohhh, I see. You're afraid of her."

"That's ridiculous, why would I be afraid of her?" Bird snapped, realizing how defensive she sounded.

"Come on, Bird. You look great, better than any of those fat old daddies she hangs out with."

Bird looked reproachfully at her friend. *So you've seen Candy, but never told me.*

"That's cruel, Jazmín. I don't like that."

Jazmín rolled her eyes. "Sorr-*y*. The strong, large, full-bodied women she's kneeling before to worship. How's that?"

Bird said nothing, just sat there. She was withdrawing into a sullen, stubborn mood. Jazmín ran her fingers through her dark hair.

"Come on, Bird. If she shows up, she'll see what she's been missing. Will you go?"

Then Bird remembered: *I told her not to tell me if she saw Candy, now I'm mad because she* didn't.

At last, Bird nodded. Jazmín, whose mouth was open, about to try another tack, blinked. *Was Bird saying yes?* She stared disbelieving at her friend. It was hard even getting her out to see a movie. Cautiously, she asked, "Really? You'll go?"

"Sure. Is it all right if I just bring bread?"

"Oh, they'll *love* your bread." Jazmín jumped up, grinning. "Let's celebrate. I'll get New York steaks for us. M-m-m-m. How long has it been since you had a good steak? I'll come get you at five." She hurried out to her car, Bird slowly following, already second-guessing her decision. "Don't forget, wear something western." She waved excitedly before jumping into her car and tearing off.

Bird watched until Jazmín was out of sight. She couldn't believe she'd agreed. She went back inside. It had been so long since she'd been to a party. How did she feel about it? She paced the length of her apartment.

Am I afraid? Of what? She reached the corner, turned right, and then paced the kitchen. *That I'll see her again and find myself back where I was when she first dumped me.* She turned around and walked the L again. *That I haven't grown at all. That I'll find she was right to move on when she did.*

Worst of all, that the last two, grindingly painful years would have to be endured all over again. And she wasn't at all certain that she *was* over her. Or that she even wanted to be.

But I can't go on like this for the rest of my life. You can't hide from pain; one way or another, it'll find you. Anyway, I kind of want to go. Barbecue; music; old friends. Anyway, get a grip. She probably won't even be there, and I'll feel stupid for all this wasted agonizing. And yes. It's true. I want to see her.

Western theme. There was actually a recipe for cowboy bread, *Pan de Campo*. It was easy. She put the ingredients together and the bread baked as she plowed through another chapter of *Anna Karenina*.

Late in the afternoon she took a shower. Then in spite of the fact that scents were frowned on in the community, she patted on some *Outlaw* aftershave—a gift from Candy—at the pulse points: behind her ear, at the base of her throat, on her wrist, and the opposite inner elbow, as Candy had shown her.

She put on her favorite cowboy shirt, black with embroidered yokes and cuffs. The cut emphasized her narrow waist and developed shoulders. Jazmín had brought it back for her from Mexico, and the detailed light blue embroidery lit up her blue eyes. Bird put on a pair of black jeans and cowboy boots. But her short dark hair looked like bed death, and there was no time for a haircut. She tried trimming it herself, made a mess of it. She brushed and combed it different ways, and was crying when Jazmín showed up.

"My hair!"

Jazmín stood behind her and looked in the mirror. She raked her hands through it and smoothed down the back, got the scissors and evened it out. She grabbed the blow dryer and blew away the strands of hair. Then she put her own cowboy hat on Bird.

"There, you look fine. Let's go." Jazmín picked up the bread, neatly wrapped in a gingham napkin, and dragged Bird out of the house.

They were early. There was only one other guest hanging out in the kitchen, stirring something on the stove.

"Bird!" Helene cried, giving her a big hug. "Ohmigod, I can't believe it. How have you been?" Then she was all business. "I'm glad you're early, I can use some help. Would you three carry the sofa into the backyard? It's not heavy. That'll give people room for dancing in the front room."

"Bird's the woman for the job," Jazmín said. "You should see how strong she's gotten." She tried to grab Bird's biceps, but Bird jerked her arm away.

"Cut it out," Bird said, embarrassed.

Bird, Jazmín, and Kahleeya, the other early-bird, bumped, laughed, and wrestled the couch out onto the deck and down the steps to the backyard. Jazmín went back inside while Bird and Kahleeya replaced the cushions and tucked the spread over the couch. When done, Bird glanced at Kahleeya's cowboy shirt and did a second take. Kahleeya laughed.

"I didn't have a cowboy shirt, so I got a plain white shirt from the thrift store and drew a yoke and horse heads with colored markers. The belt I got for three dollars in Lubbock. Isn't it cool?" It had heart-shaped conchos.

Kahleeya had long braids accentuated with glazed beads here and there. She wore an African collar of blue beads, and she had freckles that stood out against her dark skin. Kind of cute behind the big glasses, but of course, Bird wasn't emotionally available. She turned to watch the next arrivals coming into the yard.

"Are you waiting for your girlfriend?" Kahleeya asked.

"I don't have one. Why?"

"Just the way you keep looking at the gate."

Feeling busted, Bird went back inside where Helene put her to work breaking ice and filling a chest with drinks. When she carried it outside, more people had arrived and were standing in groups, talking. She saw Tori from work. A transwoman in a checked cowboy shirt and red kerchief, she looked exactly like Howdy Doody with a buzz cut. They were just saying hi when Candy came through the gate.

Bird froze; the moment seemed to stretch for an age. Her ex looked fabulous in a pink cowgirl outfit with matching nail polish and lipstick, black boots and hat. Bird had forgotten those slightly crooked front teeth, and how once she would have laid down her life for a smile.

Candy's eyes widened when they locked eyes. She stopped short. Bird's heart dropped to her gut. A moment later Candy was joined by a big, handsome daddy in a tan cowboy shirt, with a large turquoise nugget bolo, and black leather vest. Her jeans were also made of leather, and her cowboy boots were probably seven-stitch. Bird immediately felt plain and puny.

"Hi, Bird," Candy cooed.

Unable to speak for the lump in her throat, Bird gave a quick nod, and hoped she looked cool.

Candy presented the butch. "This is Max."

Of course she'd be with a "Max." Maximum. Maximal. Max-a-Million.

"So you're Bird," Max said, giving a strong handshake. *Candy told her about me?* Max leaned in, scrutinizing Bird's face. "Are you wearing mascara, ladyboi?"

Damn—crying always makes me look like I'm wearing makeup.

"No, I'm naturally beautiful," she quipped, batting her eyes at Max, who frowned and straightened. Candy laughed. Max went to fetch a beer.

Candy looked Bird over as if she was a full box of chocolates. Bird was discomfited. She looked around the yard for Jazmín. *Where is she? I should have told her not to leave me alone.*

"It's been so long. What have you been doing? Still at the hotline?"

Bird realized her hands were shaking, so she stuck them into her back pockets. "I work at the Garden of Eve now. It's a woman-owned, organic produce distributor." *At least I'm not stuttering.*

"Women-owned," Max, rejoining them, hooted. "Save your money, maybe you can take a Mexican vacation by the time you retire." She popped the beer. "Winter's a great time to go, wouldn't you say, honey?"

Candy glanced at Bird, didn't respond.

"Actually, the pay is pretty good," Tori volunteered. "And great benefits. Every year they send a few employees on an Olivia cruise."

"You two work together I take it," Max said.

Tori nodded. "Bird's a great boss. She'll finish our shift if one of us has to leave."

"You're the boss?" Candy asked. Bird nodded like it was no big deal.

"What do you do, Max?" Tori asked.

"Lawyer. Personal injury."

"Oh, an ambulance chaser."

"I hate that term," Max said.

"All work is sacred," someone stated. It was Kahleeya, standing nearby.

"Thank you, ma'am," Max said, offering a little bow. "The fact is, sometimes women need strong representation, and I'm the person to step up for them." She pulled out a business card and tucked it into Tori's breast pocket. "Give me a call if you get injured on that job." She turned to Kahleeya. "And what do you do?"

"Teach art to autistic children."

Max whistled. "Sounds like Sisyphean work."

"It isn't. Sisyphus rolled a boulder up a hill, only to have it roll back down, making his work futile."

"If you say so," Max said.

"Maybe you mean herculean, in which case, I would agree with you."

Bird envied Kahleeya's easy certainty before the overbearing Max.

"Art speaks to everyone," Kahleeya added. "It's a way to break through to some children."

Candy looked at Bird suddenly, and caught her staring. Bird flushed and cleared her throat. "Uh, are—are you a lawyer now?"

Max looked at Candy, raising an eyebrow.

"I'm a paralegal. School's on a back burner for now," Candy said, tossing her hair. "Why did you leave the hotline?"

Bird shrugged. *None of your business.* "It was time."

Music blared from the house. Helene looked out the window and beckoned excitedly to Bird. Relieved for an excuse to get away, she headed into the house. Tori followed, and to Bird's chagrin, so did Candy. Bird had done line dancing every week before meeting Candy, and together they had become the toast of the lesbian Country Western dance set.

Candy took the place in line next to Bird. As soon as Candy began dancing, the steps came back to Bird. Others joined in. Bird felt good to be dancing again; maybe she'd get back to it. The line dancing gave way to partner dancing, and Candy insisted Bird be hers.

"Like old times," she said.

Bird hesitated at the thought of having Candy in her arms again, but she feared losing face by refusing. She set her jaw, put one arm behind Candy's shoulders and went through the motions around Helene's large living room.

"He-ey, lighten up, Bird," Candy said. "You never used to be this stiff."

Candy kept looking up at her, their lips too close. *Is she* flirting *with me?* Bird wondered. If Candy kissed her—then what? She already had lost so much to this woman. She glanced around.

Where's Max? Why isn't she keeping an eye on her tarty girlfriend?

And it *wasn't* like old times, and never would be again. Not because Candy had moved on, but because Bird knew it really was over. Maybe it was meeting Max, seeing the two of them together. Bird really was out of her league, always had been. Bird turned Candy under her arm, resumed dancing.

But if Bird was honest with herself, their relationship hadn't been as idyllic as she had romanticized. Even at her best, Bird had been afraid to say much around Candy, fearful of mispronouncing a word, venturing a stupid opinion, or revealing how much she *didn't* know. Candy could be condescending. Bird used to hope her excellent listening skills made up for being boring. How was that to endure in a relationship, always wondering if the other high heel was going to drop?

Furthermore, they wanted different things out of life; Bird was a homebody, liked having a simple, serene life. Candy wanted more excitement, to go out all the time. Even more important, they had different values. Bird would never objectify someone; and she'd never leave her dangling if she was done in a relationship.

After that dance Bird relaxed, and actually began enjoying herself. She realized they danced together so well, not because they were natural partners as she had always believed, but because Bird was an excellent leader.

"I've missed you," Candy whispered. Then, "I'm *so* sorry."

Bird glanced at her, surprised to see tears in her eyes. *She means it.* She pretended not to notice, but something let go of her heart. She gave Candy's hand a quick squeeze.

I forgive you.

Bird was amazed. She had never realized there had been a lot to forgive. Any crimes of the heart Candy had committed, Bird had found a way to justify, or worse, take upon herself. She had kept the memory of their love warm—*why?* In case she came back? Although the love may have been real and mutual in the beginning, the woman had ended up using her, then throwing her away. Candy was not the woman she wanted to give her life to after all. She wouldn't give her life away again for anyone.

The next dance was a slow one and Candy made as if to dance with Bird again, but Max had finally come into the room. Relieved, Bird bowed to Candy and gave her hand to Max, then went back out to join the party.

She was quaking inside, feeling as if she had narrowly missed being hit by a car, or having a stove dropped on her. She took a deep breath, looked around at all the people she hadn't seen in so long, smiling, nodding, saying hello. But she was looking for Jazmín. All that time Bird had wallowed in isolated misery, friends had drifted away. Only Jazmín had continued to support her, patiently listening, bringing books or DVDs over, inviting her out. She deserved to hear the latest chapter of Bird's soap opera. She found Jazmín grilling at the huge gas barbecue.

"You okay?" Jazmín asked. "How'd it go?" She put their steaks to the side and set down the grilling fork.

"How was it for you, meeting the new girlfriend?"

They walked the length of the yard. Bird shrugged.

"Max is all right. I hope she treats her well."

"They're polyamorous," Jazmín said. "If you haven't suffered enough, you could always take a ride on the poly-go-round."

Bird shook her head, wondering at people who could afford to take love for granted. Just one more way she and Candy weren't compatible.

They returned to the grill. Jazmín put their steaks on plates and Bird, with sudden appetite, filled her plate from the loaded picnic table. She ate a date stuffed with cream cheese from a fruit plate.

"Jazmín, she *apologized.*"

"Oh, right. And you're just going to forgive her?"

Bird thought about it. "Yeah, why hold a grudge?" *Like I've been holding on to the sanctity of "our love" all this time.*

"Excuse me." Kahleeya held a steaming pot. Balancing her plate in one hand, Bird pushed dishes aside to make room on the table. "Try my drunken beans. I made them from scratch."

"How did you get the beans drunk?" Bird asked. Encouraged by Kahleeya's easy laughter, Bird picked up another date and held it to Kahleeya's lips. "Want a date?"

"Sure," Kahleeya replied, opening her mouth, and they both giggled.

Jazmín invited Kahleeya to sit with them while they ate, and found a place to sit in the shade of an apple tree. They hung out, talking and laughing. When they were done eating, Jazmín took their empty plates.

"I'm going to talk to Marian. I'll put these in the compost bag for you." She winked at Bird.

Bird glanced up at the house. Candy and Max were near the large back window.

"You still care about her?" Kahleeya asked.

Bird hid a smile. "Is it obvious?"

Kahleeya nodded. Bird thought about it.

"I guess, but not in the same way. It's just … this is the first time I've seen her since we broke up. Got me a little rattled, you know?"

"Understandable. She's magnificent."

Bird blinked. *Yeah, she was.*

"I don't know . . . I thought she was the love of my life, but seeing her again, I realize how different we are."

Kahleeya nodded, waited.

"Our relationship was healing at the time, but probably wouldn't have worked out in the long run." Bird was surprised at how she was opening up; Kahleeya was easy to talk to.

"I don't understand love," Kahleeya said, shaking her head. "I once waited ages for someone to get over her long-term relationship. Then, when she was finally available, I wasn't interested anymore. Isn't that weird?"

"No weirder than moping around for two years."

Kahleeya's frown made her look wise. "You weren't moping. You were taking time to grieve. Most people rush into another relationship because they're in pain, but they're not really ready for a new relationship."

Bird liked Kahleeya's insight, and added some of her own:

"Well, maybe you were grieving too, while you waited. Not being with the one you wanted. Maybe waiting is moving on too, only you don't realize it."

Now Kahleeya smiled. "I thought it was just the annoying nature of a contrary universe."

"That too," Bird admitted. "But we don't ever stand still, we keep growing."

Of course, Bird had known she had been grieving all that time. *Maybe it wasn't Candy I was mourning, but myself. For the child I was, who was criminally used, then abandoned.*

"I was such a fool," Bird said, shaking her head.

"If she betrayed you, that doesn't make you a fool," Kahleeya said. "That's on her. There's nothing dishonorable about having a trusting heart."

Wow, Bird thought. *I never thought of that.* But enough of this heavy talk; Bird wanted to enjoy the party.

"Hey, want to play a game of horseshoes?"

"Sure."

Bird glanced up at the house again. Candy and Max were out on the deck now. Candy was watching them, while Max talked to her. Bird waved goodbye, and walked to the back of the yard with Kahleeya, where Bird tossed a horseshoe and scored a ringer first try.

Of course, she had played many times and had some skill. She glanced at Kahleeya's belt.

"I once heard when you wear hearts, it attracts love. Have you found that to be true?"

"Actually I have, now that you mention it. Want to borrow it?"

"No, I think it's already working." Grinning, Bird handed a horseshoe to Kahleeya.

The Agenda

KAMRYN MET HER at a speed-dating event. Although several women had wanted to be matched with Kamryn, Priscilla had been the only one Kamryn was interested in.

From that first meeting, Kamryn began planning how she would groom her as her perfect little slave, then show her off to the SM community. Everything about her suggested submissive: she was young, partial to *Princess* cologne and flower gem stud earrings. The purses she carried were small, and she wore ballet style flats. Her pink lipstick and nail polish were a little too aggressive—if pink could be aggressive—Kamryn thought, although they did set off the girl's dusky skin.

Even her name was demure: Priscilla, Americanized from Pahila, although she wanted to be called Pichu. Her family was from Mumbai. Kamryn thought Peachie, or maybe Prissy, would be a better name for an obedient little pet, even more so because Pichu hated it. Her body was small-boned, although she was taller than Kamryn. She *liked* tall submissives. The bigger they were, the farther they had to fall. It was hard to believe Pichu climbed poles for the electric company.

That Pichu was newly out was a big advantage; she was still learning about the lesbian demimonde. She hadn't even known what "poly" meant. Kamryn would be the one to teach her all the "ropes." She would leave dates with Pichu floating on a cloud of fantastic speculation that carried her well into the night.

"Why don't you grow your hair out?" Kamryn asked, after a few dates. "I love long hair."

"I keep my hair short because I like it that way," Pichu told her. "It's easy to take care of, and it stays out of my eyes."

They still hadn't had sex after dating for a month. Kamryn was in no hurry; she was enjoying the buildup. Besides, withholding sex was part of her grooming strategy, although Pichu hadn't seemed to mind. Her game of playing hard to get—which is what Kamryn guessed it was—wouldn't work with her.

After two months, Kamryn produced a book and set it on Pichu's table.

"I brought something for you to read."

A Complete and Total Beginner's Guide to SM.

"What is SM?"

Kamryn laughed. "You're so cute." She kissed her good-night. "Just read the book."

Pichu didn't mention the book on subsequent dates. Furthermore, despite several suggestions, Pichu hadn't started growing her hair out. Kamryn was getting more and more annoyed. What's more, although their relationship had finally progressed to vanilla sex, Kamryn realized Pichu was dating other women when she called one evening and heard another woman's voice in the background, calling Pichu "sweetie."

Is that why she wasn't insisting on sex? She's been getting it elsewhere? Kamryn wondered. While Kamryn herself was poly, she would have appreciated it if Pichu had mentioned her other "interests."

Finally Kamryn decided the status quo had gone on long enough. They were on a date, downtown, holding hands, dressed to the nines: Pichu in a pretty pink tulip dress, Kamryn in high butch, a tailored black suit, purple shirt, and wingtips.

"So . . . what did you think about that book I gave you?"

Pichu nodded. "It was interesting."

Ah—so she finally read it.

"I've been dying to see the movie," Pichu said. "I heard the supporting actress gets into horrible situations, but comes up with brilliant solutions . . ."

Kamryn was miffed she'd changed the subject.

"Just a minute. I asked you a question—"

"FAGGOT!"

A big, bald ogre wearing a *Redneck 24-7* T-shirt glowered at them. Kamryn took Priscilla's arm protectively and started to hurry her away, but Priscilla stopped and glared at the man. She disengaged her arm, handed her flowered purse to Kamryn, and faced the man, fists squarely on her hips.

"In the first place, the term you want is 'dyke,'" she said. "In the second place, I think people should just accept each other, but if you don't like the fact that we're lesbians, I'll be happy to fight you."

Disbelieving, the big man, looked from Pichu to Kamryn.

"Pichu, please," Kamryn hissed. "Let's get out of here."

The man burst out laughing. "What'sa matter, *boy*friend can't defend herself?"

As Pichu marched to confront him, Kamryn grabbed her and dragged her away. Around the corner, she handed Pichu back her purse. Butch tops didn't hold purses.

"Pichu, always walk away from stuff like that," she scolded.

"Shouldn't we defend ourselves as gays?"

"No. Never, ever escalate. Weren't you afraid he'd hit you?"

"No."

Actually, Kamryn had been afraid he'd hit *her*.

KAMRYN CALLED PICHU and said she had a surprise for her. She was intentionally over an hour late. Pichu was angry.

That's what I like, a little attitude, Kamryn thought. She set a black leather satchel on the floor next to the sofa chair and handed Pichu a shopping bag.

"I was late because I was buying you some gifts. Go put them on," she ordered.

Pichu looked into the bag. "What is it?"

"Uh-uh, go change, Prissy."

"Don't call me that."

"I'll call you whatever I want. Now do as I say."

Kamryn turned Pichu around and pushed her in the direction of her bedroom.

While Kamryn waited, she helped herself to a glass of wine, and then sat in a sofa chair, savoring the wait. But it was a long wait. Finally Kamryn was about to go see what was taking so long, when Pichu came out wearing a short black maid's outfit with a full skirt, frilly petticoat, apron, and maid's cap.

Kamryn looked her over. She had spared no expense. The skirt showed off Pichu's long legs, and the black patent leather heels made them seem even longer. But Pichu wore the outfit sloppily. The dress hadn't been straightened, the belt was loose, and the maid's hat perched lopsided on top of Pichu's dark hair.

If she had done what I told her, she would have enough hair by now to attach it properly.

"So what are we doing here?" Pichu asked. "Shouldn't we talk about it first?"

"No questions," Kamryn barked. "Refill my glass. Then take off my shoes and give me a foot massage."

Pichu looked at Kamryn, taken aback.

"Do it," Kamryn ordered.

Pichu waited, glaring at Kamryn.

"My wine?" Kamryn said, tapping the glass with a fingernail.

Finally Pichu went over and picked up the bottle, raising it high above the glass, slopping wine over the table. *Perfect*, thought Kamryn.

"Clean that up."

"No," Pichu said.

It begins, Kamryn thought happily. *The games, the power struggle.*

"I'm going to spank that attitude right out of you," she said. "Go find something for me to beat you with."

Pichu glanced around, and then went into the next room. She came back and handed Kamryn a used sheet of typing paper.

"There you go, Stud. Whale away."

"Oh, a smart ass," Kamryn said, hiding a smile. "I'm going to teach you a lesson. Come here and get over my lap."

But Pichu stood her ground. She crossed her arms over her chest. "Kiss my ass."

"Well, now you're talking. You'd get your ass kissed sooner if you behaved. Right now, you're only racking up discipline, my dear."

"You know, if you want to play, we really should talk about it first," Pichu said again.

Kamryn shrugged. "Talking takes all the fun and mystery out of it."

"Well then, you should know that I'm a top," Pichu said.

"*What?* You can't be!" Kamryn yelled.

"Well, I am. And you've had your fun." Pichu took off the maid's hat and threw it on the floor, followed by the apron.

"I didn't—" Kamryn began, but Pichu grabbed Kamryn's satchel.

"What do you have in here, anyway?"

"Hey, that's private!" Kamryn reached out to take the satchel, but Pichu held it away from her. She looked inside, pulled out a black riding crop.

"You've got to be joking." She swung it through the air. "Were you going to use this on me?" She brandished the whip over Kamryn.

"Actually, it's just for—"

She slapped it against the arm rest, right next to Kamryn's hand. "Silence! Get on your knees."

"What?"

"Do it!" Pichu demanded.

"But, these pants—"

"Take them off."

Kamryn hesitated, totally disoriented. This wasn't going at all the way she had spent countless hours fantasizing. She had always been the dominator, and had never done a switch.

Well, they say you should try both roles.

She stripped to her boxers and wife-beater, feeling skinny and vulnerable out of her power suit and tie.

Pichu sat in the armchair.

"Now clean up the wine, dog."

"I, uh . . ." Kamryn's submissives did her housework. Pichu looked into the satchel again and pulled out a ten-inch yellow dildo in the shape of banana. Pichu smiled.

"Get to work, or I will use this on you."

Kamryn quickly found a sponge under the sink and wiped up the spill. Pichu was reading *Popular Mechanics*.

"The floor too," she said, without even looking up. "Then bring me a clean wineglass and pour me some wine."

After Kamryn complied, Pichu put her to work.

By the end of the evening, Pichu's floors were done and the toilet was spotless. Objections or bad attitudes were met with a swift kick to her backside or swat with the whip. And Kamryn hadn't even gotten to "service" her "mistress." Worst of all, at the end of the evening, after Kamryn was dressed, tired and sweaty, sore knees and butt and throbbing pussy, she said, "Did you like that, ma'am? Maybe next time we can do a switch?"

Pichu shook her head. "There is not going to *be* a next time, Kamryn. Thanks for the housework. Oh, and don't call me again." She slammed the door before Kamryn was barely through it.

Pichu wouldn't answer calls, texts, or emails. Naturally this made Kamryn decide she was profoundly in love. Never had a woman gotten the upper hand in their games. Pichu was truly a woman after her own heart. Kamryn hand-wrote impassioned letters, assuring Pichu she'd learned her lesson, begging for forgiveness, saying she would be her faithful slave, would even give up her other lovers for her: still no response.

Finally Kamryn hid behind a tree across the street from Pichu's house, waiting for her. Pichu showed up at last, coming down the street with a big butch. Undaunted, Kamryn bolted across the street—nearly getting hit by car—and ignoring the butch, went down on bended knee in front of Pichu.

"Pichu, please give me another chance."

The women stopped short. The butch grabbed the collar of Kamryn's jacket and dragged her to her feet. "Stand up, friend. You look like an idiot."

"Excuse me, but I'm talking to Pichu," Kamryn sputtered.

"Yeah, she told me about you," she said. "Want me to get rid of her for you, babe?"

"Don't bother," Pichu said, walking around Kamryn and going up to her porch, followed by the butch. Kamryn scrambled after them.

"Pichu, please, talk to me!" Kamryn begged. "Would you at least tell me what your resentments against me are?" She didn't think there could be many.

Pichu, unlocking her front door, paused.

"All right, Kamryn, I'll tell you." Pichu opened the door. "Wait inside for me please," she told the butch. Then she closed the door and held a hand out to the bench on her porch. "Have a seat."

Kamryn sat and patted the bench next to her, but Pichu remained standing over her.

"Aside from being a complete and total wus, I didn't appreciate how you tried to change me, bugging me about my hair, and calling me Prissy, which I told you I hate. You thought I was submissive, and then acted on that assumption, right? I learned all the terms when I read that book. I read a few other books on the subject too, by the way. But you never tried to find out if it was true. You just launched right into making me your slave. Did *you* read that book you gave me?"

"Uh—I . . ." Kamryn stammered.

"I didn't think so," Pichu said. "I might have wanted to experiment with SM if we'd talked about it first. That's what it says to do in the book.

"When I met you at that speed dating event, I found you handsome and intriguing. When we first started dating, I thought you were the silent, deep type. But when we went out, you wouldn't say very much. When you weren't off in some kind of dreamland, you behaved like you were the Goddess's gift to women.

"You hardly asked me anything about myself. If I tried to talk about something I was interested in, you spaced out. Even now, after all this time, you still don't know that I'm a Hindu, and I have a Master's in Women's Studies. I have a black belt in Amazon Kung Fu. I'm a member of the Sierra Club, and I volunteer at the food bank. I realized you were hot, but the oven was empty.

"I was thinking of ending it off you, and then you pulled that stunt with the costume. It was fun, but after that, I was done. I suspect you're all about fantasy, Kamryn. Even now, the only reason you want me isn't for who I am, but because I won't have you."

Pichu went to her door but before going inside she said, "Let me tell you something, bozo. I did not become a lesbian just so a butch could start telling me what to do. If I wanted that, I would have married an Indian man. "Now good night, Kamryn, and don't contact me again or I will get a restraining order."

Pichu went into her flat, slammed the door, and turned off the porchlight for good measure.

Kamryn walked home, nursing her broken heart and wounded ego. In her book of life, Pichu would always be the one who got away. The only woman who could top her. The only one Kamryn was willing to switch for.

But man oh man, what a woman. So adorable when she played dominant!

TALES OF
A SOUTHERN BUTCH

Johnny Magnolia

Lightning Strikes Twice

South Alabama, 1975

DEEP, DARK RUMBLING in the sky, like Titans breaking furniture in the clouds.

"Sounds like a storm," I said. I ran to the window.

Although it was high summer, heavy yellow-brown clouds were gathering over the hills. I was at our uncle's beach cottage with my older brother Andy, and cousins Ralphy and Gigi. Our parents were off golfing for the day, and we'd been sitting around bored all afternoon, Andy strumming his guitar.

"Let's go outside and watch the storm," I said.

"OK," Ralphy said.

"No," Gigi said. She was the youngest. "Are you crazy? You're not supposed to go outside in a thunderstorm."

"Oh, Gigi, don't be so uptight. Nothing's going to happen . "Come on, we can smoke some dope. I have some really great sinsemilla from California." I dug a skinny pinner joint from my knapsack. It was bent, but definitely smokeable. I went back out to the front room, waving it.

"Yeah, let's do it!" Andy said, putting down the guitar. We headed outside, except for Gigi. I paused in the doorway. "Coming?"

She shook her head. "Uh-uh, not a chance. You guys are nuts."

We headed out to the large flat area behind the house where people parked their cars. A creek surrounded by blackberry bushes boarded one side of the yard and ran down to the beach. We were about a hundred yards from the cottage. I lit the joint, took a huge toke, then passed it to my brother. I could feel the smoke all the way through my shoulders. I held it in as long as I could before finally, reluctantly, letting it pour out through my nose. Ralphy took a hit and coughed more than inhaled.

"I thought California dope was supposed to be mellow," he groused.

"This *is* mellow," I said. "You're just used to that crummy shit we get out here."

The rush was working its way up my neural pathways to my brain, which started to feel tight and tiny. The day had turned gray, the air still hot, and a wind was coming up. Everything stood out in sharp contrast from the hills. I could feel my pupils expanding in my head. We watched God's light show jotting all over the hills, turning the clouds mauve, electric blue and green.

I looked up at the house. Gigi was watching us from the big back window. Ralphy passed the reefer to me again. I pointed at it and beckoned to her. She just stood there watching us, missing that great weed.

"What's a 'gink'?" Ralphy asked out of the blue.

I giggled. "A 'gink'?" I asked. The weed was giving me the laughies. "I don't know. Where did you hear that?"

"*Dear Abby*. She called someone a 'gink.'"

"Dear Abby said *that*?" I roared with laughter. Ralphy laughed too. The weed was doing its job.

My brother exhaled a big cloud of sens that looked blue and cool to my hot, hard eyes. "A 'gink' is a moron," he said. "Kind of like us, right now."

"*We're* ginks!" I said, and we laughed so much, it was hard to smoke. The joint came to me again.

"Out-a-sight," I said, about nothing in particular. Of course, this was back in the seventies and everyone talked like that. I took another deep huff. Suddenly my eyes filled with light and the inside of my head turned white and there was a huge KAA-BOOOOM!

I opened my eyes. All I could see was sky. I sat up. I was on the hood of Andy's car. Gigi was running toward me, shirt flying. She was crying.

"I told you guys not to come out here. I thought you all were dead!" She sounded far away, like she was still inside.

"Talk louder, I can't hear you." I had to yell to hear myself. "What happened?"

"Lightning struck the beach. Didn't you see it?"

"No." Then I remembered the light and the crack of thunder. I slid off the hood. My leather vest had been blown off; my boots too. I looked around. My brother was sitting on the ground, shaking his head.

"Look at you!" Gigi shouted, pointing at my head.

I touched my head. My hair, shoulder-length and curly, now stood straight out from my head, bristling with static.

"Hey look at me!" I yelled. "I have an afro." The lightning hadn't done anything to cancel the high. My brother had finer hair than me, and it stood out from his head too.

Gigi was looking around. "Where's Ralphy?"

We both looked, calling, but he had disappeared.

"Ralphy! RALPH!" Gigi screamed. She ran around frantically while my brother and I recovered, laughing and walking around in dazes. Finally we heard groaning, and then Ralphy stuck his head out from the midst of the sticker bushes. We helped him out, all of us, including Ralphy, laughing. Except for Gigi, who had stopped crying and was mad at us now. She stomped back up to the house.

"Hey, what happened to the doob?" I asked suddenly.

"You had it last," Andy said. "Just before the lightning."

I didn't have it anymore, and it wasn't anywhere near Andy's car. We searched and searched. That most excellent joint, sent by a friend in California, had only been half smoked, and we never found it. It was the one downer that afternoon.

THAT LIGHTNING BOLT had more than just the immediate effects. For one, my hair stayed straight. Although I'd always hated it being so curly, it was actually worse now, making my stupid cowlicks really obvious unless I combed my hair straight back and wore it in a tight, low ponytail.

The other change was, although I'd had boyfriends, and swinging with married couples was the kinkiest I ever got, suddenly I was only looking at women. I'd sit in café windows and watch them pass, my meal untouched as I suffered a different kind of hunger. I studied the movement of their legs and hips and watched their breasts until my mouth watered and tears rolled down behind my dark glasses. I rode crowded buses so I had an excuse to get up close and sniffy. I wanted to touch a woman so bad, I even attended Pentecostal services where I could hold passionate women and holler "hallelujah!"

I told my mother I was a lesbian. She just laughed.

"At least you're not pregnant," she said. "Get me a beer, will you?"

I read old paperbacks of lesbian fiction only found in the porn stores of big cities. I wasted time prowling the secret bars at the edge of town. The women there knew mostly shame for what we were, like clichés in homosexual literature. I went home with them, but never stayed a whole night.

At last I checked my mother into rehab, shore off my hair, sold my dresses and books, and took a Greyhound west. I wanted to live out loud where gays own a whole city and celebrate difference by dancing in the streets. A whole month of events aimed at self-pride! Advertising ourselves with every shade of purple! J. fucking Christ—a *dyke* march! And most unbelievably: thousands upon thousands of supporters cheering us onward!

I don't smoke dope anymore. And I stay inside during storms.

Beelze-bud or, The Witch and the Fly

I ONCE RENTED a room from a witch. She lived in Berkeley and her house was a dark brown, shingled place at the end of a cul-de-sac. The garden was overgrown, the backyard fronted upon a creek, and big trees hunkered around the place like old women around a medicine kettle. But the room was large and cheap, and I had been living in my car. My girlfriend had kicked me out, saying I drank too much and was mentally ill. I didn't drink much more than she did, and what she was calling mental illness was probably just Attention Deficit Disorder, for which I'd just been diagnosed. But she was tired of dealing with me, and besides she already had a new girlfriend.

I didn't know my new landlady-roommate was a witch, and if I hadn't been distracted by shock and upset and ADD, I might have noticed the paintings of dark goddesses, the altar with a knife, bell, and chalice, the old books with cracked leather covers. Blaise was in her sixties. She was spindly, bowlegged, and hunchbacked. She had one pop-eye, while the other was squinty with a pale moon. She had large furry ears, blubbery lips, skin that was pale and crepe-y. Her long fingernails were thick and ridged like toenails. She wore big, lace-up shoes, and every week she went to the beauty parlor to get her yellowish, spider-webby hair done in a pompadour and those scary nails painted a blood red color.

Once when I got home late, I walked into a living room alight with candles and seven or eight women drinking wine and smoking. They were all dressed in black.

"Oh, I'm so sorry," I said. "Did someone die?"

The women burst into laughter.

"No, dear," Blaise said. "No one has died. Yet."

Everyone laughed again.

A woman with long, black hair with a silver streak, wearing high heels, came out of the kitchen. She loomed over me. "Is this your new roommate, Blaise?" she asked, breathing alcohol into my face. "Want to join us, cutes?"

"Leave her alone, Tab," Blaise said, taking her arm and leading her back to the group. "We have important business this evening."

Had I been in a better mental place I might have followed up on her invitation, but my wounds were still fresh. I went to hide in my room.

After a while everything got quiet. When I opened the door, the living room was empty. I helped myself to a glass of wine from one of the open bottles. I heard eerie chanting—it sounded like noooh noooh noooh, neee neee neee, noooh noooh noooh, neee neee neee—a chant I had heard Blaise crooning to herself as we watched TV. I looked out the back window and saw the women in the back yard, each holding a candle in one hand, with their other on the next woman's shoulder as they performed a spooky, serpentine dance in the dark.

Although my landlady was kind of strange, and I had found myself in a hotbed of witches who were always dropping by to exchange spells like recipes, Blaise was a good landlady. She was kind, and never threatened me with magic. I got used to full moons when the witches would gather, whispering and chanting until long after midnight, while I stayed in my room.

At that time I worked for a large vegetable distributorship. I drove a forklift and carried boxes in and out of big refrigerators. One day I found a fat little caterpillar among the lettuce. It was about two inches long, clumsy, had little fur, with pale pink skin and what looked like big, staring, cartoon eyes on its bulbous head but were just camouflage. When I tried to pick it up it reared back on its hind legs and flailed its tiny legs at me, as if warning me off.

I put it in a jar with lots of lettuce and, hoping it would develop into a butterfly, took it home. After a few weeks, the caterpillar stopped eating. It went to the bottom of the jar and seemed to melt, turning into a kind of gross mass that still had its caterpillar head and forelegs. I couldn't tell if it was dying, or if that was the beginning of its transformation. Eventually it made a cocoon and I settled in for a long wait.

Spring came, and one day I came home to find the caterpillar had emerged from its cocoon. It wasn't a butterfly. It was a dark, hairy, blue-black fly with a waspish waist, and it was big, almost an inch long. Its eyes were iridescent green. It was grotesquely beautiful.

The next day, the fly was even bigger. It had eaten everything in the jar and stood at the bottom, being very still. I didn't know what to do with it. I went to the library and looked at all their books on caterpillars and flies, especially the ones for the Bay Area and Northern California. I couldn't find anything like it. I tried to remember where that lettuce had come from; the distributorship got produce from everywhere, including south of the border. I figured it had to be non-native because insects in the Bay Area didn't grow that big. What if I let it go and it mated with another monster fly and infested the area? Most importantly, what would it do to *me* if I let it out? So I left it in the bottle.

The next day it was even bigger. It had started to move, and now it was crawling restlessly around the jar, hanging on the side with its head by the air-holes. I had to make a decision about what to do with it; creepy as it was, it was cruel to leave it in the bottle, slowly starving. I was going to have to kill it.

I took it into the yard, trying to decide how to do it. Fill it with water and drown it? Asphyxiation with insecticide?

"Whatcha got there?"

I hadn't noticed Blaise, wearing green gardening gloves, crouching among her plants. What I had thought were weeds when I first moved in, were actually intentionally cultivated herbs and flowers. She had on—I swear: a dark brown hat with a floppy brim and little pointy crown.

"A bug," I said. "I, uh, grew it from a caterpillar. I didn't realize it would turn into a fly."

I handed the jar to her. She turned it this way and that in front of her big eye.

"Well, handsome, look at you," she said. "Interesting. I've never seen anything like him." She tapped the bottle and the fly started buzzing angrily, vibrating its wings. She began crooning: "Noooh noooh noooh, neee neee neee, noooh noooh noooh, neee neee neee." The fly settled down again. "What are you going to do with him?"

"I, uh, was going to get rid of it."

"Get *rid* of it? After you raised him from a cocoon?"

"I—ummmm ... I thought maybe I'd take it to a wildlife center and see if they want it for scientific purposes," like euthanasia. "Unless ... would *you* like to have it?"

"Me? Why . . . do you mean it? I can have him?" Blaise held the jar up and turned it from side to side, admiringly. "Why, thank you, Johnny, that's so generous of you. What do you think of that, handsome?" she asked the fly. He buzzed again. This time, I swear, he sounded happy.

"I'm glad you can give him a good home, Blaise," I said, before nipping inside, because I could see Blaise was starting to unscrew the jar.

"I'm going to call you Eckstrum," Blaise told the fly.

Of course I thought the fly would take off as soon as she opened the jar, but she must have put some kind of calming spell on him, because I saw—safely through the screen door—Eckstrum sitting on Blaise's finger, and she was feeding him a blade of grass. Thus, Blaise solved my problem with what to do with that horrible insect.

At first she kept him in a brass cricket cage, letting him out once in a while to sit on her hand or shoulder. Then she started letting him out more and more, talking to him like an evil genius.

Then one full moon evening I got home, and the house was full of witches as usual. They were gathered around the table, staring at Eckstrum.

"He doesn't respond to words, so I started using hand signals, and that worked like a charm. Now watch this." Blaise made a motion with her hand. Eckstrum leaned back on his hind legs and wrung his hands.

"Cute," one of the witches said.

Blaise then made a circle in the air over the fly, and Eckstrum walked in a circle. The witches all clapped. I was stunned. I hadn't even known Blaise had been training him. I didn't even know flies *could* be trained.

"Blaise, why don't you put him on a leash?" Tabitha said. "I'll show you how." She pulled one of her very long silver hairs out and made a slipknot in it. "Now tell him to roll over again."

Blaise made a finger signal and the fly flipped onto its back. Tabitha put the loop over the fly's leg and gently closed the knot. Then she handed the "leash" over to Blaise, who tugged on it. He righted himself, and at Blaise's signal, flew into the air. The witches ooohed and ahhhed, passing him from one to another as if Eckstrum was the Devil's balloon.

I hurried to my room, locked the door behind me, and pushed the dresser in front of the door. I was doing this so much lately, I'd had to buy plastic sliders to put under the feet to make it easier. Then I put in earplugs so I wouldn't have to hear that infernal nooo nooo nooo, neee neee neee-ing all evening.

After that, Blaise let Eckstrum roam around the house all day, only putting him to bed in the cricket box at night. He tormented me, dive-bombing me whenever I came home, hitting me in the head or flying at my eyes, chasing me to my room with loud buzzing, no doubt remembering when I had him trapped in a bottle and plotted to kill him. I remained locked in my room with a rolled-up towel blocking the bottom of the door, nursing a beer while listening for that damn insect.

But Blaise loved Eckstrum and would even take him out for a walk. He'd buzz around her head or ride on her hump. She took him shopping with her at the market down the street until the manager said she couldn't bring the fly inside anymore because no pests were allowed. The real reason was because he'd land on the fruit and spit all over it the way flies do; I'd heard the employees talking about how disgusting it was. Blaise still took Eckstrum with her to the market, but instead of bringing him inside, she stuck the end of Tabitha's hair to the side of the market with some gum until she came out again. I was the one who suggested that, hoping Eckstrum would fly away. But he seemed to love Blaise as much as she loved him. She'd come out of the market and they would have a happy reunion, him landing on her cheek as if to give her a kiss. It was unbelievably disgusting.

I was hiding in my room all the time now. I didn't want to admit it, but I was afraid of that fly. I'd asked Blaise to discipline Eckstrum, but she never would. She thought it was funny when he flew at me and I ran away, covering my head with my arms.

"Oh, Johnny, don't be silly. He's just trying to be affectionate. He thinks you're his mother."

The last straw was one hot summer day, I sat in the front room watching Eckstrum with a bunch of other flies. They seemed to be flying in some kind of what had to be an intentional geometric formation. Eckstrum was facing them, flying back and forth, watching the other flies until suddenly he would dart out and hit another fly, knocking it to the floor. It would lie on its back with its legs in the air and Eckstrum would land on the floor next to him, turn him over, and they'd have a noisy conversation that involved a lot of buzzing, rubbing of each other's appendages and even fighting—no contest, since Eckstrum outclassed all of them in size. After that, Eckstrum would allow him to rejoin the army of flies, and he would return to his position in front like an infernal general.

The next day, there were more flies, and the next, even more. Although I always closed the windows, Blaise would open them in the morning, and before I knew it, the apartment would be filled with flies. Sometimes Eckstrum would lead them to a wall or ceiling, where they would land and practice marching, Eckstrum at the head like the grand marshal of the sewer parade. I was taking nips of the harder stuff to cope with the insect infiltrators. The weird thing was, they'd all clear out before Blaise got home, so she didn't believe me when I tried to tell her about them.

I was sure Eckstrum was training those flies for war. Who against, I didn't want to find out. I should have killed him while I had the chance. If I tried following Excrement around with a rolled up newspaper, he would hide in the light fixture, or in the chandelier, or high among Blaise's books where I couldn't get him. That was one damn smart fly.

Finally one day after Blaise left for work, I snuck up on Eckstrum eating Blaise's leftover breakfast, which she always left out for him now. I grabbed his leash and dragged him, buzzing furiously, to his cricket box and slammed him shut inside. I could hear him throwing a tantrum in there, banging on the sides and screeching as I carried my clothes and things out to my car.

As I passed through the dining room with another load, I realized Eckstrum was suddenly awfully quiet. I moved closer to the cricket box. A hairy arm was reaching out through the air holes, and he was working the latch free. I ran out with what I had in my arms, slamming the door behind me, leaving the rest of my stuff. I also left behind the last month's rent and the deposit I had paid, but I didn't care. Maybe Blaise wouldn't put a curse on me for no advanced notice.

I found another room, this time with a nice, boring librarian, although it wasn't far from Blaise and Eckstrum. I was just extra careful. If I ever saw her on the street, I hid until Blaise and her Beelze-bud were well out of sight. I had nightmares of Eckstrum, grown giant along with his army of flies, marching over the land, eating all the people they came across. My screams frightened the nice librarian.

My doctor put me on anxiety meds and I had to stop drinking. I also went to a sort of group therapy that I had to attend every day. I found a new job and finally began to feel more normal. I even started dating again. Then one day about a year later, I was going around a corner and ran right into my former landlady.

"Blaise!" I said, holding up my hands and backing away.

"Oh, hello dear, hello, Johnny!" she said, as if overjoyed to see me. I was surprised; all this time I thought she was mad at me for disappearing the way I had. "How are you? You left so suddenly and didn't leave a forwarding address. I couldn't contact you."

"Sorry, I had to leave. Family emergency," I said. It wasn't a lie, since she considered Eckstrum my son. Speaking of which, he wasn't with her.

"You know, it's not an accident that I ran into you," she said. "I did a 'treatment' so I would find you again, if you know what I mean."

"You did?" I asked, quaking in my boots. "Wh-why?"

"Well, you know Eckstrum passed a few months ago."

"Passed what? Oh—you mean, he died." I made an effort not to grin. "Oh, Blaise, I'm so sorry to hear that."

"Yes, thank you dear, it was difficult. Anyway, I wanted to ask if you can get another caterpillar like that. I'll pay you to raise another fly for me."

"Blaise, I'm sorry, I don't work there anymore." She looked so crestfallen I said, "But I'll ask my friends there to keep an eye out for caterpillars."

She brightened. "Oh, would you do that for me? Thank you, dear, thank you, I'll send you positive energy." She waved goodbye as I hurried away.

A friend did find a caterpillar for her, although it didn't look like the one I had found. I gave it to Blaise and told her what to do, saying sorry, but I was moving to Siberia and couldn't raise it for her.

That was the end of that creepy chapter in my life. But what remains with me about that whole experience, was how a lonely old witch and a horrid fly turned out to be so well matched. The fact that sometimes people and creatures find each other in all the wide world, helps me to have faith in the way fate works. It reminds me to keep my heart, and my eyes, open.

Unnatural Love

CALL ME CYRANO. It's not my real name, but you can probably guess by the title I had to change the names to protect the guilty because the dyke demimonde is so small and incestuous, everyone knows your business. We in-breed out of the need to survive as a community. No, this is not foreshadowing for making it with my sister. What I mean by incestuous is how ex-lovers tend to become family: my ex's best friend is my current lover, and my best friend will be my current's next girlfriend, and that ex will be my best friend after a year or two, and hers will be—you get the idea.

I don't know why I agreed to this. Yes I do, why lie. I was trying to keep my girlfriend and my best friend, and look cool even while my world was falling down around me. This is how it started: Layla (not her real name either), my girlfriend of four years, came home one day and told me she'd had a major epiphany about herself.

"My authentic nature is to be polyamorous. What that means is, in order to achieve true erotic fulfillment, I need to have more than one lover at a time . . ."

Layla had been reading all this literature on ethical polygamy. I'm sure part of what lead her to that conclusion was empirical research—she'd cheated before and thought I didn't know. This new self-realization would justify her cheating, plus she could do it in my full view. But her news flash wasn't over.

". . . So I'd like us to open up the relationship and invite other people in. And the first person we should invite in is M."

M. My best butch buddy. The only butch I'd ever gotten to know and get close to.

"She's the perfect choice," she went on. "We're all close, she really loves both of us, and we always have a good time together. M. admires us, and she thinks you're so cool." Note that Layla didn't ask if I was okay with it, nor did she invite any discussion. "Come on, Cyrano. It'll be really fun," she said through clenched teeth.

For you, I thought. But I went along with it because I'm a sucker and a wus, and because I knew Layla. She's willful and stubborn, and when she wants to do something, she does it. Also, I was outnumbered. Layla and M. had been fooling around already. I'd seen the lust-laden looks that passed between them—and heard them flirt when I was nearby.

I have to take some of the blame for this whole fiasco. I'm the one who started her even thinking about my friend. One day a few months back, Layla was looking at her butt in the mirror, complaining how fat and unattractive she was. She is neither, far from it. So I opened my big mouth and said, "No you're not, lots of people think you're a fox."

"Like who, besides you?" she said disgustedly. My opinion didn't count for anything.

Now Layla may be hot, but she's also a big pill, and lots of people don't like her. Unwary, I mentioned the first person who popped into my head. "Well, like M. She calls you a traffic-stopper in Butchtown."

"Really? M. said that?" She checked her high, firm ass one more time and stood a little taller than she already was. "Hm. That's interesting." Then she tossed her long red hair and walked out of the bedroom.

After that they started hanging around each other more. The three of us worked at a book distributorship. Layla and M.'s offices were right next to each other, while I was way out in the warehouse, stuck in a small, windowless room, hunched over a computer, hacking into their email accounts. M. was hanging out at our apartment a lot, and it wasn't long before they were doing things without me, like leaving me at work if I wasn't at the car by the time they got there. They seemed to have forgotten I still existed.

Why did I put up with it, you're wondering? Well, I was depressed. I had no stamina, no fight, and no backbone to resist the situation. So I just smiled like everything was all hunky-fucking-dory with me and tried to act jaded. Sure, fuck my girlfriend. I'm open-minded.

One Friday evening I got home from work (I'd had to take the bus) and the apartment smelled great.

"Hey, what's cooking?" I called. I heard laughter coming from the kitchen. Layla and M. had made dinner and were finished eating when I came in. The kitchen was completely trashed. The laughter died when they noticed me, and stopped talking to stare at me, as if I'd dragged in a bad smell.

"Oh hi. Have some spaghetti," Layla said. *Was that a curl on her lip?*

Just as I sat down with a plate and was pouring myself a glass of wine, they got up and started getting their jackets. "Hey, where you going?"

"A movie at the Piedmont. Be a sweetie and clean up, 'kay?" Layla said, kissing the air in my general direction, then took off into the dark with M. like a pair of duplicitous witches.

So I sat down to a lonely dinner, the kitchen a complete mess around me. There was even a spray of spaghetti sauce on the ceiling. After I ate and cleaned up (it took an hour and a half), I sat feeling miserable and sorry for myself. I was trying to read, finishing a second glass of wine, when the phone rang. It was Layla.

"There's a meet-and-greet at the Polynesian Lounge. Come on over."

My spirits lifted. Maybe she did still care! So I spiffed up, adding a tie to my shirt and exchanging my sneakers for wing tips. The Polynesian Lounge is a dive with a jungle painted on the outside and a big wooden tiki love god grimacing in the doorway, next to a fake palm tree and an equally fake waterfall fountain. A greeter handed me a name tag.

"Hello, I'm Leah. This is a single mingle put on by Yikes We're Dykes! Are you single?" I glanced over her shoulder and saw Layla talking to two butches I didn't know.

"Uh—my girlfriend is," I said. The greeter laughed like I was joking and waved me in. I stood at Layla's elbow for several minutes, but she didn't introduce me, didn't even acknowledge my existence. Finally I asked if I could get her a drink.

"Yes. Get me a Delilah Punch."

"What's that?"

"They'll know," Layla said, giving me a look that said *get lost*. So I went and stood at the bar, waiting for the bartender to notice me. It was really busy so I had to wait a long time, and as I stood there watching Layla attracting more and more attention from big, hunky butches, I could swear I was getting shorter and smaller, which must have been why the bartender kept overlooking me.

I finally got our drinks. Layla took her Delilah Punch without a pause (or thank you) and the butches closed ranks around her— literally: they sealed up the spaces between them and shut me out. I felt like a mole next to a grove of stately redwoods. I went back to the bar. In the mirror, I watched myself getting uglier and tinier by the moment. Worst of all, my nose was staying the same size—in fact, it was growing. I turned my head; sure enough, the bump was four times its normal size and the tip stuck out about four inches over my mouth, growing more grotesque by the moment, like what happens to male salmon when it's time to mate. Maybe this was nature's way of telling me to call out one of those butches. Then I heard a familiar voice.

"Hey, Cyrano, having a good time?"

M. slid onto the empty seat next to me. Layla must have brushed her aside too, and I tried very hard to feel sorry for her. Soon we were talking about stuff like sports and movies, just like old times and I started to wonder if maybe I really could be okay with M. cuckolding me. Then she cleared her throat.

"So, bro'—" She paused, and I was sure she was going to say something about my nose because she couldn't take her eyes off it. She even looked at it from the sides. "Can I ask you something?"

"Sure, go ahead. You want to know why it's so big, right?"

"Huh? Why, what's so big?"

"Never mind. What did you want to ask me?"

"Layla says the three of us should get together."

"Oh yeah? And do what?" I asked, thinking about kayaking or peewee golf.

"You know, get it on. Have *sex*."

I inhaled beer and choked. M. had to throw me over her knee and smack me on the back.

"Bartender!" she barked. "Water!" Of course, the bartender turned to her immediately. M.'s a butch to be reckoned with, unlike me, Mr. Mouse.

"No—*cough*—Delilah Punch," I said in choking agony. Might as well take advantage of the bartender's attention. Except when it arrived, M. grabbed it and forced me to drink it. She set me back on my feet.

"You okay, bro'?" she asked.

Except for the inebriated cross-sightedness, I was fine.

"So—how about it?" M. asked.

The punch, taken with beer, and no doubt the earlier wine, went straight to my forebrain, effectively lobotomizing me. I nodded in a debonair way. "Sure, why not?"

"Hey, great, bro', you are so cool!" M. slapped me on the back and knocked me over, then went to whisper in Layla's ear. She jumped up and down like a cheerleader, kissed each butch good night, and came over to me.

"I'm so glad you're going to join us," she said. "Let's go."

"You mean—you want to do it now?" I squeaked. "Shouldn't we—have another round of drinks first?" Like wine, beer, and Whore Punch weren't balls enough for me. But Layla and M. were horny and impatient. They dragged me out of the bar, back to our place. Layla and M. got naked right away. They looked like Artemis and Athena. And then there was little peon me, paralyzed and modestly clothed.

"Come on, don't be shy," Layla said. "For crying out loud, we go to the hot tub together all the time."

"All the time" was once, but being naked wasn't the issue. I was afraid if I took my clothes off, nothing would be there. They grabbed me and ripped them off. I looked down. Sure enough, my body was insubstantial, almost transparent in fact. Luckily Layla and M. didn't notice because they weren't looking at me. Layla did give me a really nice kiss, but then M. moved in.

As it turned out, the sex wasn't bad; it wasn't all that different from what it always was, except Layla had M. to kiss while I was working on her. At least I got to go first, and then I conveniently passed out so the trauma of watching M. do my girlfriend was minimized.

A little old man was running down the street grabbing his head, crying "Oh no—I'm a victim of my own philosophy! I'm a victim of my own philosophy!" until he stepped into an open manhole where I was hiding and landed on my head.

I woke up, my head throbbing like they do in the cartoons, *doo-wah, doo-wah,* swelling to twice its size with each broken heartbeat. I was alone; Layla and M. had probably gone out for breakfast. I staggered to the bathroom. I had a hangover so bad my face was swollen. Even my hair hurt. But I'd done it. I was *the man.* I flexed my biceps in the mirror.

I'm the man! I told my reflection.

But I wasn't convinced, and besides, the effort hurt. The bright light and loud Saturday morning noises like a cat mewing down the street was killing my head. I went into the kitchen and fixed a Bloody Mary before going back to bed. The pillow over my head felt like a cinder block.

AFTER THAT LAYLA and M. invited me to join them for sex a few times, but I always had excellent reasons to say no, like needing to paint my toenails. Layla was spending several nights a week at M.'s place now. Those nights I couldn't sleep, obsessing about them together; but on the nights she stayed home she giggled and cooed on the phone with M., then fell asleep with her back to me, as far away from me as possible. I was more depressed than ever, and I was avoiding mirrors like a vampire trying to hide from the knowledge of what he is.

A couple of weeks later M. invited me to go on a hike. I went to be a good sport, and we actually had a great time. I was reminded why M. was my best friend. She's sharp, witty, well-read, and fun; just because she was borrowing my girlfriend didn't mean we couldn't still be buddies. After the hike, M. suggested we go to the Crab Shack. We had beer while we looked over the menu.

"So . . . bro' . . ." she began.

Remembering another ominous conversation starting that way, I carefully swallowed and set down my beer.

"Yes?" I said.

"You and me should get together sometime."

"Yeah," I said. "Today was great."

"I mean, you know, differently."

"Uh, no. What exactly *do* you mean, *bro*?" I had an idea, but I wasn't going to say it.

She leaned into me. "Have sex," she whispered.

"Have sex," I repeated. She shushed me, even though the nearest person was on the other side of the restaurant. I studied M., drumming my fingers pointedly.

"M., are you really into all this poly horseshit, or are you just taking advantage of the situation? I know you never get anything off those straight, married women you're always falling in love with."

"No, I just don't think sex is a big deal, Cyrano. We were practically together that time with you, me and Layla. And it's not as if we're straight."

"Oh, so you mean because we're lesbians, it's okay?"

"Well, yes," M. said. "Why not?"

I ordered another beer while I thought about it. It couldn't be any worse than the other night, could it?

"Okay, sure." What I wouldn't do to make Layla happy, because this was definitely not about M.

She smiled. "Great, bro', I knew you'd come through. This calls for a *real* celebration." She signaled for the waiter. "A dozen raw oysters, please!"

"Oysters?" I asked. "*Raw?*" The only way I'd ever had oysters was in a cracker.

She winked. "It's an aphrodisiac."

I was definitely going to need that.

They arrived, disgusting, slimy things like egg whites, only gray. M. showed me how to put lemon and salt on them and a spot of hot sauce. "They're still alive, that's how you know they're fresh. Bottoms up!" She tipped her head back and swallowed it whole.

"So first I torture the poor thing with acid and chili before eating it alive?" I asked. I thought I saw one move.

"Best way." M. fixed another and held it to my mouth. "Open up!"

It went down so fast I could hardly taste it. Not bad, if you could ignore the slime. So I had another, quickly followed by a big swallow of beer.

We ate oysters, buttered French bread, and drank beer, until we were stuffed. Then M. invited me to her house, and I said yes, which meant I was drunk enough. Usually I avoided going over there because M.'s place is a complete and total sty. It smelled like a roadside bar bathroom and rotten socks. Once we got there we had another beer. The next thing I knew, we were crying and saying how much we loved each other.

"I love you so much, 'bro."

"Yeah, I love you, too."

So, holding each other up, we lurched into the next room. I tried not to look at the bed, which was a complete mess of course, the blankets dragged everywhere, the sheets old and greyish, and I wondered about Layla putting up with it. She made me change our bed every week.

We took off our clothes and laughed at each other in our boxers. Then we got in bed and started trying to make out. It was sort of like two leads trying to dance. After a couple of weird kisses, I pushed M. down on her back and started to get on top, but she outclassed me by at least a hundred pounds. She knocked me off and pinned me down, climbing on top. We started fooling around some, but it was more like wrestling—she'd start to move her hand toward a breast and I'd grab it and hold it fast, then she'd grab me in a headlock, too close to her enormous butch breasts.

Then I put my hand on her groin. It was like someone dumping cold water on my head. Suddenly I felt stone cold sober. *What was I doing?* I wasn't one bit into this. Maybe I wasn't really a lesbian. But when I thought of kissing men with their big, hairy bodies and oozing dicks, I felt sick. M. had released me and was digging around in a drawer. I looked around the filthy room. I smelled garbage, and then the walls started wobbling.

M. loomed over me.

"What's wrong?" she asked. She was holding a giant purple jelly dildo with veins and huge balls. I shoved her away and ran for the bathroom, making it to the toilet just in time. I hawked and threw up beer and whole oysters and half-digested bread. Then I let go of the toilet bowl and collapsed around the filthy commode until it was time to make another sacrifice to the chthonic gods of plumbing.

I woke up sometime around two a.m. M. was passed out, spread-eagle on the bed, mouth open and snoring like a hound dog. That purple dildo was on the floor like a mound of decanted grape jello. I had another throbbing hangover. I put my clothes on and staggered home.

M. must have told Layla what happened, because Layla said, "You always ruin everything, and you clearly don't want to work on a relationship between the three of us. So even though it's really sad, M. and I are going to have to proceed without you." But I couldn't worry too much about them anymore; I had problems of my own to work out. Not the least of which, I was drinking too much.

Not knowing what else to do, I made an appointment with a friend of Layla's who was a homeopath and a psychic. Delpha lived down the street from us. Her apartment was small but serene, painted shades of turquoise, sparely decorated except for lots of plants around the windows. She was a small woman with short blond hair who used crystals and drumming in her work. She gave me a pot of ginger tea then took my health history. After that she did some psychic work on me, assessing my aura and moving energy around.

"The first issue that has to be addressed is your depression. I can prescribe a remedy for that, but you'll have to limit your drinking. Alcohol might seem like it lifts your spirits, but it's actually a depressant. Try to have four liters of water, juice, or herbal tea every day, because you're dehydrated. Also, your work environment is bad for you in several ways: you're being stifled in darkness, obsession, and positive ions. Those, if you don't know, are the bad ones. They carry pollution. The water and herbal tea will turn that around."

The energy work left me feeling better than I had in weeks, and I now had some directions to move in. I didn't tell Layla what I was doing; she wasn't interested in me anymore. Hadn't been for years. Why hadn't I noticed?

Taking care of myself became my new mission, and ice water became my drink of choice. My general well-being improved. I could think clearly for the first time in years. I bought a car and found a job at a vegetable wholesaler in South City. They started me on the night shift, so I never had to know what Layla was doing. On weekends I had appointments with Delpha, and started hiking with a couple of new friends. Layla must have missed me, because she started leaving me little love notes. Sometimes there were notes from M. too. I ripped them all up and put them in the compost.

One day I was climbing the stairs to Delpha's apartment when her door opened and Layla came out.

"Cyrano! How did you know I was here?"

"I didn't. I'm not here to see you."

"But you brought me flowers, how sweet—" She reached out to take them, but I held them away from her. Delpha came out of her apartment then, and I handed them to her.

Layla put her hands on her hips. "What's going on here?"

A little devil got to me. "Layla," I said, "you're on the right track. Being poly is great fun."

"Excuse me . You're not poly, *I* am." She glared at us. "Delpha is *my* friend."

"M. is mine. *Was.*"

"But polyamory is about being honest with your partner. We never discussed this."

"Layla, *we* never discussed anything. You did all the talking, and I went along to make you happy. Except you're *never* happy."

"That's because you never *say* anything. You always just sit there, going along with everything. You don't even have opinions." She turned to Delpha. "You can have her. You'll see what it's like taking care of her." Layla whirled and headed down the stairs. "I never want to see either of you again!"

I had an impulse to run after her, tell her I'd been joking—Delpha was only my homeopath, and the lavender was for a spiritual cleansing—but all I could do was stare after her, going along, as usual.

Or was I?

"What just happened?" Delpha asked.

"The inevitable," I said, but the relief made me feel so much taller.

Layla moved in with M. a few days later. I cleaned the apartment from top to bottom, rearranged the furniture, and burned a sage and herb mixture Delpha had given me for cleansing and starting over. I was surprised to find that I didn't miss Layla.

THROUGH THE DYKE grapevine I learned that Layla and M.'s relationship didn't last very long. Turns out sex *was* a big deal for M. when Layla was *her* girlfriend and she was having sex with other people.

Months later I met with Layla, who told me she wished I'd been honest with her because I was the one she loved, that ours had been the important, stable relationship, while the others were just flings. Crying, she said, "I wish you had fought for me, told me that my being poly wouldn't work for you. I would have chosen you."

I doubted that, but maybe she was telling the truth. Maybe her cheating had been an act of desperation to get me to commit myself, to do *something*. Instead I'd been a wimp and a yes-man and a drunk, going along with everything she wanted, trying to be the good girlfriend. I didn't tell her our situation had been feeding my depression and self-loathing for years, or that I needed to get out of the relationship; she would have thought I was blaming only her.

ONE DAY AT the neighborhood café I saw M. She invited me to sit with her. We shot the bull for a while, and it was almost like old times. Then, avoiding looking me in the eye, she said, "I'm sorry about what happened, about my part in breaking you two up. This might be hard to believe, but losing your friendship was a bigger blow than things not working out with Layla."

I shrugged, and there was an awkward silence. Finally I said, "So, M. . . . what do you think—want to try again?

She looked up, surprised. "Friendship?"

"No, fool," I said. "Sex."

Layla wasn't the only one with ideas about radical sex.

I Am Elvis
or,
The Only Female Cross-Dresser in Memphis

I mine my partner, Rome Smith's life (with her permission) for story ideas. She wanted to be sure she got credited for this one.

August 16, 1977

THE NEWS THAT Elvis was dead came over the radio while I was on the road to Memphis. I had been doing forty mph in my heap—better slow than never--from southern Alabama, stopping only for gas and bathroom breaks, coffee, and a few hours' sleep in a road side tavern parking lot. I had the radio up loud to keep me awake. The D.J. broke into Tammy Cochran singing "Angels in Waiting" to say,

"We interrupt this broadcast to inform you that Elvis Presley, the king of rock-and-roll, has been found dead in his Graceland home. I repeat: the King is dead. There is no successor." His voice broke just before the song came back on.

Elvis? *Dead?* How could it be? He was only forty-two, our boy, everyone loved him. Except my own peers, who thought he was some boring old-fashioned has-been. I tried to tell them Elvis had revolutionized music, but they weren't interested. We were getting stoned and dancing to Led Zeppelin and Pink Floyd, and acted like nothing mattered. The seventies was a bad time for Elvis.

Elvis being dead felt like my dad had died.

Probably it was shock, but everything seemed strange after that. Like, even though I drove for a whole hour, I kept passing signs that said, "Exit for Jasper, 1 mile." A vulture sitting on the side of the road, turned out to be a tire standing on end. As I got closer to Memphis, the sky turned a putrid shade of yellow-green, forecasting nothing.

I was headed to my brother's place to find work, maybe go to college. I wanted to expand my horizons and live a little. Above all, I had needed to get out of Melon, population now 9,999. I had secrets too big to remain there.

I heard laughter and smelled dope right through my brother's front door.

"Hi, Dilford."

"Johnny! Come on in!" My brother's hair was cut in a Rod Stewart-like mullet, short at the top and long in the back. "Hey, everyone, this here's my little baby sister."

He introduced me to his girlfriend Sally and three guys, all sitting around the living room making jokes about everything on TV and laughing. I sat down, passed on the dope and Cheetos when they came around. The TV was on; a newscaster, whose name sounded like Mort Grim, was talking about Elvis. A black cat on the mantle seemed to be staring at me, but it was hard to tell with his big walleyes.

The next thing I knew I was waking up. Someone with a purple towel wrapped turban-style around his head was standing in front of the TV, hands on hips, yelling at everyone.

"What's the matter with you guys? Don't you have any respect? Elvis is the patron saint of Memphis."

Everyone but me busted out laughing. I sat up and blinked several times. The yeller had perfect features and a pristine complexion except around his eyes, which were pink and puffy. He was barefoot, wearing a black T-shirt with a pink graphic of Elvis's face, lips puckered in a kiss.

"Shelby, you're not even Catholic," someone said. Everyone laughed again.

"Hey Shelby," Dilford said. "This is my sister Johnny."

Shelby ignored the introduction. He huffed and stomped away, slamming the door to his room. I looked around. My brother and his friends were in exactly the same places, only more slumped. The bags of junk food were empty. It was six-thirty.

Someone switched on the T.V. again. After a while I went to Shelby's door and tapped. He threw the door open, looking surly.

"There's a candlelight vigil tonight at Graceland. Want to go?"

He considered me, and then closed the door. I figured he had lumped me in with my brother's friends. But a few minutes later, he came out sans turban, hair combed, black loafers. He grabbed something out of the kitchen. As we left the house, he slammed the front door. The inevitable laughter followed us.

"It's the dope," I said. "It's making them laugh at everything."

"Nothing is sacred anymore," he muttered.

On the bus, everyone was talking about Elvis. Shelby joined in, correcting facts. A couple of people were crying. As the bus made its way to Graceland, Shelby told me he was majoring in theater fashion at the Memphis Design Institute and wanted to go to New York to work with a theater or ballet company. I told him about finishing high school in a mental institution. Actually, it was a pretty cool, upscale place where Zelda had been stashed by F. Scott Fitzgerald to live out her days. I'd been sent there by my parents for "incorrigibility" (caught smoking dope), but it was the most interesting thing about me that I could tell, so I made it sound worse than it really was.

The traffic came to a standstill near Elvis Presley Boulevard, so we got off and joined the multitudes. There were lots of police, some with bullhorns, some on horses, although they weren't preventing people from putting graffiti on the walls around Graceland. Amidst the hearts and *Elvis We Love You*s, someone had written *ELVIS WHO?*

After dark, people started lighting candles. Shelby had brought a bag of birthday candles and gave me a bunch.

"It's all we had," he said.

A trio made their way to the famed gates and started playing guitars and singing a hymn, everyone joining in. When they sang "Swing Low, Sweet Chariot," everyone started bawling. Shelby and I hugged and wept. I looked up at the lighted front of Graceland and thought about Lisa Marie, nine at the time; what would she do without her amazing father?

I MOVED INTO the storage room—actually an over-sized closet, after clearing out the furniture and clothes left behind by former roommates. My brother told me to put everything out on the corner.

"This is a college town, people always need stuff." Sure enough, it was all gone within a couple of hours.

I got a waitressing gig, but had to wear a frilly pink dress uniform. No one could understand why it was always wrinkled; I didn't tell them I threw it on the floor when I got home and sometimes 'Roy—for Viceroy—the cat slept on it. After two weeks I was given the option of being fired or demoted to busboy: I took the demotion and was freed from the lame uniform.

I worked the morning and lunch shifts. By the time I got home after work, everyone was at school. This was the best part of the day. I had a collection of fifties clothes that I considered my Elvis wardrobe. At that time of tie-dyed clothes and hippy threads, you could find lots of cool, fifties clothes in thrift stores for really cheap. I had an oversized plaid jacket, mohair sweater, Hawaiian shirts, two-toned shoes with platform soles, and my prize: blue suede shoes.

I'd dress up, put on mascara and rub it around my lids to give myself those bedroom eyes. I applied stick-on sideburns, pomaded and combed my hair, and practiced pouching my lips and sneering in the mirror. The finishing touch was a rolled up face cloth that went in my jockeys. Who would Elvis be without Li'l Elvis?

Then I'd put on one of his records in the front room, and using a salt shaker as a microphone, I sang and danced like Elvis until I was so excited, I'd end the session in my room with a vibrator. I'd been doing this ever since I saw *Jailhouse Rock* when I was sixteen. I never missed his movies when they were on TV, and I'd picked up a lot of his cool dance moves.

I didn't want to imitate Elvis; I wanted to *be* him. And for those few stolen songs, I was talented as hell, scintillatingly handsome, sexy to the very roots of my famous pompadour. For roughly three quarters of an hour, I was in love with myself.

I knew about men who wore women's clothes, they were called transvestites or cross-dressers. A guy in Melon used to go out shopping in a wig and housedress, with low-heeled mules. Everybody said he was sick and warned kids to stay away from him, although he had always seemed harmless to me. I never even saw him notice children.

Because it was common knowledge men cross-dressed, made it somehow normal behavior for men. But other than being a disguise, I had never heard of a woman doing anything like that, and I was sure I was the only female cross-dresser in the world. If that poor man back in Melon was mentally ill, I tried not to think about how sick that made me. Whenever I started to feel guilty, I reminded myself that no one knew, I wasn't hurting anyone, and I sure wasn't interested in little girls. But it was also the reason I had to get out of Melon. I was afraid that sooner or later I would start appearing in the world like that, and I didn't want to end up in a locked ward. The state mental institution was just down the road from Melon, and it was a far cry from the ritzy hospital where I'd been sent in high school.

By the time anyone got home, I'd be sitting in the front room, innocently reading. Usually Shelby got home first. He'd fix a big pot of spaghetti or casserole for everyone. I'd help, chopping veggies or running to the store for him, wholesome as an altar boy.

IN THE EVENINGS while everyone was studying or stoning, I'd go out and walk the streets. "Getting familiar with the town," I told my brother. Actually, I was looking for a lesbian bar. Of course, this was only a few years after Stonewall, and in the Deep in-the-Closet South. Back then they couldn't just put an ad in the newspaper. I only found out about one in Melon from news stories of knifings and police raids. I drove around in the Deliverance-like outskirts of town until I found it: a long trailer painted yellow and black like a giant queen bee, a small hand-lettered sign next to the door saying "Bea's."

I was so excited I went in like gangbusters. Everyone stopped talking and turned to nail me with stares. I stood there nervously until the bartender and said, "Gotta ID, hon?" I handed it to her. She smiled. "What'll you have, handsome?"

Handsome! Of course I gave her a giant tip.

My feet stuck to floor as I carried my drink to a tiny table in the corner. The trailer stank of old alcohol and vomit; the air was gloomy with cigarette smoke. The windows were taped over with cardboard. On the opposite end of the bus was a dartboard, where two women smoked and played, staring at me between shots like old toms looking for a fight. The denizens were all mostly older women, wearing cut-off clothes and old cowboy hats. Most had bad or missing teeth. A woman sitting on a bar stool, legs crossed, wore platform shoes with the Stars and Bars. There were, need I say, no women of color.

I had thought I'd be welcomed with smiles and instant comradery, that I would see women I knew from Melon, and would finally know

I wasn't alone. But I recognized no one, and the atmosphere was one of suspicion, hostility, and I may as well admit it, metastasized shame.

The second time I went, the trailer was gone. Probably the owners moved it from time to time to throw off the police. Despite the unfriendly welcome I'd gotten, I was desolate. I never did find it again.

Now I wandered downtown Memphis, peeking into every bar I passed, or discreetly following women I thought might be lesbians. I was always wrong. I found a woman's bookstore, but when I asked about gay bars, the clerk threw up her hands and said, "gay bars?"

The second clerk took me to the back where she handed me an A.A. flyer and lectured me about the problem of alcohol in the lesbian community. When I asked her out, she rolled her eyes and went back to work, muttering under her breath about "drunk old dykes."

ONE DAY I was in the bathroom as Elvis, singing lines, using a blow-drier to get his wind-blown hair, when the door opened. It was Shelby. He screamed. I lunged at the door and slammed it.

I couldn't believe I'd been so careless in not locking the door. I immediately stripped off the costume. I threw all my Elvis stuff into a box, determined never to dress up again. My worst secret was out; I wanted to jump off a bridge. Shelby would blab to everyone, and how would I explain it—oh God, to my brother, Mr. "Mensa" America, who didn't even know I was a lesbian? I imagined everyone laughing and teasing me, even being kicked out for being a pervert. I felt like I'd been caught freebasing.

"Johnny?"

I rolled over on my mattress and put the pillow over my head. Shelby opened the door.

"I'm sorry. I should have knocked." I ignored him. "You scared me, I thought I was seeing Elvis's ghost." I didn't move. Finally he said, "I have a secret too."

"Don't tell me: you cross-dress too." *Two under one roof: it had to be an epidemic.*

"No. Come to my room, I'll show you."

I got up reluctantly and followed him. His queen-sized bed was tidily made up, and posters of Yule Brenner, Farah Fawcett, and the

Shirelles, and a giant one of Elvis on a motorcycle. There was a sewing machine in the corner under a window, with fabric and spools of thread piled around it.

"Sit down." He got his guitar. It was peacock blue and wasn't plugged in. He strummed a few tinny chords, then started singing:

> Well now Baby,
> Don't cha say maybe,
> Don't cha go and leave me
> 'Cause you're gonna make me die.
> If you say goodbye,
> I'll cry and I'll cry,
> Till I'm all out water
> Then I'll sit in my auto,
> Even if it's hotter,
> May as well be a grotto
> Where I'll mediate and pray . . .

He finished the song and looked at me. I didn't know what to say. Shelby's song was about the equal of my own humiliation, but he didn't seem to realize it.

"Does it remind you of anything?" he asked.

"Uh . . . the tune, it sort of reminds me of—" Just past his head was that poster of Elvis. "Elvis?"

"You could tell. Thank you, Johnny."

"Wow, Shelby. Um . . . did you write that?"

"Elvis did."

I couldn't imagine Elvis writing anything that silly. "When he was a teenager?"

"No. About three days after he died."

"You mean, *before* he died."

"No, *after*," he said mysteriously. "Do you know what channeling is?"

I shook my head.

"Have you heard about those people who are kind of like a medium, and someone who's died talks through them, with messages for the living? That's channeling."

I shook my head. Melon could be wacky, but it was normal small town things like slander, adultery, and knifings, and did not prepare one for the larger world.

"Well, I was sitting here feeling so sad about Elvis. All of a sudden I got this really strange feeling. I felt like that once before, when I had a bout of projectile vomiting. But this time something told me to get my guitar. I hadn't played in ages, but I got it, and just started making up this tune. And then the words just started coming to me." He showed me a notebook with several pages of scribbled lyrics. "They've been coming to me once or twice a week ever since."

I glanced through the pages. As far as I could tell, each song had lyrics as bad as the first.

"Here's the thing, Johnny. I think Elvis has chosen me to channel songs for him. Isn't that incredible? That means Elvis is still with us."

More likely Shelby was channeling the ghost of a dead Elvis impersonator, but maybe I was just jealous.

Later that evening I went to get my clean sheets that I'd folded and left in the laundry room, but they were gone. I looked all over the house. No one had seen them, and I knew they wouldn't have taken them because I was the only one with a twin. They were just gone. Then, after it got dark I went into my room and when I switched on the light, the lightbulb popped and flashed and went out. When I changed it, that one did the same thing.

Shelby said, "It's Elvis' ghost. He's making strange things happen to let us know he's around."

"Well, okay, but why would he take the sheets?"

"Haven't you seen pictures of ghosts? That's what they wear when they come back." I laughed, but Shelby seemed completely serious. People at the mental institution said weird things like that. I wondered about Shelby.

I WAS GOOD as God for weeks. I didn't even listen to Elvis records, and I wasn't using my vibrator. I was looking for a church to attend. I wondered if I could admit something like that in confession. I still had all my Elvis stuff in a box, although every time I went to get rid of it, something came up: I had to take someone somewhere, or I was called in to work, or I'd get a headache. I was going to take it to the Salvation Army several miles away, but my car was in the shop. I couldn't just leave it on the sidewalk; I would have felt too exposed.

Amazingly, Shelby didn't tell anyone my secret. Then one evening he wanted to take me some place, but wouldn't say where. "It's a surprise. Are you game?"

It's not like I had a scintillating social life, so I went. We drove to the edge of the downtown area, the seedy section, and parked. I followed him down a side street.

"There's a club here," he said. He turned down an alley and stopped in front of a door that looked like it was covered with aluminum paper. "Now, try not to freak out too much, okay?"

When he opened the door the sounds of music and many people talking surprised me. You never would have known a club was there.

A big guy in a leather vest checked our IDs. Shelby grabbed my hand in the gloom and dragged me to an empty table. People were talking and laughing all around us. Up front was a stage with pink satin drapes. Several women in the room had on fancy evening gowns and done up hair.

"Aren't we underdressed?" I asked Shelby about our T-shirts and jeans.

"No, we're fine."

A beautiful Asian girl came over to take our order. She wore lots of eye make-up and had on a white cocktail dress with rhinestones along the low-cut neckline. Gradually I realized there was something strange about all the women. They were either too perfect like our waitress, or goddamn ugly, with outlandish makeup.

The stage lights came on and the floor show started. A tall woman who looked sort of like Cher in a gypsy outfit, with a crazy headdress all feathers and sequins, sang and danced to "Dark Lady." She was followed by several more acts, all women, and some impersonating famous singers. Our waitress finally brought our beers. When she placed them on the table, I could see down the front of her dress. She had falsies taped to her flat chest. It hit me these weren't women at all.

"Shelby, is this a club for cross-dressing?"

"This is a gay bar, honey. And those 'women' are called drag queens, every one of them."

Amazed, I stared. "How did you find it?" Shelby, like me, was from a small town.

"Some boys from school brought me. Blew my mind, first time I came." He picked up his beer. "And that's not all, folks."

I had wondered if Shelby was gay, but never asked because I was afraid he might be insulted. Even now I couldn't be sure. Just because he brought me to a gay nightclub didn't mean *he* was gay, did it?

During intermission he said, "So, Johnny, I know the owner. Why don't you perform here? You could do your Elvis act."

Beer flowed out of my nose. Laughing, Shelby and helped me mop up with our tiny cocktail napkins.

"I don't have an Elvis act," I finally sputtered.

"Then what was that I saw the other day?"

"I—uh—" It was the first time he'd mentioned what happened. "That's my Halloween costume."

"Sure it is," Shelby said, smiling. "Don't tell me you don't sing to his records. I see them on the record player. Or is his ghost putting them there?"

I crossed my arms and wouldn't look at Shelby.

"Don't be shy. You were adorable." I kept ignoring him. He poked me with his elbow.

"Come on, Johnny, I know you're a lesbian."

I felt as if the chair had been pulled out from under me. "How—why—I mean, I'm not—um . . . you think I'm a lesbian just because I dress up as Elvis?" My voice was high and squeaky.

"No. I knew you were a dyke when I first I saw you. You're about as butch as they come, dearie."

YOU'D THINK THE shame of being found out would have cured me forever, but memories of my perverted antics kept appearing, flashing before my eyes; singing me back. The more time went by, the harder it was to abstain. I missed being Elvis. I started using the vibrator again and discovered just fantasizing that I was Elvis was enough. I quit going to church.

The next thing I knew, I was adding performing in front of actual people to my fantasies. This made getting off even hotter. But that led to me thinking about actually performing, and I was talking myself into it: how was putting on Elvis any different from those guys putting on Cher or Dolly Parton? How would I be any different from all the other Elvis impersonators, other than the fact that I was a woman? After all, no one knew what I was *really* thinking. Shelby probably thought I'd been embarrassed, not shamed. He couldn't know what I was *really* up to. Unless the Elvis impersonator ghost told him. Which I doubted.

I fantasized about it so much, that one day I found myself putting on Elvis again, and getting into it even more than before. Next thing I knew, I was back into practicing my vice several times a week. Then Shelby asked me for a favor.

"I'm going to be twenty-three, and I'm having a party at the club. It'll be in the afternoon, so it won't interfere with their evening show. Johnny, you know what I'd love more than anything?"

"What's that, Shelby?"

"For you to dress up as Elvis and perform for us."

"*Absolutely not!*" I shouted. Fantasies of doing that very thing notwithstanding, actually doing it would be like masturbating in public!

Shelby and I were friends now, and he looked so downcast, that I told him I'd think about it. And, of course, it didn't take me long to realize that my fantasy of doing it in front of a live audience had manifested. Dilford's girlfriend had told me about manifestation, a hippy theory where you visualize something so much you make it happen. Who was I to turn down a gift from the Universe? So a few days later, I told Shelby I'd perform.

"Johnny, that's wonderful, thank you." He looked radiant with gratitude, and I was glad I'd agreed. "We'll have to find you an outfit."

"Oh, I have several already." So of course he wanted to see them, which felt kind of weird, but he didn't like anything I showed him.

"Let's go shopping."

He took me to a Goodwill that had a lot of used country-western clothes. I found a jacket Elvis might have worn, red bomber-style with black piping, but Shelby barely looked at it and went off to another side of the store. At last he came rushing up.

"I found the perfect outfit. Come with me." He dragged me over to a rack with all kinds of fancy clothes with feathers and sequins. "Look at this, only seven dollars!"

I stared at a limp, one-piece turquoise polyester jump suit with printed gems, a belt hanging forlornly from a loop on the side. It wasn't even clean. Shelby insisted I try it on. It was loose on me and I had to roll up the bell bottoms, which of course, didn't stay.

"Don't worry, I can fix that," he said.

At least I found a pair of cool silvery cowboy boots to go with it. Then Selby herded me to a nearby wig store.

"But I just comb my own hair like Elvis."

"Oh, the costume won't be complete without an Elvis wig!"

The store was mostly for women: hundreds of heads with painted eyes and lips, sporting all kinds of wigs. Shelby led me to the men's section and picked one up. "Look, built-in sideburns."

As he tried several on me, I realized Shelby's idea would be more of a disguise, so in a way, I wouldn't be revealing myself at all. *I can do this for one hour,* I told myself.

At home I put on the jumpsuit and Shelby took my measurements. Then he handed me a notebook.

"What's this?"

"My lyrics book. Do you want to choose one to do at my party, or should I?"

I was already going this far, so I might as well go whole hog. The things we do for our friends. I chose a song, cringingly learned the words and melody, and Shelby and I practiced it together. We had to do it in the garage because our roommates said they couldn't study with all the racket.

The big day finally arrived. Shelby had transformed the garment. In addition to altering it, he'd sewed in shoulder pads and added tons of jeweled studs in circular patterns. He also made me a sort of padded undergarment that made my small breasts look like pecs.

"It didn't cost anything," Shelby said. "There's lots of free fabric at school, samples and remnants."

We went early to meet the owner Jim, and do a walk through. I was going to do one of Elvis's songs first, and then I would do Shelby's. His friends started showing up with cards and gifts and one brought a huge sheet cake. A woman arrived who I tried to talk to after we were introduced. She got away from me as fast as she could.

"I don't think you're supposed to flirt with butches," Shelby said. "You must have scared her."

I had a lot to learn.

There was also a woman with long blonde hair in a cute sundress. I couldn't tell if she was straight. She was in Shelby's fashion design class. Her name was Jewel, she worked part time as a tutor, and wanted to work in Hollywood.

When the party was in full swing, Shelby caught my eye and winked dramatically. That was my signal to go back and change. I wished I didn't have to make a fool of myself in front of Jewel, but I excused myself and headed to the back. Shelby met me there, and picked up his guitar.

"Are you ready? I'm going to have Jim introduce you, then you get on the stage. I'll be playing behind the curtain. Remember your cue?"

"You're not going to be out there with me?"

"No. *You're* the star. All the focus should be on you." Shelby nodded at Jim, who went out and joked with the crowd over the microphone. I listened for my name. "Now, our lovely birthday boy has prepared a surprise for you. Sorry, girls, nobody will be jumping out of a cake, but I promise you, it's the next best thing. Here's Elvis the Pelvis!"

All of a sudden I couldn't move. Shelby had to shove me out there. Jim handed me the mic. I goggled the audience while Shelby played the intro. He had to start over three times before I could sing. Finally I opened my mouth:

"*Lord Almighty . . .*"

My voice sounded weak. Jim, standing near the stage, mimed bringing the microphone to my mouth. I jerked it to my mouth. The more I sang, the more confidence I got, especially when I noticed Jewel with an expression of delight. I began dancing around the stage, hamming it up. To my amazement the crowd clapped and cheered, and I smiled and bowed when it was over. A gay boy with shining eyes came up to the stage like he was going to say something, and when I leaned over, he kissed me. I was flattered.

"Now, for my second number, I'm going to do an original Elvis song never before heard in public," I said. That hadn't been part of the script of course, but I didn't want anyone to think *I* was the author. The crowd received that song in the same good spirit as they had the Elvis classic; no one seemed to notice how bad it was.

When I got off the stage I headed into the back to change, but Shelby turned me around and held my hand as he walked me back out to the party, then raised my hand like I was a winner. Everyone said they loved the show, and several asked about the second song. Shelby proudly announced that he had channeled it. No one batted an eye.

We performed again at home for my brother, his girlfriend, and everyone else in the house. They thought the show was hilarious; one of our roommates was literally rolling on the floor. Of course it was the dope. Shelby didn't seem to mind, didn't take it personally.

After the shows, I went back to being Elvis in secret again. Shelby continued channeling the Elvis impersonator and writing songs. Then one day about a month later, Shelby asked me what I thought about doing Elvis every week at the club.

"I have so many songs now. You could do a new song for weeks."

This had gone far enough. "Sorry, Shelby, it was fun to be a latter day Elvis, but I can't do it every week. It's too much."

"Oh." He thought for a minute. "How about just once a month?"

I didn't know how to tell him I didn't want to do it at all. He would want to know why, and I didn't want to hurt his feelings. So I learned another of "Elvis's" posthumous songs and performed again at the club. That time, when I went out on stage, someone said, "Hey, it's a chick!"

Because I was one act in the whole show, I was only allowed to do one song. That, of course, had to be Shelby's song.

> My baby hasn't phoned
> So I'm a dog without his bone.
> I've never been so darned alone.
> I can't even get a loan.
> So I just stay home.

It was harder to perform that time; they weren't as receptive as an audience full of Shelby's friends. Mostly they kept talking and not paying much attention. Afterwards there was a smattering of unenthusiastic applause. Shelby was as disappointed as if it had been him up there. I felt sorry for him.

"Don't feel bad, maybe they just want to see guys up there, cutting up, and they thought a girl was kind of weird." This actually seemed to console him somewhat. I was secretly relieved it didn't go over so well. He didn't ask me to do it again.

A couple months later, Shelby said he wanted to show me something. I followed him into his room. There, on the door to his closet, hung a gorgeous Elvis jumpsuit. It was made of heavy white satin with sunbursts of topaz studs and gold embroidery. It had a large white standup collar, and a matching, wide, jeweled belt. It was nothing short of glorious, like something a modern Sun King would have worn.

"Wow, Shelby, that's amazing. Did you make it?"

"Yes, thank you," he replied. "Sit down would you, Johnny? I want to talk to you."

Uh-oh, I thought. *Now what?*

"I've been rethinking this whole Elvis performance thing. You said maybe the audience wanted to see a man up there, and I realized you were right. The reason the second performance was a dud was because a gay man would know his audience better, and what would catch their attention. Don't take this personally, Johnny. You did a great job, but I can't expect you to know exactly how the songs are supposed to be sung and performed. Anyway, I started thinking maybe there was a message for me in all this."

"A message?"

"Yes. See, the reason I got you to do it is because deep down inside, *I* want to perform. It's in my shadow." He had been reading Jung lately.

"Huh?"

"Johnny, I have terrible stage fright. That's why I got you to do it. But I have to find a way to get over it, and do the songs myself. I think Elvis wants me to. Why else would he have chosen me to channel him?"

I heaved a sigh of relief. "That makes perfect sense, Shelby." I gave him a big hug, overjoyed that I was off the hook.

I did everything I could to help Shelby get his act together. We watched Elvis movies, discussed his dance moves and choreography, and even practiced together. Shelby began breaking the stage fright ice by getting a little gig as the MC at the club. When at last he felt ready, he signed up to perform.

Lots of his friends showed up including Jewel, who sat with me up front. Shelby presented a very swishy Elvis and had a quirky stage presence that actually enhanced the terrible lyrics. The audience adored him. Shelby had been right: he *was* better at doing the songs. He had a mission, and he believed in his work.

JEWEL AND I started hanging out. I was too cowardly to come out and ask if she was a lesbian, but that was okay because I was happy just having a female friend. One evening after too much beer I told her about my Elvis aspect.

"That could be considered a form of women's spirituality," she said. She was a feminist and into women's empowerment. "After all, the women pharaohs used to perform rituals to invoke male gods. What is Elvis, if not a god?"

I liked that. After that I made it part of my ritual to light a candle in front of a picture of Elvis. I already prayed during the culmination, yelling *O God! O God!*

One day I was in the middle of "All Shook Up," when I looked out the window and saw a beautiful woman in front of the house, looking into a compact and applying lipstick. My eyes bugged—it was Elvis's wife, the sloe-eyed, sublime Pricilla Presley! (Yes, they'd been divorced, but to me she would always be Elvis's wife). You couldn't mistake her with all that big black hair and chandelier earrings. She had on a short red dress with matching high heels. But what was she doing on our street?

I stared as she put her compact pack in her purse and came up the walkway. *She must be looking for Dilford,* I thought. He was a card-carrying member of Mensa; maybe she needed him to solve a problem for her?

I threw open the door. She paused, tipping her head and studying me coyly from beneath thick eyelashes.

"Well, hello, Elvis. I guess the grim reaper can't keep a good man down."

I'd completely forgotten I was all dressed up. I grinned idiotically before I remembered I was supposed to give it a cool sneer.

"Hello, baby," I said, dropping the register of my voice. "How nice of you to drop by." By now I had recognized Jewel. "I was just practicing a song for you—" I deftly put on the breathy, "I Want You, I Need You, I Love You," and shortly after, I found out Jewel was a lesbian.

We performed this ritual about once a week after that, sometimes acting out scenes from Elvis's movies, and always ending with wild sex. Practicing our mutual perversion together had a certain bonding effect on us, and when she moved out west for a job in Hollywood, I went with her.

In L.A. I discovered a plethora of out lesbian bars. One on the edge of Hollywood, with the name Annie Hindle's, had a floor show. I was stunned the first time I saw it: six women of all ages, dressed in men's clothes and called drag kings, who danced and lip-synched popular songs with plenty of irony and nary a trace of shame. I learned that in fact, I had been following a long tradition of women who dressed in men's clothes and performed brazenly for the world.

It wasn't long before it was me up there—or should I say Elvis? I became their most popular guest. All that time in the South I thought I was a sick and disgusting degenerate, when all along I was edgy and cool: an outlaw pioneer lesbian Elvis impersonator.

The Legend of Johnny Magnolia

NO ONE IS really sure where the singer Johnny Magnolia came from. Some say it had to be Louisiana, others say Alabama. High school drop-out, two-fisted drinker, and womanizer, Johnny wasn't much of a musician in her early career. She mostly played the circuit from sleazy bar to dingy nightclub in the South, swilling beer, flirting with the women, fighting with men. That Johnny loved trouble almost as much as she loved women. White, Black, Mexican, she loved them all. When the Klan burned a cross in front of her door, Johnny went and lit her cigar from the flames. On more than one occasion she was run out of town. The story is, Johnny's the reason a certain sexual aid is still illegal in Alabama.

Johnny was handsome, and so charming she could bewitch the Devil—and many believe that's exactly what she did. There was something about her; Johnny turned women's heads around, even if they weren't "that kind."

One night Johnny beat a man nearly to death. When she went before the judge she said, "I gave him a lesson every man who beats a woman should get, and I ain't sorry for what I done." The judge sentenced her to fifteen years at Tutwiler women's prison. The sentence was much more than the crime deserved; Johnny was being punished for being an uppity dyke.

She just laughed.

"But, your Honor, how is being locked up with all those women punishment?"

"Get her out of here," the judge yelled, banging his gavel.

Johnny caused a big commotion among the women prisoners and did many stints in solitary, more to give the inmates a break than to punish Johnny. But prison had some good effects on her: she got sober and started paying more attention to her music. Every night her fellow inmates fell asleep to the strains of Johnny's guitar and heartbreaking voice. Five years passed slowly.

Then one night, an argument woke up one of the girls, Mona was her name. It was up around midnight, someone was in Johnny's cell. For obvious reasons she had no cellmate, and in any event, the other voice was a man's, dark and smokey, and it echoed through the prison. Looking through the bars, all Mona could see was a strange yellow haze coming from Johnny's cell, the only light in the whole cellblock. There was a funny smell too, like matches, only powerful strong. Mona went back to bed and said her prayers a second time.

The next day Johnny's cell was dark and the door was ajar. The inmates thought Johnny must have escaped and waited for hell to break loose. Nothing happened. At roll call Johnny's name wasn't even on the list. Later that day, two new prisoners were in Johnny's old cell.

One of the bolder girls finally came out and asked a guard, "What happened to Johnny Magnolia?"

"Who? Ain't never been no Johnny Magnolia here," the guard replied.

"'Course there was, the cute one who made all the love trouble with prisoners. And hey, didn't I see you making a love scene with her once, back in the laundry?"

"I never had nothin' to do with no prisoner," the guard shouted. "Cause trouble for me, and I'll put you in the hole for a month. Now git back to work."

Mona said, "Why, it's like the Devil hisself got Johnny out!"

That's how the rumors started about Johnny cutting a deal with Satan, that he had fogged the guards' minds and magicked Johnny out of that prison.

What happened afterward added fuel to the flames of rumor. Johnny played the same venues she had before, but it was different now. Everyone stopped drinking and talking to listen. No one could believe it was the same troublemaking Johnny who used to sing nasty songs, kiss women's hands, and pull knives on men. Her fingers had become magic, and her voice—to hear Johnny made you cry. Once—my own sister swears it's true—a mad dog lurched into town, foam dripping from his mouth, his eyes hot and crazed. Everyone was screaming and running for cover—all except Johnny. She got her guitar and headed out the door.

"Johnny, where you goin'?" my sister screamed. "Come back!" But Johnny stood in the street, playing her guitar and crooning sweetly about an old blue dog. That mad dog stopped in front of her, cocked his head like he was listening, then laid down right where he was and peacefully died.

Johnny's music cast spells over you, made something change deep in your soul. Women were crazier about her than ever, but Johnny's heart seemed to have hardened. Some thought it was prison that done it; others said that was the deal she'd made with the Devil—exchanged her heart of flesh and blood for one of stone. Others said the Devil *was* a woman, and took her heart because if Johnny wouldn't love only her, Johnny wasn't going to love no one.

Horse pucky to all of that, I say. If you knew Johnny at all, you'd know she'd never quit women. She'd probably even romance the lady devils and cause pandemonium in hell. No, Johnny just changed her public style. Even though she still wore men's clothes, being cool to women made her appear rehabilitated even down to her "orientation." The public liked that. Johnny'd play for the crowds, then meet her latest girlfriend in secret places where only lady lovers go. Just ask any Southern lesbian.

Johnny became an overnight sensation. She started playing all the big nightclubs and swanky venues, even opera houses. Every night sold out. And with a voice like an angel, it wasn't long before the churches were asking her to sing, but Johnny always refused. People say that was just more proof she was in the Devil's pocketbook. Especially when after many years, she finally agreed, and the first time she did it, was also the last time anyone saw her.

There are lots of different stories about how Johnny Magnolia disappeared. People with no imagination say she retired to Mexico with her wealth. Others say she was murdered by old enemies, who fed her body to the alligators. There are even people who say an angel took her. But the most popular story is that by singing to God's glory at that revival, she broke her promise to the Devil. He picked her up afterwards in a big black limousine that huffed fire and burned brimstone. Hundreds of people saw that car, but no one saw who was in it. Makes a fitting end to the mystery that was Johnny Magnolia.

But that's not what happened.

It was one of Johnny's many girlfriends who got her to sing at that revival. She was a dark-haired, Southern beauty named Savannah, who had come in second in the Miss Old South contest. She was actually far more beautiful than the young belle who won, but running around with Johnny naturally started rumors about her being a lesbian. And Miss Old South judges couldn't have a lezzie winner; might say they approved of that behavior. But I doubt she really was, because something about Johnny made straight women want to walk the wild side.

Anyway, Miss Savannah's church was sponsoring a revival. The bishop asked her to ask Johnny to sing for them, and to everyone's surprise, Johnny said yes. My guess is Johnny couldn't say no to that amazing face.

The revival started in the early evening. The preacher was preaching, people were singing, but it was like everyone was just holding their breath for Johnny. Finally she came on stage wearing a dark red suit that matched her hair and set off those blue bedroom eyes. Everyone went quiet. In that silence, Johnny strummed her guitar and sang into the mic:

"Mine eyes have seen the glory of the coming of the Lord!"

Battle Hymn of the effin' Republic of Northern Interference. Wasn't it just like Johnny to sing a Yankee song at that most sacred of Southern institutions. Well, the crowd didn't care. They went insane. Johnny had people weeping and testifying, calling on the Holy Spirit and speaking in tongues. Many reached out to touch her and swore they'd been healed. Womenfolk swooned and had to be carried outside. I'm quite sure what was passing for sanctity in those women had a good dose of another, less holy feeling. There were more conversions and souls saved that night than that particular preacher ever had. He was closely questioned later, after what happened.

Now, among the crowd was a woman who was sick with love for Johnny. I don't mean crazy like girls are for a rock star without ever even meeting them. This woman had known Johnny since they were teenagers, when Johnny was a callow boi, putting on Elvis. Her name was Lil Queen, and she was a root woman's daughter. Johnny had been her first love, and they'd been inseparable as children. They'd sworn to love each other always, and Lil Queen believed in that love.

L.Q. stayed faithful all those years in her heart, where it most counted. She kept the home fires burning for Johnny when she was gone on circuit, tended her wounds when she came home—both physical and emotional, mind you. But L.Q. was tolerant of all Johnny's tomcatting.

"It's not as if I never hook up," she said. "A woman gets lonesome. No one knows better than me that it don't mean nothin'."

Johnny said she'd come home one day for good, and that she wanted Lil Queen and no one else. That's how Johnny always had someone to fix her a meal when she happened to be around; someone to iron her shirts and warm her bed. And when Johnny was doing time (for a crime committed over another woman), Johnny had someone writing and sending care packages, even though Johnny rarely wrote back.

Lil Queen's friends told her to forget Johnny, find herself someone who would be true and stick around, but L.Q. kept waiting. What no one could tell her was that Johnny was gone from prison. She found out when her letters were returned stamped "NO SUCH PERSON." Worried sick, Lil Queen took a greyhound all the way out to Tutwiler, only to find no Johnny, and no record of her ever having been there. Lil Queen was beside herself, wondering if they had killed her Johnny and then hushed it all up.

Then one day she saw a poster in town. There was Johnny Magnolia staring out at her, big as life in a blue sequined dinner jacket, holding her guitar like she would a woman. Johnny was alive and well all that time, but there'd never been a visit, not even a phone call. But was Lil Queen angry? No ma'am, not a bit. She was overjoyed.

"I knew in my heart Johnny was OK." L.Q. was sure any day now, Johnny would be home. More years passed.

So when the first revival Johnny ever sang at was held on the outskirts of her town, she went. She believed Johnny was just under the spell of success, and if she could just see Johnny, she would remember all they'd meant to each other. But though she stood in front with all the cripples and wheelchairs, Johnny never paid her any mind.

As soon as she could get away, Johnny slipped out the back of the stage, headed for a black limousine, but Lil Queen stepped out in front of her, stopped Johnny in her tracks.

"Heard you got out of prison, Johnny," she said.

Now Lil Queen was dressed to the nines in a royal blue lace dress that set off her pure, dusky complexion. Johnny caught her breath, no doubt surprised to see her old sweetheart looking so fine.

"Miss Sugar," Johnny said, using the old nickname she used to call her, and she took Lil Queen into her arms. "Oh, my Miss Sugar. How've you been, baby?"

The sun rose in Lil Queen's heart. Hugging Johnny, she wept for joy. She had known everything would be OK. Then the limousine door opened, and a low, sweet voice called, "Johnny-Boy?"

Lil Queen could feel a change come over Johnny as she raised her head to look over her shoulder. Johnny forgot all about the woman in her arms. L.Q.'s tears of joy became those of rage as Johnny left in the car with Miss Savannah.

Lil Queen's impulse was to blame Miss Savannah until she realized even her unearthly beauty couldn't make Johnny faithful. She saw heartbreak ahead of the younger woman, and L.Q. found herself feeling sorry for her. Instead, Lil Queen cursed that faithless butch.

"Someday you'll pay for what you done to me, Johnny Magnolia!" But the limo was gone.

Now, during the day, Lil Queen helped her mother in the shop, prescribing root treatments. In the evenings she worked in a lesbian bar outside of town. That evening the place was romping, just what L.Q. needed to keep herself distracted. Suddenly everyone was at the windows looking out. A red Mercedes was pulling into the parking lot.

"Why, it's Johnny Magnolia."

Someone whistled. "Yes it is, and look at the woman on her arm!"

Johnny came in escorting Miss Savannah. A couple gave up their table to them. Lil Queen stared, unable to believe her eyes.

"That's your table, Lil Queen," the bartender said. "Go on, hold your head up and do your job."

Lil Queen went to the table and Johnny, looking her full in the face, gave their order, acting like she didn't know her from Eve. L.Q.'s humiliation was complete. She brought their drinks throughout the evening, and Johnny never looked at her again. All she felt had turned at last to hate. But what she didn't realize is that hate is just love having revenge.

About eleven, L.Q. asked for a round of drinks for Johnny's table. "This one's on me." The bartender noticed an odd look in her eye, but was too busy to think about it.

Sometime after midnight Johnny excused herself and stumbled off to the bathroom. Nobody was surprised when they heard her being sick, as Johnny's drinking of old had been legendary. She looked terrible when she came out of the bathroom, and she and Miss Savannah left.

No one ever saw Johnny again. Next day, Miss Savannah came into the bar, desperate, asking for Johnny. A day after that, the police came asking questions. Normally, they wouldn't care about an old dyke, but Johnny was a star and everyone—her agent, the club owners, fans, church people, even the mayor—was asking for her. But nobody knew anything, and everyone knew better than to say anything about Lil Queen, standing there with a perfectly innocent look on her face. That was the end of Johnny Magnolia, and a chapter in lesbian history drew to a close.

Except two people *did* know: the bartender, and Lil Queen herself. The bartender gave L.Q. a ride home after work, where they found Johnny passed out on her doorstep, her royal blue guitar dropped in the grass a few feet away. Lil Queen stepped over her and went into her house.

"That cheatin' dog dyke can stay right where she is, because I'm done handing out pussy and cleaning up after her. Get her out of my yard."

The bartender touched Johnny and gasped. "Lil Queen, Johnny's dead!"

L.Q. didn't bat an eye. "Well, I guess the demon rum finally claimed her sorry ass. Too bad."

But the bartender knew it wasn't alcohol killed Johnny, because Johnny had only been drinking grapefruit juice and soda water that night.

Lil Queen lit a cigarette and stood at the window, looking up at the scythe moon. Her hands were shaking. After a while L.Q. said, "I guess we should call the police or something?"

There would be an investigation, and no doubt Lil Queen would be charged with murder. She was a root woman's daughter, and Big Queen had taught her all the remedies and solutions for the troubles in life.

"Someone was bound to kill Johnny sooner or later," the bartender said.

They say real love is when you accept a person for who they are, in spite of what they do. The bartender, who deeply loved Lil Queen, didn't ask any questions. She just found a shovel and spent the rest of the night digging a hole in the woods behind Lil Queen's house. She laid Johnny in the grave just before dawn and wrapped Johnny's arms around her guitar. L.Q. declined to pay her respects, so the bartender kissed Johnny on the forehead.

"Thank you for the beauty you brought to the world, my butch brother," she said. She covered her up and said a prayer for Johnny's lonely soul.

I USED TO hate Johnny Magnolia. She took all of Lil Queen's love and left nothing for me. L.Q. would throw me a scrap of loving now and then, and I'd scramble for it like a damn dog, even knowing she'd be thinking of Johnny the whole time. Johnny didn't deserve her enduring loyalty. Everyone knew what a cheat and terror Johnny had always been. I believed the rumors that she'd sold her soul to the Devil. What else explained her luck with women and money?

A buddy and I went to New Orleans, to one of her concerts. We sat up front so we could heckle her with questions like, didn't she kill a man once, how'd she get sprung from prison, and was she sucking the Devil's pecker now? The lights over the audience went off and everyone hushed. A spotlight came on, and Johnny appeared like St. Michael with a guitar. Her skin under the spotlight looked like a marble statue in a sunrise. She was handsome one moment, beautiful the next, and I hated her more than ever in that moment.

"Hey, Johnny," I called. "Saw you with a ho' last week!"

There was laughter, but Johnny looked right at us in the dark and smiled.

"Hi, fellas," she said in her soft, strong voice. "Thank you so kindly for coming out to see me tonight." Then she played a chord so lovely, anything we were going to say died in our throats. And in a voice so changed I couldn't believe it was old Johnny Magnolia, she began singing.

I tried to harden my heart when I heard Johnny's songs about pain, sorrow, and regret, and the price of self-hate. Every song was about salvation—and not the kind you get in church. Tears started leaking from my eyes. I whipped them from my eyes, but they wouldn't stop. I glanced over at my friend, hoping she hadn't seen, and there she was, sobbing into her handkerchief.

One thing I learned that night: that music did not come from the Devil.

Afterward we didn't feel like drinking and carousing like we'd planned, being in New Orleans and all. Bad behavior comes from not liking oneself. We walked around, took streetcars to see the sights, and just talked. I felt new. The tears had washed away the hate and jealousy, but also a shame so old I didn't even realize it was a part of me. I wonder if it wasn't Johnny I was so jealous of, so much as her having the courage to be an out and proud dyke, who knew no fear or shame for being a woman who loved women. I understood her gift and curse was having too *much* love. So I took a page from Johnny's book and loved her right along with all of her fans, and I'm not too butch to admit it.

Often, we get what we wish for, but in ways we hadn't expected. L.Q. had wanted Johnny to come home and stay with her always, but I doubt buried out back was what she had in mind. I had always loved and wanted L.Q. for my own. Sure, I wish Lil Queen had chosen me of her own accord, but I accepted what was given me.

I wonder sometimes why Johnny came to her house that night. Had she come to ask for forgiveness? For an antidote? Or was she coming home to L.Q. at long last? I suspect Lil Queen wonders too.

We never mentioned Johnny again. I proved my love that night, and every night since, staying with Lil Queen even though I knew what she'd done. I held her through the bad dreams, the crying and trembling. I sat up with her nights when she couldn't sleep at all, when she was afraid to be alone with Johnny's ghost.

Whether it was that terrible secret, or Johnny's actual spirit, it felt like she was living there with us, a third presence who I fully welcomed. And sometimes, in the long, sweet Alabama evenings, I believe I hear the distant strains of Johnny's guitar, letting me know she's still around.

Hello, my butch brother, I love you dearly.

LESBIANS IN MAGIC, FANTASY, AND THE SUPERNATURAL

Enchanted!

HER EYES FOUND me from across the room. Wherever I looked, there she was, her eyes unblinking, compelling, catching mine, pulling me in. If I turned away, I could feel them, boring into the back of my neck.

I had seen her around the community; she was probably fifteen years younger than me. I had thought she looked hard; not particularly good-looking, though an interesting face. Now, she was a knockout. I couldn't stop staring. My girlfriend's hand slipped from mine.

"Lupe? Honey?" she said. But I was making my way, across the room crowded with lesbians, to the other woman. I'd been faithful to Maria for a long time, despite a bad romantic track record before that. I had settled down; matured. Now I didn't look back, didn't even think. I just had to have her—what was her name? It came to me, clear as a mermaid's song.

"Ravina Giuliana," I said, tasting her name.

She smiled. "That's me."

I leaned against the wall next to her and inhaled her scent: smoke and incense. She wore a long, crushed velvet dress with a leopard print, black and red, the same luscious color of her lips. The fabric flowed over her skin like wine. I could see down her cleavage, she wasn't wearing a bra. *Uy*—my lips and fingertips tingled. Dark amber eyes stared deep into my own. I hadn't felt like this in years. I reached out and tangled one of my fingers in her long, red-hennaed hair.

"Hello."

She didn't respond, only looked at me with those deep, deep eyes. I tried to remember the last time I'd seen her—just last week, at my monthly gig. Sitting alone. I realized she had been at the one before as well, alone again and—I was sure, the one before that as well . . . how far back?

I studied her lips, and my mouth went suddenly, desperately dry, so I kissed her. She fed my thirst like sea water, quenching the immediate desire while leaving me with a worse need. When I surfaced, I noticed a silence had fallen over the room, everyone was staring at us.

"Let's get out of here," I said, taking her hand.

I left the party like I had no conscience, no responsibility to, or history with Maria. Ravina led me to a metallic green Jaguar, put the roof down, and we roared away with the cool evening wind blowing through our hair. I hadn't had a sexual adventure in years. She could have been a vampire for all I knew, but what a way to go.

Finally we ascended a winding road and plunged into the driveway of an old Victorian. Beyond the house was a wood. When she cut the engine, I could hear crickets and tree frogs.

"Let's go," she said.

I followed her around the side of the house, down three steps and into a door, where we were swallowed by darkness like a viper swallows a mouse. Ravina had disappeared.

"Wait—Ravina, where are you?"

"Come," she called. Her voice echoed. It sounded like it was coming from deep in a cave.

When my eyes adjusted, I saw there were high, narrow windows, but they didn't light the depths of the darkness. I oriented myself with fingers on the wall, found stairs with my feet. I climbed down seven steps, reached flat ground. *What was I doing?* I didn't even know this woman. I was suddenly terrified. Yet something compelled me onward. I stepped carefully, tapping the floor with my foot, all the way through a hallway and finally an open door. A match was struck, Ravina was lighting a candle.

Her dark form was suddenly outlined with light. She stood before an altar, head bowed, seemed to be praying. On the table was a statue of a black goddess with red lips and fiery orange hair cascading down her side. I thought I saw the eyes glisten and flicker with intelligence: she was looking at me. But when I blinked, the illusion disappeared.

Ravina had me sit on the floor, then put on strange, slow music with a drum, then she left the room, returning with a hot tea. "It has damiana and chocolate, among other herbs. Drink it, it has aphrodisiac properties."

She danced for me then, bewitching, a dark goddess; Nyx. Scents engulfed me: perfume, herbs, and her own womanly odors. She knelt ceremonially before her altar, raising her arms and whispering prayers. She turned to stand before me. My terror fled—or rather, I moved right into it as fear ignited into overwhelming excitement. I couldn't remember taking my clothes off, but there I was, naked, on my knees before her. She slid the dress off her shoulders; it sighed into a sumptuous mound around her feet. How could I never have noticed her before, this woman with her enormous goddess eyes, and powerful, wiry hair; that luscious, full-figured body, the big nipples that were an old dyke's gush-dream? Shaking like a drunk with gin lust, I rubbed my face into her smooth, full stomach, her feminine scent filling my head like witch's mead.

LATE SATURDAY MORNING I stumbled out of bed, punch drunk from sex and only a muzzy recollection of it. My bladder was bursting. I found the bathroom, sat peeing, leaning forward, holding my head. *Ay caray.*

I washed my face with the icy, underground water coming out of the spigot, scooped some and took a long drink. I looked up and caught sight of a dripping, frightful face and yelled, until I realized it was *me*. I was unrecognizable; looking shell-shocked, wrung out, and shrunken. I squeezed my eyes, opened them: I was back to normal ugly. I took a deep breath.

Mirror, mirror on the wall,
Is this woman my downfall?

I ran my fingers through my hair. What was I doing here? *Maria*—had I really just abandoned her at the party? Had I really just walked away from our relationship of six years for a roll in the hay? There was no more time to think, Ravina was calling me.

"Lupe? Where are you? Come back here."

I went to her. She was on her side, wrapped in rumpled sheets, her long hair draped quite fetchingly over her shoulders.

"Where were you?"

"Bathroom."

"You were gone a long time. What were you doing?"

I couldn't believe she was asking. "What do you *think* I was doing?" She pulled up the sheet, exposing that amazing body.

"Make love to me again," she ordered.

So I did, as she saucily told me exactly what and how she wanted it, and I was only too happy to oblige. Maria and I had settled into that sexual familiarity stage that was comforting and warm; no more surprises. I'd been perfectly content. But *this* was all surprise. I dived into hot sensation.

Afterward, Ravina wanted to go to brunch. We went to a popular dyke-owned restaurant. We entered, Ravina holding my arm proprietarily. The talking died down. I ignored the staring, glaring, judgmental diners, many of whom I knew. I said hi as we passed them, but no one said hi back.

Bet you wish you *had the ovaries . . .*

"Get a Ramos Fizz," Ravina said. "They're great."

"Actually, I don't drink."

"Why not? Don't tell me you're an alcoholic."

"No. It's just that my music is better when I abstain."

"Oh, well, you're not playing today are you?"

"No, but . . ." Since I couldn't think of any other reason not to, I got one, along with *Huevos Rancheros*, hot and spicy with refried beans and extra jalapeños. I was too lost in Ravina's lovely eyes to put on the brakes.

Then, back to Ravina's bed. Afterward, she napped, and I writhed in post-sex, post-gastronomic agony. I had forgotten the number rich, spicy food did on my stomach. It woke her up, but she didn't seem to mind. She made me more tea, a different concoction with a lot of mint this time and a medicinal under-taste. She gently massaged my stomach with baby powder and fingertips, and I felt better.

Sometime later we got up to take a bath in her claw-foot bathtub. We raided her refrigerator. A second night passed. I felt like I was in Dreamland.

New relationships are always great. The highs, the feeling of being so present, so seen by your lover; that wonderful, breathless "in love" feeling without actually being so. Taking loans out against love's bounty, because lust is not love. For that, we'd have to wait and see. Just because I was acting crazy, didn't mean I actually *was*.

I finally checked my phone: several messages from friends, and one from Maria. I didn't listen to them. Ravina had come into the room, wearing only a sheet.

"What are you doing?" she asked.

"Checking to see who called." Ravina dropped the sheet and wrapped herself around me. Reluctantly I tried to pull away.

"What's wrong?"

"Nothing. It's just . . . I should probably go home and face the music."

"What can you say that she doesn't already know? You're mine now."

An objection to her possessive statement rose in my throat, but she was flicking my ear with her tongue like the snake of paradise. I didn't go home that night either.

I'd never had so much sex in my life. My senses were on overdrive, and every touch, every look, seemed weighty with emotion and obsession. After that weekend my circuits were blown, and I had what can only be described as a love hangover. I felt groggy and disoriented, out of my body. Ravina put on soft music and used aromatherapy to ground me again; put warm towels on my forehead. I was late to work that day.

I stayed at her place all week, barely managing to get to work each morning. Ravina drove me and picked me up again in the evening. She didn't have to work due to some trust fund set up by her grandparents.

I asked, "What do you do all day?"

"Take classes, visit friends, museums, read. Whatever I please."

She also did esoteric things with herbs; they hung like dried, dead elves from beams in her dark little kitchen, their earthy, cloying scents suffusing my head and giving the room an underworldly feeling, like a conjure woman's cave.

The following Sunday, Ravina invited me to move in. I said yes, because I was as good as homeless now. Maria wouldn't take me back, after how I'd done her. The next day I called in sick at work and Ravina took me to get my things, when Maria wouldn't be there.

We pulled up in front of my apartment building, and I said I'd see her back at her place. She said she'd wait.

"I can take some things for you," she said.

My Mustang had a ticket from street sweeping day, but otherwise seemed all right. Inside I gathered my toiletries and clothes; quickly, so I wouldn't feel the sadness: CDs, knapsack with laptop, journal and library books. Ignoring my cat Horsey, as he followed me around, meowing needily. I put my electric keyboard, guitars and amps in Ravina's car, which was all it could take. Still she waited; keeping an eye on me, or to make sure I followed through and didn't stay.

I left my books and DVDs, my music system, furniture, espresso machine, and Horsey. He was getting old and probably wouldn't do well with the move. Besides, Ravina said she didn't like cats. I took the apartment keys off the ring and put them in the mailbox. Didn't leave a note. What would I say? "Got my stuff, it's been nice"? So I just slunk away like the craven *bribón* I was.

The Mustang packed, I sat there, staring up at the apartment window where I'd spent so many happy hours with Maria, for whom I'd grown up. Horsey nosed apart the curtains and looked down at me. I saw his silent, anxious cry. I tried to ignore the clutching in my stomach. Was I doing the right thing? Everything had happened too fast to think. A honk made me jump. Ravina. I realized tears were pouring down my face. I wiped my face on my sleeve and took off, Ravina tailgating.

Ravina had the whole bottom floor of the Victorian, in a big U, with several rooms she didn't use at the far end of the U. I stowed my clothes and music equipment there. After everything was inside I said, "I guess I'm officially a U-Haul dyke now."

Ravina whirled around. "What's that supposed to mean?"

"Whoa, Ravina, just that I never moved in with anyone so fast before. You know the joke, what does a dyke bring on her second date—"

"Who *doesn't* know that lame joke, spread by jealous faggots?"

I was shocked. "Ravina, that's a terrible—"

"Don't try to change the subject. Tell me you never got into a relationship with someone after one date. I know your reputation."

Yes, I'd been a *mujeriega*. I'd had my share of relationships that were faster than the speed of bullshit, but that was when I was young, a bum, and full of come-ons. Three months was a long-term relationship back then.

But how long had she been keeping tabs on me?

"Ravina, what's wrong?"

"Don't you think people know when they've found their soul mate?"

Oh yeah, the "soulmate" ticket. I'd had those too; most of those fly-by-night "relationships" fell apart within weeks, if not days.

"I'm sorry, Ravina, it was a really bad joke," I backed down. We had some kind of compelling connection, but soulmates we were not.

She locked me out of the bedroom so I lay on the couch all that night, wondering why she was so offended. Was she pissed off that she'd been a fan for so long, but I'd never hooked up with her?

In the morning, like magic, she acted like she'd never been mad at all. I was back in her good graces and her bed, where she more than made it up to me.

Now, I have a lot of mileage on my holster due to my musical avocation. I write sensitive and sincere songs, and I've sincered myself into lots of beds. But I'd never been with anyone like Ravina. The nature of feminine sexuality is a gift that allowed us to go for hours, and we often did. Ravina had lots of toys; throw in a little kink and lots of play, and we enjoyed Cupid's smorgasbord.

Sex with Maria had been sweet. She'd put on one of her satin vintage nightgowns, perfume, and jewelry. I'd wear my best boxers and a tie, set the lighting, put on romantic music. I never felt like I was supposed to impress her. Now it was all I could do to keep up with the ravenous Ravina, who tore up the sexual rule book.

One evening I got a call from the pub where I had a gig. It was the bartender.

"Lupe, what's up? You coming?" she asked. "You're usually here by now."

"Huh? What day is it?" I looked at Ravina's confusing moon calendar. It had become a new month without my even noticing. "Damn—I'll be right there."

I flew through the bedroom, past Ravina, into the back, and came charging through again, dragging my instruments and equipment.

"Where are you going?"

"The Lavender Club. It's first Thursday."

"Well, I'm not dressed."

I almost said *it's* my *gig, not yours.* "You look fine."

"I'm not going like this. Wait until I change."

It would be at least an hour of waiting while she changed and put on make-up. But I didn't want to start an argument either. I just grabbed my keys and headed for the door.

"Can't wait. Meet me there."

She crossed her arms across her chest. "You're going without me?"

"Yes. We're not Siamese twins you know." It was the first time I was salty with her.

I took the steps three at a time and jumped in my car, arriving five minutes before starting time. When my music filled the club I started feeling like my old self again. I actually forgot about Ravina until I saw her glaring at me from the back of the bar. I had to admit, she looked smashing—she had redone her make-up and wore a green outfit that set off her hair. She made her way up to the front. Unbelievably, two people left a table just as she got there, as if making way just for her.

Ravina gave me one, constant evil look that told me I was in trouble, although when I took a break, she came up on the stage and stuck her tongue down my throat: staking her claim. I felt embarrassed, more for her than for myself. After the show she followed me home, and didn't even wait until we got inside before she started yelling at me.

"I can't believe you just left me here like that," she stormed. "You're not even serious about music. You never practice."

"But my playing bothers you—"

"You have that gig just so you can flirt and pick up women. You wore that color to be sexy, didn't you? Huh? Because it sets off your eyes?" She pushed me.

"Stop it, Ravina. You know I didn't have time to change."

She ignored what I said. "Women would never be interested in you if you weren't a musician, you know." She then proceeded to tell me I was a dilettante, skinny and ugly, had a comical nose, and wasn't very smart. We argued for two hours and only stopped because I promised I would quit that gig.

I went to sleep on the couch, but Ravina pulled off her top and threw it in my face. Then she headed toward the bedroom, unzipping her skirt and dropping that too. Clad in only panties and boots, she looked over her shoulder coquettishly, one large breast in profile. She could change so quickly from cold to hot. I forgot how pissed off I'd just been and followed after her, my tongue hanging out. I didn't realize until much later, sex was my reward for caving.

The next morning as I stumbled out of bed, short of sleep and yawning, Ravina grabbed my arm. "Don't go to work today."

"Have to. I've been absent too much lately."

"You owe me for last night."

"I'll make it up to you later," I promised. But wait—I *didn't* owe her—I was giving up the gig for her, and that in itself was *huge*. She propped her head up on her arm, breasts displayed very fetchingly above the bedclothes.

"I can support the two of us you know," she said.

I turned my back to put my jeans on so I wouldn't be distracted. I wasn't going to live off a woman, and I didn't dare be late yet again. I did tech support for a software company, and I was making too many mistakes lately.

As it turned out, I was fired anyway.

"Lupe, you used to be our best techie. You're not using drugs are you?" My boss asked.

Of course, I couldn't say I was mainlining a new woman.

Ravina was thrilled I was on "all days off" now. But after a few days of inactivity (except for the games she thought up), I started going to the library every day to spruce up my resume and research jobs—and to have some time to myself. I didn't dare tell her she ran interference on my brain, and the sexual funhouse didn't help.

I applied to every job I saw, but strangely, couldn't get an interview. It didn't make sense. Tech support was in demand, I was good at it, and had plenty of experience. I'd never had trouble getting a job before. It was like I'd been jinxed.

One day on my way to grab lunch, I saw a hand-written sign on the window of a busy Mexican buffet: *"Necesitamos ayudante de camarero. Aplicar adentro."* Desperate—I'd been unemployed two months—I applied for the busboy job and was hired on the spot.

"You're joking, right?" Ravina said.

"This will give me a little cash until I get something permanent."

"I wanted to do some traveling with you."

"Sorry. I couldn't enjoy that without a job to return to."

"Do you love me?"

"Too soon to say, Ravina," I hedged.

"It wasn't too soon to move in with me."

That had more to do with sex and convenience, but I couldn't say I was just making the best of it with her. What was passing for love was drama, histrionics, and sexual intensity. I knew better than that. Aging had made me careful about throwing that word around. Real love is about responsibility, commitment, and being bonded, and that's serious stuff. Why didn't I think about any of that when I left Maria for her?

The longer I was with Ravina, the more I realized what a bad fit we were. I tried the saber fighting martial art she did, but thought it impractical. Her taste in books ran to sensational, tattletale biographies and sex-filled crime thrillers, which made me squeamish. The only movies she wanted to see were about horror, sex, and murder. I visited her yoga class; too painful. She did shamanic meditation and insisted I join her, but when I did it, my so-called power animals were all cartoon characters. Eating, drinking, and sex were pretty much all we had in common. That was okay when I was twenty, but I was in my late forties.

And she was jealous. She hung on me when we went to lesbian events, and watched me to make sure I wasn't ogling other women. She didn't even like a tattoo I had of a naked woman in high heels on my thigh, head tipped and lips puckered in a kiss toward my crotch. I'd had it put on decades before when I was stoned.

"Who is she?"

"No one, I just liked the graphic. It's iconic."

"Well, it's disrespectful of women."

That was actually something I'd wondered about, but just hadn't done anything about it.

"You could have my name tattooed in a banner under her," she suggested.

One minute it was disrespectful, the next, she wanted to *be* that woman. We went to a tattoo parlor and I told the artist to put a black bikini on the little lady, but I wouldn't have Ravina's name on my body no matter how much she begged, cajoled or pouted. That would be like a permanent commitment.

Ravina loved conflict, and was an expert at put-downs and getting the better of me. She'd pick on me; the way I combed my hair, or my clothes. She called my musical technique naïve and imitative. She made fun of the books I read, called them trite, and me a literary snob (*The Handmaiden's Tale*, big deal). Then she'd say she was only teasing. She bought clothes for me and dressed me; I looked spiffy, but my true style ran to T-shirts with flashy logos and jeans. Where had I gone?

She pouted when I got a phone call, and if she thought I stayed on too long, would start talking to me and interrupting. She even complained about the way I cleaned, never mind that between visits from a housecleaner, she would rather go out to eat than wash a plate. She made mountains out of molehills, called that communicating, and thought it was healthy.

I have to admit I was no angel. I *did* ogle other women, and although I had promised to quit my music gig, I didn't do it. I kept putting it off, using one excuse or another: it was a special occasion, or there was a wedding reception at the club I had to do, or they hadn't found anyone to take my place yet. Also, she had a food allergy: peanuts. It wasn't life-threatening, but if she had peanuts, they would give her flu-like symptoms for twenty-four hours. I would "forget" and put them in something like cookies. She would be sick for twenty-four hours, and I'd have a break from her.

But I also tried to please her. I waited until she left the house to read or play music or go for a run. I didn't see or talk to friends anymore. I tried changing habits she complained about, although it wasn't fast enough for her. I gave into her whenever we had a fight. Then I wondered why I tried so hard, since I didn't really like her very much. Yet it didn't occur to me that I could leave.

In secret moments, I thought guiltily and longingly of my serene years with Maria, how that stability had allowed me to develop my musical avocation. Maria had insisted on processing all the time, which I had tolerated as a quirk of hers. Now I realized that was why our relationship worked so well. I had learned to own and talk about my part when we argued. But when I did that with Ravina, she heaped on the guilt and blame. I wondered again what had possessed me to leave Maria.

I OPENED MY eyes and gasped. A naked, blue-grey woman with crazed, black eyes danced on top of a dump, ridiculing me with a long, lurid, bloody tongue. It wasn't a dream: it was an Indian statue on a nightstand, messy with books, empty bottles, and scraps of paper. I sat up. My head reeled. I looked around—where was I? Nothing looked familiar. I felt like Rip Van Butch.

I rolled over and looked at the woman next to me. Memory returned with an awful, sinking feeling. Granted, no one looks great in the morning, but Ravina was the gorgon's distant cousin, her hair snarled and snaking across the pillow like flowing blood, dried saliva on her cheek. She was snoring loudly; her teeth looked like old Chiclets. I wasn't sure who was scarier, her or Kali. I slid out of bed, and quietly picked up my jeans and shirt.

I stuck my head under that icy faucet, and then walked through the apartment rubbing my head with a towel looking at everything as if for the first time. Strange I'd never noticed how low the ceiling in this place was; how dank and dark the rooms seemed, how high and narrow the dusty windows. Or that Ravina's portrait was hung right over her altar.

I went outside with my phone and cigarettes—another bad habit I'd resurrected with Ravina—and headed into the woods. My message box was full with calls I'd never listened to. I needed to talk to someone, and I knew Stef, formerly Maria's and my best friend, got up early. I called her.

"Lupe?" she asked. "I can't believe it. How are you?" It sounded so good to hear her voice, like warm honey filling my soul. "You never returned any of my calls."

"I'm sorry. Uh . . . she gets upset when I talk on the phone." I chuckled lamely.

"Possessive. Yeah, I haven't heard good things about your girlfriend. Is she controlling too?" Stef had worked at a domestic violence hotline and looked at relationships through that lens.

I laughed. "Well, she *is* pretty bossy."

"She's not hitting you, is she?"

"Of course not, I wouldn't put up with that."

"No threatening behavior, like pushing?"

"Well, yeah, she pushes me sometimes, and she throws plates, but it's mostly in fun."

"Mostly," Stef repeated. "Fun."

"Come on, Stef, I didn't call you to get the third degree. How are you?"

"You're right, sorry. I'm well, I got new car, electric. It's great. Oh, and I moved out of that crazy house. I have one calm roommate now, she's Philippina, and she has a great dog, Star. You have to come over sometime, so you can meet them. What about you? What's going on?"

"I . . . I don't know, I just woke up in a strange mood. It's like . . ." but I couldn't bring myself to say I'd woken up to find I was in someone else's life. My eyes filled with tears. "I miss you, Stef." *I miss my old life.*

"I miss you too, Lupe. You know, at first I was pissed at what you'd done. It was like you did it to me too. Then when I never heard from you, I started wondering if something else was going on. I mean, it's been a year, Lupe."

It had been a whole year?

"I'm sorry, really. I'll keep in better touch now, I promise." There was an awkward pause. Finally I asked, "Stef, um . . . how—how's Maria?"

"Well, not bad despite having been humiliated and abandoned. But she rallied. She has a show of her paintings at the Yerba Buena Café, you should go see it, if chickie will let you out of your cage," Stef said, rubbing it in. "Let's see: Maria got promoted to senior research assistant at work, she loves it, and she's making more money. She's taking that women of color film class, and she's making a film about *curanderas*. Oh, and Lupe, I'm sorry, but Horsey died."

It was a blow. I took a long moment to absorb it. "When . . . when was that?"

"About a month after you left. Maria thought it was of a broken heart. He missed you, Lupe. He would sleep in a sweatshirt you left, always sniffing it. Then one morning, Maria found him curled up on it, dead."

My tears spilled over. *Good goddess, what have I done?*

"Hey, buddy, I have to get ready for work. But I'm glad you called, stay in touch. That isolation isn't good for you."

She seemed to think I couldn't take care of myself with Ravina, but I didn't mind taking advantage of her compassion to renew our connection. *"Buddy."* It had been warming to hear her call me that again.

Maria. Horsey. I hated that I hadn't been there for them. Maria had adored Horsey. I wept over losing Maria, over Horsey, Stef, my old friends, and everything else I had thrown away. I'd been selfish and entirely self-absorbed. Did Maria have a new girlfriend? If so, I had only myself to blame. I howled to the indifferent trees.

Ravina was up when I got back, wrapped in her black dragon kimono, smoking a cigarette and bouncing her bare foot, which meant sky-rocketing impatience.

"Where have you been?"

"For a walk."

"Bare-footed?"

"Yes, bare-footed, Ravina. What do you think, that I was upstairs, having wild sex with the old lady?"

The idea wasn't a bad one, actually. The "old lady" was in her late fifties, not really so old. She had her own business as a house painter, was healthy, interesting, and really nice. Probably why Ravina tried to keep me away from her.

I brushed past Ravina toward the bathroom, stripped, and got in the shower. I didn't want her to start giving me the third degree about my red eyes. She didn't like the fact that I'd had a life before her; she was afraid of my friends, my memories, my past, and I think she knew that, deep down inside, I didn't really love her. She came into the bathroom, slipping naked into the shower and tried to put her arms around me. My skin crawled.

"Cut it out, Ravina. I have to be at work in half an hour."

"It's just a service job, they can get anyone to fill in. Call in sick."

The last time I went down that road, it led straight to the unemployment line. I got out of the shower half washed and wiped the soap off with a towel. I quickly dressed and left her underworld digs.

One good thing about being a busboy, it's straightforward work, which left my mind free. Normally I'd obsess about Ravina, our most recent fight, and how to rectify it. Today I was wondering how the hell I got into this mess.

Lots of women had come on to me during my relationship with Maria, usually fans. I'd flirted—it was part of the job—but I never even considered the bait. After decades of unsatisfying, unhappy, and abbreviated relationships, I'd been overjoyed to find Maria and finally settle down. I adored her.

So why had I so easily tossed her aside? Was it ennui? And why had I chosen Ravina? She wasn't my type at all. Was it a mid-life crisis? I thought about the cliché of men going through them; I knew gay men in long-term relationships who simply redecorated their apartments. Why hadn't I just bought a Porche, or started a lesbian meetup? I would still be with my Maria.

Near the end of my shift, the manager said the evening busboy was out sick, and asked if I could stay on for dinner, offering me double-time. It was a perfect excuse to stay away from Ravina. I grabbed a quick meal and a cigarette and went back to work. My phone buzzed fifteen minutes later.

"Where are you?"

"At work. It's Cinco de Mayo season, so I'm taking another shift. Gotta go."

"Why didn't you let me know?"

"When did you become my parole officer, Ravina?" I growled, hanging up on her and turning off my phone. An hour later she came into the restaurant, beautifully dressed and made up. I said hi, and then ignored her. I was sick of her always checking up on me and hoped she wouldn't make a scene. When I was clearing the table next to her, she grabbed my arm.

"Lupe, are you mad at me?"

I jerked my arm away. "No."

I was mad at myself.

She had beer and a meal, waited a while, but the place was packed and rowdy, and I was immune to her. To my relief, she finally left.

She was up, reading and smoking when I got home. I gave her a noncommittal wave and went to the liquor cabinet. I took out the tequila and stared at the bottle. *I drink to deal with Ravina.* I suddenly noticed dark sediment at the bottom. Herbs. Ravina must have put them in there, she was always doctoring things. My stomach turned. I put the bottle back.

Ravina put down her cigarette. "What's going on, Lupe? You've been distant."

Oh, now that I'm reconsidering the relationship, you want to talk.

"Ravina, I'm exhausted, okay? I just want to chill."

One harsh word, and I was out of here, I would sleep in my car if I had to. I grabbed the remote and threw myself on the couch. The energy between us was different, and Ravina didn't push. Instead she made me chamomile tea and massaged my neck. She spoke gently. Why wasn't she like that more often? I closed my eyes, and she put a blanket over me and turned off the light.

When she was gone, I stretched out on the couch, glad I didn't have to sleep with her. It had been so easy to reclaim my power. I hadn't always been such a wimp. Sex had made me hand her my *cojones* and self-esteem. It was almost as if she had put a spell on me.

I sat up in the gloom. *The ritual on the first night I'd come here. Black Aphrodite on her altar. Ravina's books on witchcraft. Had* she cast a spell on me? Would she do something like that?

Of course she would.

I turned on the light. No sound from the bedroom, Ravina slept like ten dead elephants. I went over and closed the door anyway. Then I looked through Ravina's witch books. I read all about love magic, then came across this:

> *... Magic can't make anyone do anything they don't want to. They have to already have the inclination ... It is important to remember that love spells eventually wear off. All they can do is attract someone's attention. While he is under the influence of a magical enchantment, you should be working your own natural charms on him. Hopefully by the time the spell wears off, he will honestly be in love with you. However, be aware that the person may leave you when the spell burns itself out.*

Ravina had cast a spell on me, and it had just worn off; that explained how different I was feeling. I went over to her altar. I'd never looked at it closely before: there were goddess statues, dried herbs in vases, candles, something disgusting that turned out to be a snake skin, an incense burner, even a Christian cross. I knew I shouldn't touch anyone's altar, but this was a matter of life and liberty.

As I reached out to pick up a box with runes on it, I knocked a jar with dark glass off the altar. It broke at my feet. I froze, listening for Ravina, but she didn't stir.

I squatted to pick up the pieces. Among the shards, there was a little doll, hand-sewn, with some black hairs glued to the head, a plaid top, and simple denim jeans. The plaid looked like a shirt of mine that went missing sometime before Ravina and I got together. And everything was tightly wrapped and knotted with strands of long, dark red hair. The doll was supposed to be me.

If Ravina had put a spell on me, might she have done others? Like making me lose my job, or unable to find another ... my mind boggled. There would be time to think about that later. I grabbed Ravina's scissors off her desk and snipped through the red hairs, freeing the little guy. Then I lay down again and began planning.

The next morning I pretended to sleep until Ravina left for her early morning yoga class. As soon the Jaguar roared away, I got dressed and started carrying my stuff outside.

Ravina came in as I was getting the last of my music equipment out of the back room.

"What are you doing?" she asked.

"Moving out."

"Just like that? Without talking about it? Why?"

I took the little doll out of my shirt pocket and shook it in her face.

"You shouldn't have done it, Ravina." She blanched and tried to grab it, but I stuffed it way down into the front pocket of my jeans. She put her hands on her hips.

"You were snooping through my things!"

I just laughed. "Nice try, Ravina. I know you'll agree that 'all's fair in love and drama.'"

I wasn't afraid of her anymore, and I was disturbed to realize I'd been living on pins and needles for months. I picked up my amplifier and guitar and shoved past her. She followed me out of the crypt of horror.

"Wait, Lupe, you're right, I shouldn't have done it. I'm sorry." It was the first time she'd ever apologized. "I wanted you so bad, I got desperate. You were always giving me the brush off."

"Ravina, I wasn't *available*. I was in love with Maria and living with her." I put my equipment in the car and found places for the things I had hurriedly set around the mustang that morning, trying to get everything out before Ravina got home.

I was about to head back into the apartment to see if there were any last things of mine, but stopped. I wouldn't put it past her to lock me in one of those empty back rooms, and turn me into one of those horror stories she was always reading.

"Please, Lupe, let's talk about it. Maybe we can see a couples' therapist."

"No. I don't love you anymore, Ravina. I'm not sure I ever really did."

I didn't want her to try and twist my brain around so I didn't know if I was coming or going. Even more important, I didn't want to waste another minute of my life. Speaking of which, it was time to leave. I checked around the car to make sure I wasn't leaving anything.

Ravina started crying. "I don't understand. We've been so happy together."

"Maybe *you* have," I muttered.

"But we've had such a great time together. You can't deny how compatible we are sexually. Admit it."

It was true, no matter what had gone down, the sex had always been great. Maybe I'd miss it, but I was looking forward to getting reacquainted with my hand. I got out my keys. She stood there, crying and wringing her hands like a garishly made up spinster from a nineteenth century novel.

"Everyone . . ." she sobbed. "Everyone leaves me in the end."

Gee, I wonder why, I thought but didn't say. No need to be cruel. She wasn't a bad person; just no one I would ever, in my right mind, choose.

I took one last look at Ravina, all in black, as if already in mourning; but maybe I was flattering myself. She'd probably have a shot of *Strega,* then start scheming on her next victim. I honestly hoped they would be more compatible. All of a sudden, I realized what a little shrimp she was. I couldn't believe I'd never noticed before; big breasts, big hair and high heels had made her seem big. Illusions. I got out my cell phone and took a picture of her. She gave a little cry.

"Why did you do that?" Good old Ravina again.

"To remember you, of course." Later I would compare it with the other photos of her, to see if she really was as small and unattractive as she appeared right now, or if that was just the manifestation of dislike. I jumped in the car and rolled down the window.

"Good-bye Ravina, nice knowing you, and thanks for all the fish." I took off before she decided to come after me on a broom or something.

As I headed to the edge of town to find a cheap residential hotel, I thought about Maria. I didn't know if she would take me back, if she would buy the story about my having been under a spell. It even sounded crazy to me.

I couldn't put all the blame on Ravina. The spell might have given her an advantage, but deep down inside, I'd had the "inclination." I never put the brakes on. I abandoned Maria and Horsey. I had taken my job for granted, messed up, and gotten myself fired. I allowed Ravina's insecurities to limit my life and interests, instead of asserting myself. I'd been on a Wild Zipper ride for the last twelve months, but my feet were back on the ground now, wobbly as I might be.

I had kept the doll so Ravina couldn't do any more hocus pocus on me, but maybe it would be useful for starting over. I patted my shirt pocket, and was reassured by the crackle of paper: spells for a new job, to receive forgiveness, and bring back a former lover, all copied from Ravina's books.

It worked for her, why not me?

Horsewoman

The Xtaybay (sh-TY-by) is an ancient Mexican female monster, associated with the sacred Ceiba tree (Kapok or Silk Floss tree). This story pays homage to the ancient feminine entities, and the profound love and appreciation women have for one another.

THE WOMAN STOOD at the very end of the bar, head turned slightly, staring out the oval window at the setting sun. Leah, who had been there more than an hour, wondered how she got there, how she came in without her noticing. And she *would* have noticed. The woman was of Amazonian proportions, tall, broad of back, muscular arms, powerful hips. A thick mane of black hair fell down her brown back, bare to its middle, and set off by a backless white dress. Leah could tell from where she stood the hair was strong and coarse; imagined what it would be like to touch it, run her fingers through it, and breathe in its scent.

The memory of Margarita and their sudden breakup passed through her mind. The agony still fresh, Leah had been unable to face the weekend alone. She got in her car and drove south for hours, ending up in this town on the Mexican side of the border.

She had wandered aimlessly through streets crowded with Americans down for the weekend. In an effort to participate in the festivities, she went into a popular bar and ordered a silly drink: Bananarama. No one talked to her, but it was still better than being alone. Then when Leah looked around after paying for her second drink—Dos Equis this time, the woman had appeared, almost by magic.

How did I not notice her?

The woman stood, leaning against the bar, a monument of graceful stillness in the rowdy room, radiating energy. Leah thought about going over, starting a conversation, but the impulse died at once. This was not a woman to approach casually.

Leah stared, trying for a glimpse of the woman, but her face remained averted. A drink stood on the bar next to her, and she was holding a cigarette. It had seemed to just appear in the woman's strong, supple-fingered hand. Although Leah hadn't had a smoke in more than ten years, she felt a sudden, baffling craving for one. There was a cigarette machine by the bathroom. Leah tried the coins in her pocket and found it accepted American money.

When she got back the woman was still there, although she had put down the cigarette and shifted position. The sun had gone down, and Leah realized she could see her own reflection in the window, darkened as it was by the street beyond. But try as she might, she couldn't see the woman's face in the glass, only a darkened shadow framed by that wonderful hair. It was as if she were veiled.

Leah lit a cigarette and inhaled reverently, eyes still fixed on the woman. A former lover, another Latina, had a theory that when someone lights a cigarette in a film, one should look for the underworld.

"It's a marker," that girlfriend had told her. "I think most of the time it's unconscious on the filmmaker's part." Since then, Leah had noticed many times this was true—a cigarette was lit, and what followed was often profound: if not the supernatural, then something meaningful, scary, psychologically twisted; at the very least, bizarre. Or maybe it was just the films she watched. But tobacco had once been sacred to the native people of the so-called new world, to be used only for healing, ceremonially, or as an offering to the gods or spirits. Its casual abuse had brought the curse of cancer.

The longing to see the woman's face turned into a longing for the woman herself. It was a painful, urgent, and hopeless feeling that triggered the memory of all the women she had known and lost. The woman seemed to shake herself, tossed her head impatiently. Was she waiting for someone?

Leah signaled the grinning Mexican bartender.

"What's that woman drinking? The one at the very end of the bar."

"The woman with the two men?" he asked, indicating a woman way too small for Leah's tastes.

"No, the tall one in the white dress. At the very end of the bar. She's alone." The bartender looked again, turned back perplexed.

"Señora, no one is there. That end of the bar is empty."

"She's got her back to us. The magnificent woman with the long black hair," Leah insisted, unable to believe he didn't see her. The bartender looked for several long moments, his smile fading. He turned slowly back to Leah.

"No one is there, I tell you." He stared at her. "Señora." He lowered his voice. "If you are seeing who I think you are seeing, leave her alone. I am serious. Do not follow her."

Leah wondered if he meant the woman wasn't a lesbian, or if he was displaying some kind of macho protectiveness of his Latina countrywoman. As if that woman couldn't protect herself.

"I mean no disrespect. She's a fine woman. I just want to buy her a drink." Leah was surprised when a look of anger and fear crossed the man's pleasant face.

"I think you've had too much to drink, lady," he said, no trace of his former heavy accent. "Go back home." He paused, glaring. "You gringos come here thinking Mexico is so much fun, that the Mexicans are so wonderful and nice and easy-going, but you come with no understanding . . . this can be a very dangerous place."

Someone yelled for him.

"You're eighty-sixed, lady. And don't come back here, if you know what's good for you." And throwing one last, baleful look at her, his grin returned, sardonic now, as he left her.

Leah felt foolish and guilty. She knew her attraction to Latina women was probably racist, unconscious though it was. One Mexican-American girlfriend had leveled a similar accusation against her:

"You think it's cool to have a woman of color for a girlfriend. We're a fetish to you. But you don't care about who I really am. You don't care about my culture. You just want someone who can cook Mexican food for you!"

Ashamed, Leah started reading about the history of the Mexican people, the immigrants to the U.S. and their struggle to survive in this country. She got a cookbook and learned to make her own food. She even resurrected her high school Spanish skills, but it was too late for that relationship. She'd kept up with the readings and Spanish, but even that was probably just to impress the Latinas she met. Feeling sheepish, Leah glanced at her watch. If she left Mexico now, she'd be home by midnight.

Just as Leah turned to leave, the black-haired woman moved toward the door and walked out just ahead of Leah, her beautiful hair lifting and flowing in the sudden breeze from the street. Leah caught a scent of musk and something organic, like hay. Did she work with livestock, with horses? Maybe she was a v*aquera*—a cowgirl. She certainly looked strong enough.

The woman headed into the crowded sidewalk, self-assured, arms free, no purse, no apparent jewelry, clip-clopping down the street on white *guaraches* with chunky heels. People stepped aside for her, even as the crowd enveloped Leah. Leah struggled, wallowing among the tourists as if in a dream, desperately determined just to see the woman's face before she left the border town. She was dragged back, like a receding wave; yet no matter how far behind she fell, Leah could still see her up ahead, ever more alluring.

Near the edge of town the crowd thinned, and Leah was released. She hurried to catch up. The woman turned left into an alley. Leah's impulse was to be chivalrous and escort the woman in what could very well be a dangerous part of town, then wondered about her *own* safety. Yet the lure of the woman was almost painful and drew her recklessly forward. It was like running from a threat in a dream, when you can't seem to move fast enough. The far end of the ally emptied out into the desert beyond the town. The woman trotted quickly, fluidly into the dark, her clopping steps now making no sound on the sandy dirt.

A brilliant moon lit the wide open space, making the vastness of the valley almost bright, cacti sending long shadows like desert spirits. A warm whisper blew toward her from the desert, and Leah could swear it said, "*sígueme.*" The woman knew Leah was there—she *wanted* her to follow. Then Leah's feet began to move of their own accord, as if she was sleep-walking. She no longer seemed to have a choice about it. She followed, the lights of the border town's main drag now a memory.

What is happening to me? Leah wondered. *Who* is *this woman?* Too late she remembered the bartender's words:

If she is who I think she is, stay away from her . . . do not follow her.

Leah remembered suddenly a legend she'd read, something about a sexy spirit who lured inebriated men into the jungle. No matter how fast you went, you couldn't catch up to her. When at last she turned around, she was revealed to be some kind of monster, who then pounced on her pursuer and devoured him.

Leah knew now, it wasn't a legend. This was happening, to *her*. The woman stopped about ten feet away. Leah stopped too, her heart pounding.

I know you've been following me.

Her voice was high, not the kind of voice she would have expected from such a large woman. Furthermore, the voice hadn't seemed to come from the woman in front of her, but from her own head. And it wasn't English or Spanish; and yet Leah had understood.

The woman turned slowly, her muslin dress catching and billowing in the light breeze, her black hair blowing ribbon-like across her face, hiding her features. Then she tossed her head and at last Leah beheld the face, painted in moonlight, that she had pursued. The sight of her was a shock, but not of repulsion—not for Leah. She was ugly in a way that made Leah want to stare at her for a thousand years. Her face was long and strong, with powerful features, big, snorting nostrils and full, sensual lips, and her eyes—they were large, lustrous, and preternaturally fierce. Her hair, wind struck, flew around her head. The woman seemed to grow. Leah felt she was in the presence of something terrible and sacred, a high priestess . . . an ancient, chthonic goddess. She wanted to prostrate herself, but couldn't move.

The woman paced slowly, menacingly toward Leah, who decided to simply give herself over to her fate with this woman. Fear left her, she straightened her spine. The woman paused. Pointed ears at the top and sides of her head turned forward, as if suddenly curious.

"Usually it is men who follow, who think they will rape and conquer me, but no matter . . ." She tossed her hair. "Do I repel you, *gringa?*" she asked contemptuously, taking another step forward.

Leah could feel the woman tense, as if to spring.

"Tell me: Am I not the ugliest creature you've ever seen? Run, why don't you? See if you can outrun *me*." The woman bared pointed, carnivorous teeth.

Leah suddenly found she could move again, but she did not run. She fell down on one knee.

"No," Leah said. "I won't run from you."

The horse-woman stood still, her mouth open, her large eyes blinking rapidly in surprise.

"You . . . *what?*" A moment of baffled silence, then, "Have you no fear of me?"

"No." Leah swallowed. "Maybe I'm a fool, but I don't care. You are . . . you are the most beautiful creature I've ever seen."

The creature was still as an ancient statue. "No one . . . no one has ever . . ."

She raised an arm, caressing her long hair almost coquettishly. Suddenly she threw it back.

"You are lying. You are trying to distract me. I will kill you!" She loomed menacingly over Leah. Yet still she hesitated, and Leah could sense the woman's terrible need to hear such words; could feel the profound loneliness and longing that all creatures share.

"Then kill me," Leah said. "I give myself to you. I am your willing sacrifice. But first, let me say the only reason no one told you how very beautiful you are, was because . . . because they must have been struck dumb in absolute awe."

She was trembling, more frightened than she'd ever been in her life, and yet never so real, so present. If these were to be her last moments, she wanted to suffuse herself with this wonderful, incredible presence. And though touching her might mean death, she reached out, her hand tentatively touching the hip, fingers spreading. The woman gasped, allowed her touch. Slowly Leah stood and moved even closer, closing her eyes and inhaling her scent, touching the creature's glossy hair that blended with night. The touch made Leah breathless and brought tears to her eyes. Leah stroked the hair then brought her hand forward to hold the woman's strong chin. She knew what to do.

"Let me love you," Leah whispered.

LEAH WOKE THE next morning in the desert outside of Mextitlan, the sun pounding down on her, a dull ache in her head. A dream came to her, so powerful it could have been real—riding a horse across the desert, bareback, her hands clutching the thick main. *Only a dream, only a dream*, though Leah could still feel the pounding in her thighs.

Leah felt something tangled in her fingers. It was a long, coarse black hair.

It came rushing back—the woman in the bar, the encounter in the desert, and the wild ride across the desert—or had it been the sky? And how the night mare had set her down finally, and they nuzzled for a long time, Leah weeping, knowing the horse-woman would leave her soon, and she'd never see her again.

Just before dawn the magical creature snorted, tossed her head and backed away. She spoke English now, as if they hadn't shared that strange, silent language all night.

"Just remember the *Xtaybay*, baby."

And then she galloped away.

Queen of the Cats

This story is based on an old British folktale, King o' the Cats. I wondered what that story would be like told from a woman's point of view. This is my version. I included this story because the two females end up together.

NIGHT WAS COMING on fast as it does that time of year, when the harvesting is almost done, the trees are losing their leaves, and the evenings grow longer and colder. I had stayed too long at Mrs. Kemper's. Though she pays me well for the extra help, my husband Jack hates me not to be there when he gets home. Too, he'd see the bundles of food and make me throw them out, saying we don't accept charity.

I reached the crossroads where one goes around the forest, and the other disappears into the woods. If Jack were to see me coming out of the woods he'd give it to me but good, but it takes thirty minutes off my walk when I don't have to go all the way around. The woods are said to be haunted, and there's a heathen graveyard in the middle where witches dance naked with ghosts. What Jack is really afraid of is I'll see, and get ideas. He doesn't think it's fitting for a woman to have those feelings. He needn't worry; I don't have them for him anymore. Not since he broke my heart: the day he broke my head.

I picked up my skirts and moved quickly through the woods. I reached the graveyard, nothing to be afraid of, just an old, overgrown place with tall, leaning stones. I was so concerned about getting out of the wood, I didn't notice it at first—an eerie keening. It was many voices, but they weren't human. The hairs on my body rose up. Frightened but curious, I slipped behind a tree.

A light grew from between the trees and then cats emerged, walking orderly in a procession, but not like normal cats. They stood tall, on two feet, carrying tapers like unholy priestesses, their eyes glowing in the flames. Then came six cats, carrying a long black box with a tiny golden crown on it. They stopped when they reached a hole in the graveyard, and gently settled the box down into it.

As two cats shoveled dirt on top of the coffin with tiny wooden shovels, the cats began crying and wailing, "Regina Grimalkin is gone—our beloved queen is dead!" and tearing their fur out in grief.

I came to my senses and realized the time I gained coming this way would soon be lost, and I was in far more danger from Jack than I was from a gaggle of howling cats. I snatched my skirts up again and dashed the rest of the way through the woods.

I was in luck. Jack wasn't home, and Grizelda, my faithful red cat, was waiting on the step for me. I gave her a quick greeting stroke and opened the door. Once in, I put on an apron and hurried to put on water and stoke the fire. Then I laid the table with the bread and cheese Mrs. Kemper had given me and fed the cat some of our mutton stew lunch. Grizelda was a fine cat, large, hale and hearty with the reddest fur I'd ever seen, the largest yellow eyes, the longest and finest whiskers. She gave me much comfort on nights after Jack had worked me over. I should leave, but it wouldn't be fair to subject Grizelda to a life of uncertainty. When she finished the stew, I poured her some milk and set it down on the hearth, where she would be warm.

"Grizelda, you'll never guess what I saw—"

There was a thump, and the door slammed open. Jack saw what I was doing and his face turned uglier.

"Wasting good milk on that damn cat," he said. I quickly moved the saucer off the hearth and away from Jack's sight.

"Well, Jack, you're home. Let me get you some beer." When evenings started out like that, it might mean a beating later, but better to distract him from the cat. She was my one comfort, and I couldn't do without her. I don't know what I'd do to Jack if he hurt her.

"Husband, you'll not believe what I saw on my way home this evening," I said, pouring the beer. He ignored me as usual, but I went on. "I saw a procession of cats, and they were carrying a long, black box. It had a tiny gold crown on it!" I set his beer in front of him. He grabbed it and took a long drink. "I think—I think it was a coffin. There must have been a dead cat inside."

He wiped his mouth with his sleeve and looked at me suspiciously. "And where might you have seen this procession, Missy?"

"Why—on the road alongside the forest," I lied. "They turned in front of me and must have gone in toward the graveyard!" I glanced at the cat, and then looked again. She seemed tense, her bright eyes sharp, her milk forgotten. She seemed to be listening too.

"So?" Jack said.

"Oh, well they were wailing something fierce!"

Jack set the beer down and began working off a boot.

"They carried—can you believe it? They were carrying candles that lit up the trees!"

Jack glared at me balefully. The boot finally came off, and he threw it to the floor. He would not set anything down gently if he could slam it. Sometimes at me.

"Go on."

"Well, the cats were crying and carrying on."

"Yeah, you said that." He began working on the second boot.

"Oh, yes, I did, didn't I," I said nervously. I glanced at Grizelda, who was still as still could be. "Well . . . they were standing tall, on two feet, like humans, and they wept and cried out. They said, 'Regina Grimalkin is dead. Our beloved queen is dead!' and they put the box in that hole and buried it."

"What?" Jack cried. "So you *were* in the wood, weren't ye, you lying hag?"

But I was staring at my cat.

"Jack, will you look at Grizelda?" She seemed to have grown to twice her size with her fur on end. And with the fire shining through it, she looked like the very sun.

"Damn that cat," Jack roared, wrenching his boot off and throwing it at Grizelda. I screamed and reached out to stop the boot, but Grizelda reared up on her two hind legs and caught the boot in her two front paws. She threw that boot right back at Jack, where it caught him square in the face and knocked him backwards off his stool. Jack was aghast, his mouth open and speechless for once.

"Damn yourself, Jack," Grizelda spat. "You mean old sot. God's curse on ye for being mean as a dog, and the devil of a bully!" Her eyes burned hot and yellow, I'd never seen her look so majestic or fierce, standing there on two feet, planted well apart. Then she bared her teeth and hissed, "Regina Grimalkin was my mother, and if she's dead, then that means I'M THE QUEEN OF THE CATS!"

With that, my cat gathered herself as if to jump, but just before she did, she turned her wild, magic eyes to me.

"It's now or never, Missus!" she cried. "You can stay in misery and torment with *that*, or lead a life of wonders with me and mine."

And then she did jump, and when she did, I moved just as quick, grabbing her tail and up the chimney I went with my queenly cat, and we never saw the likes of Jack again.

Tammy Lynn

This young adult story was inspired by the ancient Scottish story Tam Lin, only the narrator and leading man of that story are here cast as lesbians.

Nov. 2 ALL SOULS DAY

SINCE I'VE BEEN excused from classes for the time being and I'm under lock and key and under psychiatric observation for MENTAL ILLNESS I'm writing down everything like the doctor told me to, so I'm starting from the very beginning so I'll never forget—*as if.*

What eventually happened in a way started way back with Kathy Rosen. Before our teacher Ms. Sandoval made us work on a lit project together we were academic RIVALS. When we were forced to work together, we determined to get the best grade in the class and we decided our project would be on stories with female heroes so we read about a 100 fairytales, myths and folktales and that's how we became Best Friends Forever. We explained the different types of stories and presented statistics and ratios about them to our 8th grade class and we both got A+'s, the only ones who did, and kids tried to bully us and called us The Goody-Two Shoe Sisters because they were jealous, but we decided to change our image IN SPITE of them to be WITCHES because in stories THEY were the WOMEN OF POWER and we wanted to make everyone be afraid of us. So Kathy shortened her name to Kat and made some velvet ears to wear on a headband. I dyed my hair red on one side and green on the other because I couldn't make up my mind what was witchier and changed my name from Janet to Jet and wore a T-shirt with a really rad cartoon rocket on it. Jets aren't exactly witchy, but KAT and JET sound cool together. First thing we did was cast an anti-bullying spell we found on the internet and IT WORKED! But to tell the truth, no one was really scared of us.

Of course my parents threw a tantrum when they saw me until I told them it was only Kool-Aid. They blamed Kat (like I can't come up with MY OWN BAD IDEAS) and PUBLIC SCHOOL although I don't know what that had to do with it. They called us INCORRIGIBLE because we stayed out late ALL THE TIME but actually it was ONE TIME, just because Kat and I went to a double zombiefeature and didn't get home till midnight. How were we supposed to know we'd get out of the movie so late, and we had to get our money's worth and see both movies, right? Or that we'd be STARVING so we had to go to an all-night diner and eat root beer floats. I don't know what the big deal was, after all it was summer.

Next they caught us DRINKING although that was actually THEIR FAULT because of a cocktail party where THEY were boozing with all their friends and dancing and yelling and keeping us awake. Kat was spending the night and after everyone left we snuck downstairs and drank what was left in everyone's glasses then put on music (it wasn't THAT loud) and we were laughing and dancing like crazy and woke them up. I don't know why they got all hysterical when it was exactly what THEY had been doing. They said Kat wasn't a good ELEMENT like she was a chemical or something. I know it was really because she wasn't CATHOLIC or RICH and they're prejudiced against anyone who's pagan and she's Jewish.

I overheard mom gossiping about me to my dad (actually I was spying on them). She said She's fifteen, boys are next. Well maybe it was just a MAGICAL COINCIDENCE, but Kat and I didn't happen to like boys, except maybe someone majorly cool and cute like Prince who's dead anyway. So my dad jumps to conclusions and starts saying Oh no we're not having UNWANTED PREGNANCIES in this house like I was a big ho! The next thing I knew I was enrolled in St. Joan of Arc's Catholic boarding school for girls! I couldn't believe it! We're Catholic, but we don't go to mass very often and my parents don't even LIKE the church, which goes to show what complete and total moral hypocrites they are. I called up Kat crying What kind of witch goes to a Catholic school? But she said That school has an excellent rating and furthermore, I heard St. Joan's is where all the LESBIANESE go (which was a code name we made up for OUR KIND). So I told my parents and I said If I turn out to be a lesbian from going there you're only going to have YOURSELVES TO BLAME. (Actually I was secretly preparing them for MAXIMUM GUILT when I CAME OUT someday.) Of course they didn't believe it because lesbianism is a SIN and they think the nuns wouldn't allow it (as if the nuns aren't all doing it too) and they just laughed and said You're still going. Kat said I'm going to ask my dad if I can go to St. Joan's too so in the meantime KEEP YOUR EYES OPEN FOR REAL LESBIANS. We didn't know what true lesbians were like except for pictures on the internet and we didn't believe there were so many perfect looking movie star and Playboy Bunny Lezzes.

I went to St. Joan's website to and found out it's the oldest Catholic girl's school in the state and in Napa right next door to the state INSANE ASYLUM about five miles away so I think there's a connection between them. When school started I hated it and I secretly cried at night over my ruined life but my roommate Fumiko must have heard because she said I was forced to go here too for disobedience but it's not too bad. It has a really fun art and athletics departments and most of the nuns are really cool.

Anyway, I heard about Tammy Lynn in the gym locker room. A couple of girls were talking about a scandal, a girl named Tammy Lynn who disappeared. I pretended like I wasn't listening so they would keep talking and they said people believed she was murdered by the nuns and was buried somewhere at St. Joan's. So first chance I got I looked her up on the internet but there were lots of Tammy Lynns so I asked Fumiko and she said her name was actually Tamara Bird Lynn and it happened hundreds of years ago, like in 1940 or something, and rumors got started about DEVIL WORSHIP at the school and I believed it because I've seen movies about nuns dancing around with the Devil and kissing his butt and poisoning nuns they didn't like, but the police never found a trace of Tammy or satanic practices and the nuns hushed it all up to save their reputations and the school's too.

I found a section devoted to the school in the old Jane Carter Hall Library so I looked through the yearbooks for Tamara Bird Lynn but her pictures had all been cut out with a mat knife (probably censorship). So then I got the idea to look at the public library on a Saturday, which was our free day and we could go out. The librarian got me the story on microfiche which is what people had to use before technology came out and I read about how Tammy Lynn first came to

St. Joan's on a special scholarship for orphans. It had lots of pictures of all her athletic achievements and WOW Tammy Lynn was a complete and total BABE!!! Short blonde hair, bright eyes with long, long lashes and Beyoncé lips. I finally got to the story about her. In her senior year when she was the school's star pupil and town hero and she had at least three famous women's colleges bribing her with complete and total scholarships so she would pick them to go to, she DISAPPEARED. The police questioned everyone but no one knew anything except to say she didn't have a boyfriend and she wasn't unhappy at St. J's. All they found out was that some girls were playing a game the night before and Tammy went to the bathroom and that was the last time they saw her. They thought she went to bed and didn't even know she was missing until the next morning. It was HALLOWEEN so that must be where the satanic rumors came from.

Then there was a BUNCH OF DIRT! It came out Tammy was close with a nun who was supposed to be her "mentor" complete with photos but she denied "anything untoward" in their relationship which means there WAS something "untoward" that's why she was being questioned and EVERYONE KNOWS nuns lie all the time and furthermore there was something VERY SUSPICIOUS about her because she was a STONE FOX (but not as cute as Tammy) so what was she doing at St. Joan's instead of on the cover of a magazine? There was another story about her being sent away to a nun-jail where BAD NUNS are sent to be re-brainwashed I bet (ha ha) which PROVES her guilt. The police searched the grounds with dogs and even the FBI was involved and even a PSYCHIC who said Tammy Lynn was in a place no one could reach her and would never come back, and she was right because they never did find her. The school's OFFICIAL STORY was that Tammy Lynn ran away, but that didn't make sense with all those great scholarships howling at her door and that totally hot NOT nun-advisor of hers (when you're a lez you learn to read between the lines).

Of course the more I read about Tammy the more I fell TOTALLY IN LOVE with her. But Tammy Lynn was long gone, plus it was a long time ago, and there was nothing for me to do but crush in secret. I couldn't even talk about it because:

a. I couldn't tell if anyone else at St. J's was a lesbian and would understand and

b. There was no one there I trusted to tell something like that and

c. I didn't want anyone to think I was absurd, me all in love with a picture of a girl (even though a witch could have a ghost girlfriend, but I can't tell them that either.)

So Halloween comes and the nuns held a vigil in the chapel with everyone having to pray against the PAGAN festivities that were going on everywhere in the world except at boring St. J's where the most exciting thing that ever happens is maybe someone tells A LIE. In church Fumiko whispered This is a tradition that started after Tammy Lynn disappeared. After saying a WHOLE BORING ROSARY and being tortured because we had to do it on our KNEES, we went back to our room and I put on my nightgown and Fumiko her pajamas when Nina comes over and says Georgie says to come up! She's a cool senior with her own room on the 3rd floor and she and Georgie are good friends. So we snuck up even though it was AGAINST THE RULES and kind of spooky up there. So we're sitting around talking about ghosts and stuff, it being Halloween after all, and all of a sudden Nina says If you say TAMMY LYNN three times looking in a mirror, she'll appear and KISS YOU. "A GIRL" kisses you? I say like I'm all disgusted because I was only like 10% sure that any of them was a lesbian and Fumiko says Yeah, a GIRL! smiling with all her big teeth and no one else was offended and that 10% jumped to 99% (leaving a margin for error.) (By the way, lesbians look like REGULAR PEOPLE, that way we can hide in real life.) Then I was all ears because aside from Tammy Lynn being my SECRET HEART THROB I finally had EVIDENCE of St. J maybe being a HOTBED OF LESBIANS (maybe even hot beds WITH lesbians!) after all and I had to memorize what I heard so I could report it all back to Kat who would kill me if I forgot.

That's about when Sister Pam showed up with red wine and potato chips and she gets into the conversation laughing and saying, That's a myth. And I started to say Actually, it's an URBAN LEGEND but I closed my big mouth just in time because it's a very bad idea to correct a nun, even if Sister Pam was the youngest and coolest of the nuns. She visits Georgie anytime she can give the slip to the other nuns. So Georgie says Hey, let's see if it works! And Sister Pam gets all teacher-like and says I FORBID SATANIC PRACTICES, but because she hung out with students she had kind of lost her authority over us, and Georgie says It's NOT satanic it's a GAME (actually it's a ritual) and they start arguing. Then in the middle of it, Fumiko says Hey it's midnight, I'm going to try it as a SCIENTIFIC EXPERIMENT and goes into the bathroom and closes the door. I thought I heard her say Holy (something). A few minutes later she comes out with her eyes all big: It worked! It totally worked! TAMMY LYNN CAME AND SHE KISSED ME! Sister Pam just laughed like she didn't believe it and guzzled some wine. I was wondering if it really worked or if Fumiko was just trying to annoy Sister Pam when Nina says I'm next and runs into the bathroom and slams the door. She comes out a few minutes later with her eyes giant and her hand over her mouth saying OMG! OMG! It TOTALLY WORKS and SHE IS THE MOST AMAZING KISSER! And Sister Pam looked mad and like she was getting ready to FORBID US from doing it again (probably really to keep GEORGIE-GIRL-FRIEND from trying it) and I'm like REALLY JEALOUS now, Tammy Lynn kissing everyone in the student body except me so I said all bored I have to use the bathroom, which I did, because I was going to do the Tammy Lynn spell.

When I closed the door it was all dark because only a distant light came in from the moon coming through the tall narrow window and looking in the mirror was creepy because it was streaked and peeling and all ancient. I couldn't see my reflection, just the dark shape of my head and shoulders and I was getting more and more scared, but then I thought of Tammy Lynn and how I would do ANYTHING to be kissed by her and that gave me the braveness to look into that spidery mirror and say TAMMY LYNN three times. Nothing happened at first, then a weird light showed up over my left shoulder, but it wasn't over my shoulder, it was ACTUALLY in the mirror. I kept staring because I was so jazzed, because suddenly I was inside the mirror, and TAMMY LYNN was there in front of me!!! I thought she was so pretty in her pictures, but in real life she was ABSOLUTELY TO DIE FOR! First of all, she was all lit up like she had a saint's halo, only all over her body. Her hair was light blonde and punked, shaved on one side and soft and longish, hanging down from the part. And she had the MOST AMAZING EYES with a kind of light in them. Then I saw silver tears rolling down her cheeks. Tammy Lynn, what's wrong? And Tammy Lynn says I weep for you Jet (she knew my witch name!) and for the girls who summon me every Halloween. I will kiss you, as you wish, but first, I must warn you of the terrible danger you attract when you recite that charm to summon me. And I'm so shocked I just say Really? How did you end up in here anyway, are you stuck? And she told me the whole story.

Many years ago tonight, my friends and I performed this same ritual, calling another name, believing it a game. We did not know Halloween is when magic is at its most powerful, nor that mirrors become a door into the underworld at midnight. We did not know that magic, evil people on the other side could see us, or that they sometimes take humans to dally with. This was how the queen of the underworld took me for herself. Now she thinks it a lark when I am called, and orders me to fulfill the ritual. Because of my girlish folly, I am now a slave to that witch in her decaying castle.

At first I didn't mind so much, it was a strange and wonderful world, the queen was beautiful beyond dreams, and best of all, I was her darling.

For a time, because I soon discovered she had so many darlings and favorites, I never knew who had not been with her. Worst of all, there is a price to pay for all the magic that holds the underworld in place. Every seven years the underworld rulers pay a tribute of human souls to the Devil. Now I suspect she is tiring of me, of my jealousy and sadness and pining for my old world, and that she will soon choose me for the tribute.

So by now this sounds like one of the fairy tales I read and I'm sure I'm dreaming so I'm not one bit scared, and I want to keep dreaming with gorgeous Tammy Lynn, and as long it was my dream I say How I can help you? as if I was a big hero, but I was thinking I could get masses said for her, but she looks at me with those blue crystal eyes, twinkling with silvery sad tears and she looks amazed and says No one has ever offered to help me. Would you really do it Jet? And I answered YES of course, because I would have done ANYTHING for her. She says There is a way, but it is fraught with peril. So I say I don't care, I'll do it. And she says Then take my hand, and I did and suddenly we're whooshing together down like a really long well, then we're standing on a dark wet street corner in a place that smelled like moss and mud, but I didn't pay attention to where I was, I only had big eyes for Tammy Lynn, because she was glowing in the darkness all in white leather with an eight point gold star on her chest. She reminded me of the paintings at school of St. Joan in her white armor.

Watch for me at midnight, Jet. I will be in the queen's entourage; all of us will be dressed alike. You will know me because I will wear only one glove. You must pull me from my place in the procession and hold onto me. The queen will use her power to get you to release me. Pray, (I wonder if that's what gave me the idea later) do not let go, no matter what you see, no matter what happens. Now I must take my leave, she will be looking for me, wanting to hear of my romps with young women who can never have me, because I belong to her. Tammy let go of my hand and just like that, she disappeared.

I was, like, all dizzy from the ride down and confused from everything happening so fast. I looked around and I was wondering where I was and what did I get myself into now. I wanted to do whatever I could to save Tammy Lynn, but I wasn't bold or brave, especially without Kat. How was I going to save Tammy, and get us out of this place? Everything was really weird, the bricks and stones the place was made of were crooked as if they had been there for a thousand years and moss and mushrooms were even growing out from between them and it was dripping like rain, yet it was steamy and almost warm and there was a strong earth smell. There were these balls of fire at street corners and hanging by these flying buttress-type walkways that were over the street that led to higher walkways. The buildings were all strange and leaning over precarious-wise, kind of like the way Dr. Seuss draws buildings, tall and thin and crazy, and far above everything there was a ceiling where all these pipes and ducts all connected to each other, some blowing steam others sucking or making other kinds of noises. I thought it must look like that under a city with pipes and sewers and tunnels and stuff. The place was like a wet and foggy San Francisco, if it was night and had spooky smoking fireballs instead of streetlights, and giant trees holding it all up, and it was in a dream. The trees—they were big and gnarly and ancient here and there right among the stone walls as if the people had built their houses and walls right up to them, then continued on the other side instead of cutting it down like we would up in the daylight world, in the world of no magic. Because I just knew that's where I was, in a magical world of darkness and that dreams and stories were made here and sent up to us as a reminder of what we've lost by being all modernized. There were branches hanging down with what looked like beautiful dark fruit and smelling so strange but delicious and ripe and it seemed like they were begging for me to pick and eat them and I reached up to a big fat dark red one like a hanging heart, but then I remembered one of the myths Kat and I read was about a girl who ate fruit while she was in the underworld and was condemned to go back there every six months and of course, EVERYONE KNOWS what happened to Alice Wonder in the underworld so I snatched my hand back and wouldn't even look at them, but I wondered how they grew without the sun then realized I couldn't see the tree tops among all those overhead pipes and stuff, so they must grow through the ceiling all the way up to the sun and in fact these were actually root-trees and root fruit. I had only walked about five feet and there were all these wonders so far. I was standing on one of four corners and there was an old sign that said Miles & Cross Roads, but there were other signs around with words in letters sort of like you see in those old leather books, written by ancient nuns and monks—we have one in a glass case in the library—and I kept trying to read them until I realized it wasn't the English alphabet.

In the very middle of the crossed roads was a big huge black tower thing with a top in the shape of an upside-down beet, and four long legs that made archways. It looked like iron but when I crossed over to it and touched it, it was actually black clay, and I remembered from the stories fairies are allergic to iron and this must be Fairyland (although maybe all magical beings can't touch iron). There was a well underneath the tower, and as I was looking at all the whorls and curlicues and faces in the clay, all of a sudden steam started coming out of the well and the water was making a churning sound and I ran back across the street. There was a long low CHOOO sound and water rose up and flooded the well and spilled into a channel that divided the street. Watching that dark water made me think of a myth where a girl fetched water of death for a goddess who turned it into the water of life. I wondered if this was that same water, or something like it.

On the tip of the beet's spire was a clock with three weird faces that overlapped each other like a Venn diagram, one was a crooked moving spiral like it was trying to hypnotize you, another some kind of mirror with a mouth and an eye, and the third had numbers or letters scattered all disorderly across the face. There were people passing by too, I guess you would call them that. Everyone seemed to be wearing something on their head, whether it was some kind of mask or helmet or even a big rusty can with eyes cut out and holes poked through for the mouth. One person even had what looked like an upside down boot on his head, although it had to be the shoe of a giant. He was looking at me through the shoelaces with the toe part jutting out over his forehead and he had smeary eyes and a sharky mouth. Some masks had giant frog or cat or bird heads. Another looked like a rat-boar, with a hairy pointed face and curly tusks. Then I wondered What if those aren't masks but their actual heads, and they're monsters? Only they didn't come after me like monsters do in movies or dreams. They were gawking at me when they passed as if *I* was the weird one. It was probably because I was really obvious. They all wore dark clothes as if they wanted to blend into the damp dark walls and there I was all in white like Baptism and Holy Communion Day at the same time, my nightgown wet from all the dripping off the ceiling and fog and steam and dragging around on the ground. Or maybe they were staring because of my bare face practically glowing and making me stick out. My hair had frizzed out and was straggling down my back so I pulled some hair forward and twisted hair like dreadlocks down in front of my face to make a sort of mask that I could see through and was at least as good a disguise as that stupid giant shoe mask. There was so much to see right from one spot I didn't wander very far and I was afraid to anyway because I didn't want to miss Tammy. What time was it? I was still wearing my watch but the hands were zooming around the face. How was I going to know when midnight was? Was time different in that place? That strange, layered clock was no help.

The guy with the rusty can on his head was talking to a woman-insect saying I just saw the ugliest thing ever and I don't even know what it is and he was looking right at ME, and I was about to say who are you calling UGLY? when a voice coming from the clock said IT IS TIME PREPARE TO STAND IN AWE OF AND WORSHIP and I looked to see where it was coming from and it was the mouth in the clock mirror and the eye had opened and a really skinny arm that looked like a slug with fingers was pointing repeatedly to one of the strange numbers. Then I heard bells tinkling and a sound like machinery, all sinister like and I turned around and there was a procession coming slowly down the street toward us. Everyone had turned to face the street with their arms crossed on their chests and stood completely still, so I copied them. The procession drove slowly by all wearing that white leather with stars, everyone glowy like Tammy had been, all pretty much the same except for their helmets which were kind of like knights used to wear only with studs and gems and stars and spikes, but also turning wheels and clicking gears, little propellers and even wings. Each person was upright and still and looking straight ahead and I wondered if they were actually manikins, all sitting on some kind of flying silver motorcycle-like conveyances only with no wheels, floating about a foot off the ground, some on fire, some with wings or tails but I was too nervous and scared to really look, the whole parade was amazing, but hypnotizing and distracting so I forced myself to look mainly at hands as they went by, except for the one who must have been the queen. She was higher than everyone else on an invisible horse—at least she was seated on horse-shaped armor with nothing inside it—and she was surrounded by what looked sort of like sea horses (but must have been earth horses) with big spikes sticking out all over and huge wide open blazing green and red eyes, flying along beside the queen, their long, gross wormy tails with bright crystals all along the length rippling behind. Her long delicate silvery hair floated out behind her as if a wind were blowing it, and there was a silvery mask that looked like a wonderful moth with enormous eyes in the wings that were like clear eyeballs and moved around looking at everything. Its head had lots of antennae that were moving in different directions, as if picking up and transmitting information. The mask-moth-butterfly flew in front of the queen's face just enough so you could see around it to how perfect and fantastically beautiful she was, like you would do whatever she said because of it and no wonder Tammy fell in love with her. Even though she had been completely still like everyone else, the queen turned her head slowly as she passed me, and she and the mask eyes all looking at me, it must have been that stupid white nightgown announcing my existence as if I was an escaped prisoner with a searchlight on me. But I stood still as a graffitied cartoon on a wall not even moving my eyes or breathing, hoping she'd think I was just another creepy underground citizen who happened to find a white rag to put on. Behind her and the earth horses were more motor-flyer processioners and I kept watching their hands and I started getting panicky that Tammy already passed while I was looking at something else and I missed her, then I saw her sign: ONE BARE HAND so I didn't even think about how scared I was, I just ran over and pulled her off the floating motorcycle thing and her helmet with goggle eyeholes and turning wheels and dials, fell off and bounced and IT WAS TAMMY! All at once I heard a thousand voices screaming like those creepy cicada bugs and one second Tammy was laughing, and the next she was a big squiggly slippery salamander like those gross giant ones they have in Asia, but Tammy had told me to hold on to her no matter what so I slipped my arms all the way around the salamander and grabbed my own wrists with each hand, which is how mountain climbers help each other up, just in time because then I was holding a giant, hairy spider that was waving its gross arms around and snapping right at my face with human teeth among fangs, but I focused on holding tighter. Then she became a huge roaring struggling monster cat with wide open shark jaws with sharp ugly teeth all around its mouth and I was so scared I thought I was going to pee! So I focused on not peeing and squeezed my eyes shut so I wouldn't give up. Then she got really still and suddenly I felt hot and I opened my eyes and Tammy was a big branch on fire that was sweeping over the leaves toward me and I didn't want to find out if it would actually burn me so I ran over to that well and jumped in, dragging branch-Tammy with me. When we surfaced, Tammy was her regular self again only she was all naked, hanging on to my neck like women do to the HERO when she wants him to save her and she was crying into my neck out of fear or relief, and I was afraid the water would chuff and rise and throw us out again at the queen's feet, and then what would I do?

Up above us crowded all around in the archways were the helmet heads of the other riders all quiet now, looking down at us. Then the queen pushed them out of the way and socked away her mask, which flew up over her head whimpering like a poor, kicked dog. The queen's face was all red and her eyes were squinched up and she bared her teeth like Cerberus and she was STILL beautiful as can be. She glared at us and yelled DAMN YOU TAMMY LYNN IF I HAD KNOWN WHAT TREACHERY WAS IN YOUR HEART I WOULD HAVE SPOILED YOUR INNOCENT BEAUTY I WOULD HAVE RIPPED OUT YOUR LYING TONGUE AND PUT A SNAKE IN ITS PLACE I WOULD HAVE PLUCKED OUT YOUR FAITHLESS PELLUCID EYES AND REPLACED THEM WITH ASHES I WOULD HAVE GIVEN YOU TO THE

DEVIL A CURSE UPON YOU AND THE WHORE WHO STEALS YOU FROM ME!

Well I wasn't going to just let her put curses on us so I yelled back SHUT UP BI-ATCH! YOU'RE the ho' with so many lovers you can't scratch without bumping into one and anyway YOU STOLE Tammy from her life and you're just mad because someone is actually rejecting you, how does it feel? Her huge eyes got bigger and her amazing mouth fell open, she must have been shocked someone was talking back to her, then I remembered she was dangerous--me and my big mouth--so before she could do anything I made a big sign of the cross in the air between us and said really loud: IN THE NAME OF THE FATHER AND THE SON AND MARY THE MOTHER AND THE HOLY GHOST WHO IS THE SHEKHINA ON EARTH (which is a subversive Catholic prayer I made up to replace the sexist one) and there was an even WORSE shrieking than before, then everything vanished and there was that whooshing wind again and the next thing I knew we were inside the mirror of Georgie's bathroom, Tammy still holding me against her CREAMY DREAMY body! She said Jet, you did it, you saved me! I'm free! Thank you! And she hugged me and then she KISSED ME, and it was the most amazing thing that ever happened to me! I almost passed out in her arms like a SWOON in Sleeping Beauty but I stayed conscious (I wasn't about to miss THAT for anything). We kissed like that for a while and I would have gone on and on kissing Tammy for the rest of my life but she stopped and smiled and that was nearly as wonderful. Tammy wasn't perfect or bright like Joan of Arc anymore, like when she first appeared to me. She was more ordinary cute like humans are supposed to be, but it made me even MORE IN LOVE WITH HER!

Through the mirror I could see it was morning out there and I sort of heard Fumiko and Nina and Georgie in the other room talking with voices raised like something was wrong and Sister Pam was walking around and waving her arms. So I said all excited Let's go out there because I couldn't wait for them to see that I'd found Tammy and brought her back and to tell them the whole amazing story. But Tammy said Wait Jet, stop (her voice was normal now too) when we go through the mirror I'm going to turn to dust, and I said NO! Yes, she said back, If I had lived an ordinary life, I would have died two decades ago. The queen showed me a mirror where I saw how and when I would have died. So I said Then I'll stay here with you, but Tammy said That would be like living in the vestibule of Hell. We'd always be trying to hide from the queen, and sooner or later, she'll catch us and send both of us to Hell. Jet, you'll have to be brave one more time. You have to return to your life, and let me go to my final rest.

I put my head against her chest and she let me cry and cry. Then we kissed one more time and I looked at her again, touching her face and hair so I would always remember what it was to hold her. Jet, she said, don't be sad. Because of what we've been through together, we'll always be connected. Whatever that means. It was like we were breaking up, only without the relationship. Finally even though I felt like I was killing her, I held her hand and stepped through the mirror and pulled her back into the world. As soon as she passed through I felt her hand collapse in mine and she turned into a sparkly dust, floating in the air for a minute before disappearing. Even though I knew it was going to happen it was a complete and total shock and I didn't even have time to process when Sister Pam was all in my face and shaking me yelling WHERE HAVE YOU BEEN ALL NIGHT YOUNG LADY WE'VE BEEN LOOKING FOR YOU EVERYWHERE and no one even noticed the silvery dust that was Tammy Lynn floating around us and winking out. Then everyone crowded around hugging me and asking what happened and Sister Pam examined the bathroom and out the window and knocking on the walls and ceiling and floor tiles as if she was looking for a secret passageway, me crying the whole time.

I was crying so much I couldn't talk so Sister Pam took me to the infirmary and told the nurse-nuns I had been engaging in a FORBIDDEN ACTIVITY and got a fright. The nun-nurses talked about calling my parents to come and get me but I said NO! Even though for the last 2-1/2 months I would have done ANYTHING to go home and be with Kat again all of a sudden I had to be where women honored women, ESPECIALLY LESBIANESE. St. Joan had been staring at me from paintings and stained glass all over this place and HELLO?!! She was a COMPLETE AND TOTAL DYKE WHO WENT TO HEAVEN! Therefore lesbianism CAN'T BE A SIN. Probably men only made up that rule because they wanted women ONLY to have sex with them, which I figured out because of my Feminist Critical Thinking class.

So the nun-nurses didn't call my parents but made me talk to a shrink who would know what to do. She was a nun-shrink but turned out to be really nice. She asked me where I had been and I told her I fell asleep in the bathroom all curled up in a corner behind the john and no one saw me and I had a scary amazing dream, because it really *was* pretty scary when I thought about it. I said that because if I told her it was ALL REAL I would end up in the asylum (and now I know its connection to the school). She gave me a journal and told me to write everything down and said I didn't have to show it anyone, not even her, but doing it might make me feel better. So that's what this is, and even though it makes me keep thinking and crying about Tammy, doing it makes me feel better.

I got to stay out of school for the rest of the week and I hand wrote a letter to Kat (they don't allow computers or phones in the infirmary) but I didn't end up sending it because everything was just too amazing and awesome so I have to tell her in person. Even though I TOTALLY FAILED at being a witch by using a Catholic prayer blessing instead of magic to save Tammy, I knew Kat would totally get it and say something cool like We get to use whatever we have to save ourselves.

Nov. 12

I'VE BEEN BACK at classes now for a week. Everyone keeps looking at me as if I was that evil fairy queen. Students and teachers and Jesuits, even the lady janitor. They're all being super nice too. I thought it was because they didn't want to upset me and make me go postal, so it was really annoying. Then Fumiko told me it's because I'm different somehow, and everyone's been talking about it. She said "You used to be average, but now it's like you're glowing somehow, like a saint, only without the halo. It's like an awesome maturity, almost numinosity. (I had to look that up. It's like mystical.) That must have been a really powerful dream, Jet."

I feel different, but I didn't know other people could see it. I wonder about that water we dove into, maybe it was magic after all, or because I spent some time in the magical underworld. Or maybe a magic love just makes you totally changed.

I'm talking to my teachers and I've really knuckled down in my classes. I have to make up for all the weeks I was pissed off and not doing my homework because I was at St. Joan's, and falling behind. Even though I'm still really sad, I want to excel again. I want to live up to that magic people are seeing in me, and one way to do that is to KNOW LOTS OF DIFFERENT THINGS. Also, I have to stay because Kat convinced her parents to let her come here!

November 20

I MIGHT HAVE gotten Tammy Lynn away from the queen, and figured out how to escape her, but I'm not a hero. After all, Tammy told me exactly what to do, and although she went through all those weird changes, they were just illusions, otherwise that spider or tiger would have gotten me. Also I suspect if Tammy had come through the mirror alive, she would have been really old, and then the age difference between us would probably have been a problem. She might even want to be with that nun mentor of hers, if she's still alive, and I couldn't blame her, because they had an actual relationship.

The main characters in fairy tales always live happily ever after, but I wasn't so lucky. I couldn't save Tammy in the end. I still cry about it all. Do people ever get over a broken heart? Maybe I don't want to, since it's all I have left of her.

December 21

I DIDN'T REALLY lose Tammy Lynn after all. I understand now what she meant when she said we'd always be connected. She's been coming to me in dreams! And they're just as real as when I was in that spooky wonderland with her. We hold hands and wander through those scary streets. We hold each other and kiss again. Sometimes we have adventures, and if the queen or some other monster shows up, we get out of it by my waking up.

Dreams are the place in this world where magic is still real. Those and stories, of course.

The doctor was wise, telling me to record everything. It's as if everything was flying around crazily in my head, and writing put it all in order and stable again and calmed me down. It's also a way of keeping Tammy Lynn, and remembering that magical, amazing world.

I even put drawings (thanks to the great art classes here) in the margins of the wild amazing things I saw, like that weird architecture, those monsters, and that poor butterfly mask the queen just knocked away. She obviously took Tammy and creatures and love for granted.

My parents are coming to get me today to go home for Christmas break. I wonder if they'll notice a change in me.

Kat and I are going to have SO MUCH FUN! We'll have to behave so my parents will let us be together. I can hardly wait to tell her the WHOLE STORY!

Ode to Jimmy Jean

Another version of this story, *The Haint on Cryin Baby Bridge* was published in *Haunting Muses*, an anthology of lesbian ghost stories (GusGus Press, 2016). That version is a real ghost story. Many stories and films with lesbian themes kill off the evil, seducing dyke at the end, leaving the female protagonist free to return to a man and "real" love. The message is "the only good lesbian is a dead one." Not wanting to follow the homophobic tradition, I came up with a different and more satisfying ending. *Ode to Jimmy Jean* is the new version.

YEAH, I'VE HEARD the song about Billy Joe. Who hasn't? How he jumped off a bridge, and nobody cared because he was just a dumb hillbilly. It was a song by Bobby Gentry, not even based on a real person. Created a big stir because it was so mysterious and symbolic and everything, and everyone wanted to know what it meant.

Weird thing is, that song came out just before someone I knew who really did jump off a bridge. My friend, Jimmy Jean, called J.J. We were in seventh grade when we started doing stuff together. Don't know why J.J. took a shine to me. Maybe she could tell there was something different about me too. Knew it before I did. She wore backward baseball caps before it was cool and taught me the proper names of bugs and trees. We'd catch snakes and turtles and go swimming on hot days, but J.J. didn't ever go in deep. She was afraid of the water on account of almost drowning when she was little.

Otherwise she was the bravest person I knew. She didn't take guff and would fight boys bigger than her even if it meant she was going to get whupped. Once in the children's section at the library a man was playing with his weenie. Most of us kids were peeking and laughing, but J.J. got mad and went after him with a bat. He only got away on account of a lame foot J.J. had and she couldn't move too fast.

We talked about everything. She explained the difference between plain old naked (like when you go skinny dipping), buck naked (you still have something on, like socks), bare-ass naked (every last thing off), and nude (how models get for artists, and it's not nasty, it's how we learn). She told me how to get a baby, and we both took vows we'd never let a man do *that* to us. That led to practice kissing—my idea—so we'd know how when we went on dates. Even though J.J. didn't like boys, she always volunteered to be the boy. Kissing leads to fooling around, J.J. told me, and fooling around is sex play and makes boys think less of you, but women never think less of men for doing the same thing, and it's no fair.

People saw her go off that bridge, but they didn't see why. I knew. I was with her when it happened. It was summer, getting late one evening. We were walking across the Teleme Bridge, just hanging out and talking. About halfway across, Cash and Eli, two hoodlums about seventeen years old, show up. They hated J.J., were always calling her dyke. I didn't know what that was, thought it had something to do with the geography of Holland. J.J. stayed away from them. They'd done something to her once, she wouldn't say what. She let it slip once that they'd tied her up first.

So J.J. sees them heading toward the bridge and says oh great. Of course we were near the middle. We turn round, and start walking back the other way, fast as J.J. could go, which wasn't very. You run, she told me. Don't wait for me. I looked back. They were smiling, not hurrying, and I thought maybe they would be nice this time. What about you, I say. Go! she yells. *Now. Do it!* So I ran off the bridge, but once off I looked back. J.J. was getting closer to the side of the bridge. When they caught up with her suddenly Eli starts to grab J.J., but she twisted away from him and got to the very side. I screamed *No!* when I saw what she was going to do, but she jumped, cannonballing like she seen me do, down into the muddy, dark water of the Telame.

We all stood staring at where she went down, me holding my breath like I was doing it for her. J.J. didn't come up. I scrambled down by the side of the river, staring at the water, running into it, screaming her name, but she was gone.

You killed her you idiot peckerwoods! I screamed. We weren't goin' to do nothing to her, Eli yelled back. She didn't have to jump. They came off the bridge at me so I took off running. You better not go spreading any lies about us, Cash yelled after me.

Couple of kids fishing saw J.J. jump, pretty soon everyone knew what she done, but not Cash and Eli's part in it. They acted like they had tried to stop her from jumping and they were some big heroes. Sheriff talked to me too, asking what I saw, if she'd been depressed, had she ever talked about killing herself. I thought that was like putting the blame on her somehow. Yet I never told what happened. I wasn't brave like J.J., I was afraid of those two big bullies.

Sheriff said until we found the body, we couldn't even say she was dead. That actually gave me a secret hope that maybe she hadn't drowned. Maybe she survived somehow and lost her memory. At least it gave her a chance.

Ma said Jimmie Jean wasn't too smart going around looking like a boy, competing with them and everything. She drew attention to herself. You can't do that if you're different. Did she think this was California? My brother said people like that should tiptoe, but carry a big stick with a nail in it. So you see this story is a lot like that song. That's why I couldn't listen to it whenever it played on the radio. And they played it a lot, it being a top ten hit in the South by one of our own women.

They dragged the river but never did find J.J. I heard people talking, saying she probably got stuck in some place deep under submerged trees and eaten by fish and crawdads. Just to look at a fried catfish made me feel like throwing up.

I stayed home, feeling awful and mopey till Ma made me go out with other friends. So I went to see Mary Sue Parsons down the road. She was real nice, she knew about me losing J.J. of course. But somehow it made me miss J.J. more.

School started but I couldn't concentrate no more. I was still shocked from watching my friend die and mad at myself for being a chicken shit. First I betrayed her by leaving her, then by keeping quiet, even if it wouldn't have served a purpose to say anything. Eli and Cash actually *had* tried to keep her from jumping, even if they did it in a mean way, but I didn't know what made J.J. jump into deep rushing water that scared her so.

Halloween came around and I went with Mary Sue to chaperone her little sisters trick-or-treating. After we went to everybody's house for candy and apples or popcorn, they said can we go out to Cryin' Baby Bridge? That's a nickname for the Telame Bridge. Story is someone left a baby there and no one found the poor thing till after he was dead. Some people claimed when it was real quiet, you could hear it crying.

I hadn't been back there since it happened, but I put on a brave face. The girls were all excited and kind of scared about maybe hearing the baby ghost. The moon was big and the black, leafless trees looked like long, skinny fingers were scratching the sky. The little girls talked about Casper being a little boy ghost. When we got there, who should we see but those jackasses, trouble-makers Eli and Cash, standing on the middle of the bridge smoking. They see us, that we're just four girls, and Eli says hey let's beat up those kids and take their candy. Mary's sisters screamed and started running, and Mary was calling me and begging me to go with them and Eli and Cash were coming toward me—but I couldn't move. I just stood there with my mouth falling open because I couldn't take my eyes off the other end of the bridge.

It just appeared out of the darkness, a girl, soaking wet, wearing a big, muddy T-shirt plastered with leaves. She had something, a fishnet I guess, tangled around her head and sticking against her face, and through it you could see her eyes were big dark hollows and her mouth all bruised purple and bloody against her white face. She had sad little cherub wings, and she was holding her hands clasped in front of her like she was praying. Her head and shoulders were the only part of her lit up. Mary Sue screams it's Jimmy Jean! and Cash and Eli look too, and there was J.J.'s ghost floating toward us, pointing now at them standing there with their mouths flapping. Cash says, what is it? Then the ghost said in this chokey, watery voice The Devil says you are goin' to hell for all you done.

Eli yelled It's a haint! and he grabbed Cash's jacket arm and they ran away screaming into the night like a pair of ambulances from the scene of a crime. Me, when I could move again, I ran across the bridge crying and calling J.J.! But just like that, the light went out and she disappeared. No one was at the other end of the bridge. By the light of the moon I could see muddy footprints on the wood, leading nowhere.

When I got back to Mary Sue, her little sisters were just standing there, hiding behind her, holding onto her dress with cartoon-big eyes, so I knew they all seen J.J. too. We all run home. Me, straight to bed. I stayed there crying for three days. Ma had to bring in the negro root granny. Soon as she laid her warm hand on my forehead I started feeling better. She looked in my eyes and said Girl, you've had a powerful fright. She prayed and blew tobacca on me from her corn pipe. That night I dreamed of J.J. laughing, just as fine and happy as can be. Next morning I got up and ate for the first time since Halloween. I heard if you dream about someone dead, they're really visiting you. I figured J.J. was telling me she was just fine in the afterlife, and I set about trying to accept what happened.

Well, the ghost of J.J. put the fear of God into those two no 'counts. They didn't have so much in common anymore. Eli suddenly found some ambition and started working on his brother's farm. Cash studied his Bible and eventually became a deacon at the Methodist church. Neither ever said what caused their profound changes.

One day a few months later I got a letter with no return address. I immediately recognized J.J.'s fast, sloppy writing and thought she had written me from Glory. I tore it open and read,

> How did you like my Halloween prank? GUESS WHAT! I aint afraid of water no more! It carried me a ways, and just when I thought I would have to open my mouth and breathe water, it bobbed me right up! I am as floatational as a piece of driftwood! Been staying with my aunt Ricky down river. Miss you something fierce.
>
> J J
>
> PS, My address is at the bottom but don't tell anyone I'm really alive!

J.J. survived that jump. She'd been alive all this time! It was like I came back to life too. I started paying attention in school and doing my homework again. I helped around the house without being asked and didn't fight with my brother no more. I was so good, Ma thought I was a changeling.

I kept J.J.'s secret. We exchanged letters, and J.J. talked about moving out west, the only place that was safe for people like her. I started taking after-school jobs and saving my money so I could go with her.

That song about Billy Joe may not have been about a real person, but I think what Bobby Gentry was saying is that all people need sympathy, even if they're just a dumb hillbilly, or dyke, or colored, or old, whatever. Without it you jump off a bridge, or become a hateful hoodlum. As such, I made up my mind to always try to have sympathy for people. It hasn't always been easy, but I have learned it's the mean ones who need it most. And it makes the world a kinder place.

Prayers for La Llorona

1

THE FIRST TIME I saw La Llorona, I was six. It was on my grandparents' ranch on the outskirts of Los Angeles. Of course I'd heard of her; even white people knew who she was. She was a lady ghost who haunted the waterways of Mexico and sometimes the American southwest in search of her children.

We were by the canal, hanging out with my cousins, and a couple of boys on bikes from a nearby ranch. An owl landed on the top of the telephone pole on the other side of the canal. It was huge, and it watched us steadily with yellow eyes in the early twilight.

"Look at that bird," I said.

"That's an owl," my know-it-all cousin Nicky said, as if an owl isn't a bird.

"Mom says they're bad luck," Rochelle said, my favorite cousin.

"No, they mean someone's going to die," Nicky said. "But that's just superstition."

The kids on the bikes hooted at it, but the owl just stared at us. We went back to what we were talking about before: the boys had told us if you see the streetlights go on, they'll give you a hundred dollars.

Nicky said, "That's stupid. How are you going to prove it? Anyone could say they saw the lights go on. And who is this person that's going to give it to you anyway?"

When I looked at the telephone pole again, the owl was gone, but there was a woman on the pole, wrapped around it like a cat holds onto a tree, still staring at us. She wore a long white dress and her hair was loose, blowing in the warm, twilight wind. She had large, sad eyes, they reminded me of a horse, and she seemed to be looking just at me. I stared back, falling in love. The woman was Mexican and beautiful, even more than my mother, who of all her pretty sisters, was the beauty in her family.

My sister saw me staring and turned around to look, and right then, the woman called to us, "Come to me, my children." Her voice sounded far away, like it was coming from the ocean, which was a couple miles west from us. Too young to know better, I started walking toward her.

My sister's hand came clamping down on my shoulder. "Stay here, you. You're not supposed to talk to strangers."

"I'm not," I said, but I couldn't take my eyes off the lady. She smiled, and beckoned me with her hand. I stared at it. The hand looked old and yellowish, with big veins and really long, scary fingernails, a witch's hand.

"Your mother told you to come with me," she crooned.

My sister's fingers dug into my shoulder. "You don't know our mother," she shouted. "Stop looking at us, or I'll call the police." Rita was four years older than me and pretty streetwise for her age. Bossy too.

"Come on, we're going back," she said, turning me around and dragging me away. "You too, Nicky and Rochelle. *Now.*"

She marched us back to the ranch house. I glanced back. The two boys on bikes were still there, looking toward the canal. I couldn't see the lady on the telephone pole anymore.

We were shocked when we heard one of those boys had drowned. He was a good swimmer, but the sides of the canal were straight up and down.

"I found his bike by the canal where we were," Nicky said, looking white and stunned. "I rode it around for a while, then took it over to his house. That's when I found out."

"The owl!" Rochelle said. "It was warning us, just like I said."

"*I* said," Nicky corrected, not too stunned to demand credit.

"Maybe that lady killed him," I said.

"What lady?"

"The one who kept looking at us. With the long black hair."

But no one remembered her, not even my sister. I thought they were pretending, teasing me like they did sometimes.

The drowning was a terrible, sad event, and we all went to his funeral. My mother forbade us to go anywhere near the canal after that. I obeyed, although for days I stood in back of my grandparents' house and stared out toward the canal.

2

"MOM, TELL ME about La Llorona again."

My mother told really good stories. She was putting me to bed in the spare twin in my grandparents' room, while the adults were still up, watching TV and eating barbecued corn. After lighting the chimney candles for the saints on the dresser, she came over and sat across from me, on my grandparents' bed.

"Well, it happened a long time ago in Mexico," she began in her storytelling voice. "There was a woman named Maria Luisa—"

"Did you know her?"

"No, this was before I was born, I only heard about her. She lived in a little *casita* near Lake Cuitzeo. She was as beautiful as a queen, and she had an important boyfriend, a Spanish general. And she kept having children, first two boys, then a girl. She thought that would make him marry her, but he didn't."

"But how did she have children when she wasn't married?"

"Never mind, you'll understand when you get older. Listen to the story. Maria Luisa did an *hechizo* on him—"

"Was she a witch?"

"Some people say she was, but I think they said that because of the terrible thing she did. Anyway, Maria Luisa put a magic potion in his food to make him be in love with her forever, but it didn't work. He just got very sick. I think it was also because he was *muy Católico*, and went to church every Sunday with his family, and never with her. I think that's why people said she was a witch, because she didn't go to church."

"But that's a sin."

"Yes, it is. That's probably why she did what she did, because she was making a sacrifice to the old gods who used to live around there, until Jesus and the priests chased them out like St. Patrick chased the snakes out of Ireland."

"Did she ever turn into an owl?"

"No, because she's a ghost. Ghosts don't turn into owls, only witches from Mexico do that. Not the witches here, they're different. Anyway, Maria Luisa's witchcraft didn't work very well, so she probably couldn't turn into an owl if she tried. So where was I? Oh yeah. So one day, her boyfriend never came to see her again. It was because he had found someone else to marry."

"Another lady, Mamá?"

"Yes, of course another lady, what do you think, a *mujeriego* like that is going to be interested in another man?" she said crossly.

"Oh yeah. Go on."

"Well, Maria Luisa was so mad, she got all dressed up in a white wedding dress with a veil and everything and stood outside the church." Here, my mother stood up and put her hands on her hips, like it was her, waiting for that cheating boyfriend. "And when they came out, Maria Luisa shook her fist and yelled, 'you'll never be a man again when you see what I'm going to do!'" My mother squinched up her eyes like she was really mad and shook her fist, making me laugh.

"And all the people just laughed at her. Of course, they all thought Maria Luisa was just going to do more witchcraft on him and weren't worried, because none of her other spells had worked. But instead Maria Luisa went straight home and took a big knife, and killed all three of her children, and chopped them up into little pieces"—With her imaginary knife, she viciously chopped the air, sending *escalofrios* over my skin— "and threw them all in the river."

"I thought you said she lived by a lake." Of course, I was asking lots of questions to keep my mother talking, and there with me.

"Well, how do you think lakes get their water? From rivers. Now do you want me to finish, or not?"

I nodded, my lips pulled in between my teeth to remind me not to talk anymore.

"Maria Luisa stood there staring after them for a long time. Then when she finally calmed down and the *coraje* left her heart, she realized what she had done, she couldn't believe it. Why had she taken it out on her three innocent little children? *Pues*, it was because she was *loca de rabia*, and it made her not think right.

"So she starts walking in circles next to the river and pulling her hair and tearing her wedding dress and screaming, *'Ay, por dios santo, ¡mis hijos! ¡mis hijos!'* And when she heard horses galloping, getting closer and closer, she knew it was *los federales* coming to get her, so she jumped into the river and drowned herself.

"Her ex-boyfriend was so sad and sorry about his three children, he put three little crosses next to the river where it happened, and everyone in the town cried and prayed for the little ones. But no one did anything for Maria Luisa. Everyone hated her, and called her bad names, and spit when they talked about her as if they never thought about doing the same to their kids.

"And to this very day, her ghost can't rest, regretting what she did." Now my mother lowered her voice all scary. "She goes by all the rivers and lakes and beaches, looking for every piece of bone, every strand of hair, every drop of her children's blood, crying and screaming ¡mis *hijos!* the whole time. Some people say that her screams are so loud, the earth shakes. And that's why they call her La Llorona, which means The Woman Who Cries." She sat down again, putting her arms around herself as if she had scared herself.

I ventured another question. "Does she come looking for her children here too, in California?"

"People say they've heard her here, too. So if you hear screaming that's near water, nine times out of ten it's probably La Llorona." She stopped to think. "Or maybe it's the other way around *aquí en los Estados Unidos*: Only *one* time in ten it's La Llorona, the other times people are just drowning for no reason.

"La Llorona got a bad deal, if you ask me. People act as if she's the worst person who ever lived. No one says a word about *el cabrón infiel*. What she *should* have done, was go after him, sneak into his room at night and strangle him. Boyfriends behave badly, and the women take it out on the children, or the other women, or themselves. It's terrible, *pero así es*." She sighed. "Okay, that's enough now, go to sleep."

My mother turned off the light and closed the door behind her. I snuggled under the covers, thinking about La Llorona and ghosts. I wasn't afraid because the candle of the Virgin of Guadalupe was lit, and I knew I was safe with her. I looked at her, and after a while she looked like a skull, her eyes caverns and her smile was horrible grinning teeth. I sat up and looked again. She was back to the gentle Mary again. I knew the Devil had made her like that, trying to scare me. I crossed myself.

"I'm not afraid of you, Devil."

The saints' candles shed a lot of light in the room. I looked around, especially at all the little china figurines on the wooden pelmets over the drapes, and on the shelf-molding around the room: ladies, birds, animals, and a beautiful little glass boy angel that I knew was my grandmother's favorite, given to her by my cousin who died. I believed that the figurines danced and moved around when everyone was asleep, although Rita had told me that was silly and couldn't happen. I prayed to the Lady of Guadalupe to make them come to life while I could see.

I lay still for a long time pretending to be asleep, but secretly watching them through skinny eyes. Sure enough, I saw them start to move. An owl turned its head. A rabbit raised its ears. A black Halloween cat with orange eyes and a top hat, twitched its tail. Then a lady on a horse moved jerkily to the end of the pelmet.

I sat up. "I saw you move," I told them. "I knew it. You move around when you think no one can see you."

The figurines looked down at me, then at each other. Some started growing. The lady on the horse jumped down to the floor, and after that, most of the others started coming down from the shelves like a rain of china, even a horse's head, the flat bottom of his base rippling to inch him forward like a slug. Once on the floor, they started running around the room and talking in funny, screeching, sometimes ringing china voices. Some had become as big as a foot high.

I got out of bed even though I could get a spanking for it, but it was so wonderful that the figurines were showing me their real selves, I didn't care about consequences.

But they were playing, and galloping all around, and ignoring me. If I tried to touch them, they ran away from me and hid under the beds. The girl on the horse jumped up onto my grandparents' bed and rode around, tracking mud everywhere she went. The rabbit, a fat Buddha, and a dog, all big now, climbed up too, and started jumping on the bed until I heard it break. The horse's head, a foot high now, started chewing the drapes and then pulled on them until they fell down.

The black cat climbed up on top of the bureau and lit a cigar, throwing matches everywhere, which smoked on the rug. He knocked all my grandmother's holy cards off onto the floor.

"Hey, stop it, those are holy!"

The cat just narrowed its eyes and bared his teeth at me, hissing like a devil. I picked up the cards and tried to put them back, but the cat grabbed them and jetted them all over the room, flattening himself like a paper cutout cat behind the chimney candle when I tried to get him, snarling and scratching at me. Then he started pushing the Guadalupe candle until it tilted precariously, and I was afraid he'd spill the hot candle and start a fire.

This wasn't fun at all, and I knew *I* was going to get blamed for the mess. Then the little boy angel, the only one left on the pelmet, fell off the end, batting his crystal wings, but he didn't fly, he hit the ground, and his head and wing broke off. All the figurines went quiet, staring. I tried to put his head back, but it wouldn't stay of course, and he started crying, a high plaintive bleating sound. The tears became crystal splinters that littered the floor around him in a sparking pool. I stepped on his broken wing and cut my foot, so on top of everything else, I started getting blood all over the floor.

All the figurines got scared because of the blood and started panicking, running in a circle around the room, squeaking and ringing like a rusty, crooked merry-go-round or roller-coaster, going up and down the beds, pulling the covers onto the floor. Some started jumping back up on the shelves but they were in the wrong places and when they tried to move, fought with whoever was already there. The noise was deafening.

Some wouldn't go back up on the shelf at all. The girl had gotten off the horse and taken all her clothes off. When I looked at her again she was naked and had put on her horse's head and hooves, and was walking around with her front hooves on her hips, showing off her cherry boobies. When I looked at her again, she was pulling at her horsehead and shaking it like something was wrong. I tried to help her take it off but she kept galloping away from me and snapping at me with sharp teeth.

I was standing by the window and thought I saw something move out there in the darkness, so I got right next to the window and looked out, and I saw two big, unblinking eyes looking right back at me. *The Devil!* I ran screaming out of the room.

"¡*Mamá!* ¡*Mamá!* ¡El *cucúy!*" I was amidst my aunts and uncles, crying. "A *cucúy* was looking in the window at me!" Everyone went quiet and stared at me.

"*No seas necia.* You're old enough to know there's no such thing," Amparo said, my least favorite aunt. She wore a black dress and her grey hair in a tight bun on top of her head. She always sat tall, and she wore a white neck brace that made her look like those paintings of mean Spanish queens.

"*Hora veras*," my uncle said. He had lost a leg in the war, and he was sitting without his prosthesis, the empty pant leg hanging from his knee all scary.

"But I saw him, right outside—" I looked around for my mother. She must be in the kitchen.

"Go back to bed!" my father snapped. He acted like he was going to take off his belt, then my fifteen-year-old cousin, Imelda from Mexico, got up from the couch.

"I'll take her."

Imelda was everyone's favorite. She had big, crooked teeth, a bunch of curly hair, and a dark mole on her chin. She always brought us Mexican candy when she visited and told good stories. I let her take my hand, but then I remembered the mess in the room.

"No–"

"Don't worry, I know what to do about *cucúys*. Come on, I'll teach you."

She led me back into my grandparents' room and put me right to bed, ignoring the mess that was all around us and even on the walls.

"Okay, where was the cucúy?" she asked.

I pointed at the left window. "Out there. He was looking at me. His eyes were this big!" I made an oval of my thumbs and forefingers.

Imelda got the crucifix that hung on the wall over my bed. "Okay, this is what you do." She went over to the window and unlocked it.

"Don't! He might be hiding under the window!"

But she opened the window anyway and stuck her head out.

"Óye,¡cabrón! *El diablo de cucúy, ¿qué estás haciendo aquí? Vete al infierno con los otros diablos donde perteneces.* ¡Ándale!" She held the cross up outside while she cussed him out with bad words. Then she came back inside and slammed the window and locked it.

"He's gone. Now watch, so you know what to do to keep him out." She made the sign of the cross in front of each window, then got a little bottle of holy water off the dresser and scattered some in front of each window, the door, and on me. Then she put the cross back on its nail over my bed.

"*Mira,*" she said, looking at the clock. "No wonder you saw the Devil. It's midnight, *la hora de la bruja.* That's when he comes out."

I hoped I would grow up to be like Imelda, she was so brave and strong, and wasn't at all afraid of the cucúy. Right then I heard distant singing.

"Imelda, do you hear that?"

We both looked out the dark window. The singing seemed to come from the hills that stood over the ranch. There were no words, just o-o-o-o-o-o-o-o. It was beautiful and hypnotizing, and it floated down to us through the clear summer night. It made me think of the lady with the sad eyes.

"That's a witch who sings every night at this time," Imelda whispered. "It's bad to listen to her." Yet we both continued to sit quietly, listening.

"Is she La Llorona?"

Imelda pondered this question as she stared out the window. At last she said, "I don't think so, because La Llorona usually screams or cries. She never sings, that I know of. Sometimes she calls little children to her, and she makes you want to go to her. If you ever see her, don't go with her, because you'll never come back, and no one will ever find your body."

"I won't go with her," I promised. I didn't tell her I almost had, and probably would have, if my sister hadn't been there.

"Have you seen her, Imelda?"

She nodded solemnly. "*Sí*. I saw her once, outside of *Tijuana*."

"Tell me!"

"My family was at my uncle's ranch. It's right next to a river. One night I saw a woman passing by there."

"Was she screaming?"

"No. She didn't make any sound, but I knew it was La Llorona because she was crying and looking in the water for her children."

"What does she look like?"

"Well, some people say she's an ugly old *vieja con* big wrinkles down her face from crying so much. But the woman I saw was beautiful, all white, like a ghost, except for her long, long black hair, with white flowers, that floated out behind her."

"Were you scared?"

"No. She was sad, so sad, that it made me cry, too. After that, I wasn't afraid of her anymore," Imelda continued. "I felt so sorry for her. It was wrong for her to kill her little children, yes, but everyone knows she was *loca*. When you're crazy, you can't help what you do, and it's not a sin. I don't know why God punished her like that. It wasn't fair."

Imelda stopped talking and we listened to the last strains of the song. There was one light on the hill, and I thought that must be where the witch singer lived.

The next thing I knew, I was waking up and it was morning. My grandparents were snoring in the next bed. Then I remembered all that had happened the night before, but when I looked around, I saw that the figurines had cleaned everything up and were all back in their exact spots. Even the broken angel boy was completely well again. I wondered if Guadalupe had made a miracle for me, so I wouldn't be blamed.

After that I would say "hi" and "goodnight" to them, but I never wished they would come to life again.

3

WHEN I WAS almost twelve, I went to stay with my cousins near Lake Cuitzeo. It was the first time I visited, and from the outside of my aunt and uncle's home, it just looked like a tall, dirty old adobe wall with an old door stuck in it. But when you went inside, there was a garden open to the sky, with spindly trees and birds in cages, and a fountain in the middle of everything. All the first floor rooms opened up onto that garden, including my cousin Araceli's. She was two years older than me, and I slept with her. On hot nights we kept the door open and talked late into the night, and when we finally went to sleep, she liked to cuddle, which I loved. It made me feel like we were the best of friends.

I loved Mexico, there was so much to do. There were always vendors selling *churros, raspados,* or hot, fresh and salted *chícharos* on the plaza, where we would hang out, meet my cousins' friends, and talk to boys. We went down to the lake, or up to the waterfall on the side of the mountain. There was even a crowded graveyard with all kinds of above ground graves, where we would go and explore and find things, like old statues or crucifixes. Once I found a little broken hand that I think belonged to *La Virgen.* We'd wash them in the wobbly graveyard spigot and set them on random graves.

On market day my cousin and I went with my aunt to get the vegetables and meat we needed. I was fascinated with the large, airy warehouse with tall piles of vegetables and fruit, and arrays of sugary candies in huge baskets. Araceli would take me around, showing me things, like baskets of fried insects people actually ate. She'd hook her arm in mine, and we'd walk around like that in public, very familiar and intimate, and no one blinked an eye. I would have been called gay if I tried that in the U.S.

The least fun thing was having to stop everything in the middle of the day to take a siesta. That included any other relatives our age, and even friends who were visiting, although they had the option to go home if they wanted. Moaning and complaining, we were sent up to big, dim second floor rooms where we pulled out mats and pillows to sleep for a couple of hours. But sometimes we sat around talking instead. They told me about witches who turned into balls of fire, *la mano*, a ghost hand that would appear to people sometimes, and the axolotl, a monster salamander.

"Do they eat people?"

"Yes. They live in lakes that have no bottom, because they're connected to the underworld, and they come up to eat people."

"I saw one once," Carlos said, a neighbor from across the road. "But it was a baby. It was about this long—" He held his hands about a foot apart.

They also told me about *chupacabras*, who were aliens.

"'Suck goats,'" I translated for myself. "Why are they called that?"

"Because they suck all the blood out of goats, then leave the carcass," Araceli told me. "People have been finding a lot of dead goats, and sometimes dead cows or dogs down by the lake. That's how we know the chupacabras are coming here."

"A lot of people are afraid they're going to start eating people," Lalo said, Areceli's brother. He pulled a chain from inside his shirt. "That's why I always wear this." On it were a couple of medals, one of St. Jude and the other St. Teresa, and a brown scapular that had been taped over. "The chupacabras can't come near you if you wear these."

I told them about Bloody Mary, who I had heard about at a slumber party. "You go into the bathroom at midnight and brush your hair with your left hand and eat an apple with your right, then say her name three times. Bloody Mary will appear and tell you'll how you're going to die."

"Why would anyone want to know that?" Lalo asked.

"I don't know. Maybe that's why no one ever does it. Anyway, I fell asleep too soon." I had almost volunteered to try it that night because I secretly wanted to see Bloody Mary, but I didn't want to know how I was going to die.

One naptime, I asked about La Llorona. "My mom told me she came from here. Do you ever see her?"

"No, she came from Mexico City," Concha said, Araceli's best friend. "That was a long time ago, hundreds of years ago."

"She was a whore," Lalo said carelessly.

I was shocked. *"Puta"* is a swear word. My sister had told me what it meant, and never to use it because it was an insult to all women. It even sounded like someone was spitting.

"No she wasn't," I said, but everyone nodded in agreement. Araceli giggled nervously.

"She used to throw her babies into the river and drown them because she didn't want to take care of them," Concha said, who had lived in the capital, and was very sophisticated.

"No she didn't," Lalo contradicted. "She gave herself *abortos* by putting a knife inside, to kill the babies, then threw the pieces into the river."

"Que asqueroso," I shouted at him. "Anyway, I don't believe you. A woman wouldn't do that."

"They do, sometimes," Areceli assured me in a whispery voice.

"It's very sad," Concha said, nodding. "It's only the poor women who can't afford more children who do that. And then they both die."

"She wasn't poor," I said, as if I was the expert on La Llorona. But I realized that if she could kill her children and herself, maybe she *would* do an aborto. I was suddenly mad at everyone. In a huff, I lay down on the mat and turned my back to everyone.

"It's just a legend," Lalo said. "Maybe it's not even a true story." But I knew in my heart the story of La Llorona *was* true. I didn't want to talk about it anymore and pretended like I was asleep. Eventually, everyone settled down and the room was silent.

I didn't sleep. I was scared and grossed out. It was almost as if they wanted to upset me. Lalo was the oldest one of us, and becoming really *grosero*, which is rude and mean. My mother said it was because he was a teenager, and they all act like that.

I didn't know why I was so mad, or why I had defended La Llorona. I was still thinking about the beautiful lady I had seen by the canal so long ago, the experience no one else remembered, and now seemed like a dream. I felt a sudden stab in my stomach: the realization that I had a crush on her. I was ashamed. It was bad enough that I liked girls too much; who would ever have a crush on such a monstrous woman?

There was a little ceramic holy water font with a picture of Mary and her baby on the wall, right next to the door. Everyone was fast asleep. I got up and went over to it, but the little basin was dry. I dipped my finger in and touched the bottom, and used the ghost water to bless myself. Then I went out, closing the door quietly behind me. I tiptoed downstairs and through the crookedly tiled garden, expecting to get yelled at any minute: *¡acuéstate ahora mismo!* But no one was there. I went all the way out the door to the street.

The streets were dead; all the shops closed. I didn't even see a dog. Of course at that time, everyone in the little town was taking a *siesta*. Off the main street that ran in front of my relatives' house, was a narrow little lane next to a building. It was shadowy with a flowering vine and seemed magical, and it led down to the lake. I headed that way.

This was usually the hottest time of the day, but the sky was overcast and blackish yellow; the air seemed thick and smelled different from the rotting fruit scent I had come to associate with Mexico. I wondered if there was going to be a storm.

The lake was completely deserted; there wasn't even a boat in the distance. Everything was as still, as still could be. I was sure there weren't even any chupacabras out. At least, I didn't see any dead animals.

That part of the water was covered with a curly, bright green plant with a purple flower my *tia* told me was *jacinto*. It was so thick it looked like a mat you could lie down on; like a raft. My cousins told me people had gotten bogged down underneath and drowned because of it.

I sat on the bank and looked out at the lake. I could see the mountains all around, grey-blue in the distance. What would happen if I called La Llorona? Would it work, or did it have to be at night, in a bathroom, with a mirror and all? Would she come and tell me how I was going to die, or could I ask her something else, like what *really* happened with her children?

I squeezed my eyes shut and thought her name three times, then remembered it was supposed to be with your eyes open and out loud, so I did it again. Nothing happened. I looked around for a while, then decided to try once more.

"La Llorona, La Llorona, La Llorona," I said, louder this time, cupping my hands around my mouth and calling out across the lake.

Nothing.

As I sat there, a light wind started up, and the clouds were darkening. I waited a while, disappointed and bored, and was just getting up when I noticed something, movement on the far side bank. It was whitish and irregular-shaped, and it seemed to be blowing up the long length of the bank, toward me.

Lake Cuitzeo is the biggest lake in the Mexican state of Michoacán, and the far bank was maybe a half mile across at that end, so I couldn't really see what it was. A curtain or sheet being blowing around. It seemed to fold and turn as it rolled in the light wind. Sometimes it almost seemed as if it was wrapping around a shape, a body, but then would loosen and continue its travel. I stared as if I was hypnotized. Suddenly it turned and started blowing across the water, toward me.

In the middle of the lake it crumpled and flattened on top of the water, yet it continued to move swiftly, in my direction. How was it moving? I stood up, trying to see better, and I stumbled forward and tried to step on the jacinto mat, but I fell straight down into water over my head. I floated down for a moment, looking around at the silent, dim world. Then I saw something from the corner of my eye: it was coming toward me, through the frogs and tiny fish and trailing jacinto roots. It was shaped like a hammock or an early moon: fish-like, whitish-grey, translucent. I thought it was a mermaid, because I could see eyes through the watery gloom, and long, long blood-colored hair, undulating behind her. The eyes were fixed on me, and as it got closer, I saw they were wide and bloodshot and furious, and the mouth—it was red too, as if it had been feeding on a fresh kill. The creature was sobbing. My water-filled ears heard, not screaming at all, but a creepy, watery, familiar whispering past my ears:

Come with me—come with me—come with me!

My feet touched the muddy lake bottom, threatening to suck me in, and it was like I woke up. Always proud of my swimming abilities, I kicked up with all my might, arms straight above me, rushing back up toward air, right into the dense forest of long, dark, purplish finger-roots of jacinto that seemed to close around me even as I felt something else, horrible and slimy, wrapping around me. I could see spots of sunlight shining through the conspiring plants, and I focused on the largest of these openings, steadily churning my way toward it.

Reach the light, reach the light, I coached myself, ignoring the slime that weighed me down, and quickly and systematically shoving aside tangled roots. Suddenly I broke through and gasped air. The bank was only a couple of feet away. I pulled my legs tight under my chest, cannonball style, and gave one last, mighty kick, gaining the rocks. The momentum of adrenaline drove me on until I scrabbled wetly out and threw myself on the bank. I thought I felt something slip from an ankle.

I heard someone calling, "*Oye,* ¡*mensa!*"

"¡*Ayuda!*" I yelled. Something was still holding onto my feet. I scrambled over onto my butt and sat up, but it was just a big gob of plants caught on my shoes. I ripped them off.

Lalo leaned over me.

"Didn't we tell you not to walk on the plants? It's a good thing I saw you. Stupid girl."

I lashed the plants at him, sweeping water at his face. "Stop calling me that!"

"¡*Vaya!* ¿*Qué te pasa?* I was just joking."

"*Pues, tus bromas apestan.*" *Your jokes stink.* I'd had about enough of him.

Resting, still gulping air, I looked back at the bed of plants. There was an opening in them where I had floundered, already being covered again with plants. I stared into the watery shadows, fearful, yet somehow wanting to see those terrible, sad red eyes again. But everything seemed back to normal.

"How did you know where I was?"

He shrugged. "I woke up and you were gone, so I came looking for you." He started talking about someone who had drowned there, but I wasn't listening. I stood up and turned my back to him, squeezing out my hair and shirt.

I was thinking about how I had been terrified, then somehow calmed myself and had known what to do, even when I felt long, wispy hands wrapping around me. But they hadn't been very strong, and I hadn't panicked. It was sort of like that first time I saw her, and escaped her, even if that hadn't been my doing; I had eluded her once, I could do it again.

"La Llorona's children are in the church that's in the cemetery," Lalo said.

"What?" I said, startled. "You mean, buried there?"

"No, statues of them. La Llorona will never find her children *sabes, porque* God sent an angel to gather them up, and take them to heaven."

It was typical of the Catholic Church to set up an impossible task, just to keep someone in misery, especially a woman, especially *la pobre de La Llorona*.

"Want to go now? I'll take you there. By the time we get home, you'll be mostly dry. No one will know you fell in."

He was being really nice now, trying to make it all up to me.

"Is there one to La Llorona too?"

"*De ninguna manera.* Who would pray to her?"

"No, to pray *for* her."

We walked over to the cemetery, my clothes keeping me cool, tennies squishing with every step on the silent street. The door to the church was cracked open and no one was there. We stood in the cool gloom, lit only by candles in a stand, and a single one in red glass, on the side of the altar. When we reached the front, Lalo pointed to a niche in the transept.

"There."

Statues of two boys, and an angel holding a little girl. We sat in the pew closest to them, Lalo waiting while I studied the tableau. The statues had real-looking eyes, creamy white skin, and dry blond hair that had turned kinked and brassy. They were dressed like angels, in flowing white, with painted gold flourishes, and wearing metal haloes. They looked old, probably made about the same time as the *La Virgen de Merced*, just around the corner from the niche: Our Lady of Mercy. What part had she played in La Llorona's story? Clearly, no one had asked *Her*.

Feeling heartbroken about the waste of lives, I went over to the stand of candles in the front of Our Lady and dropped some coins in the donation box. I prayed, lighting a candle for the shunned mother who had become the infamous, lonely Llorona.

MEMOIR

The Pooka

MY IRISH HUSBAND Connor (now ex) took me to County Tipperary, Ireland, where we stayed out in the country with his parents. One evening he invited me to hike out to an ancient site where he used to go with his siblings when they were children.

"It's unexcavated. We used to find things like broken pieces of pottery or old clay pipes." There were a lot of old sites like that all over Ireland, he told me. "They're called 'fairy rings.' It's believed they're haunted or cursed, and you'll die if you bulldoze them."

Why he wanted to go exploring in the middle of a dark and cold December night was beyond me; maybe it was fate. We bundled up (winter nights in Ireland are very cold), and headed out. There were no streetlights, but the sky was starry, and we could see a glare on the horizon from the nearby town of Clonmel. I followed Connor up a *boreen*, twisting country road, that we followed until he suggested we take a shortcut.

"We'll get there faster through this field."

He helped me climb over a split rail fence. The rough ground rose slightly under our feet. After we'd been walking a while, my husband stopped and looked around. I waited, we continued on. After another while, he stopped again.

"Are we lost?"

"No." He appeared to be listening.

After the third pause I finally asked, "What's going on?"

"I thought I heard something."

My husband was not the type to scare or tease me, and I became a little anxious.

"People?"

"No."

The night was still, I hadn't heard anything at all. I kept my pace near him through darkness lush and cold. Connor stopped again. I stopped too and this time held my breath, listening carefully. I heard something like a subtle sort of wind, and could just feel the fairy kiss of air against my face. The night was very quiet; there was no wind; where had it come from? The hairs raised at the back of my neck.

"What was that?"

"A horse," Connor said, his voice low.

"A horse?" I repeated doubtfully. "I didn't hear anything. Wouldn't we have heard hooves?"

"It's the horse that lives in this field."

"Wouldn't the horse be in the barn at night?" Connor didn't answer. "Should we turn back?"

"No, she knows me. Let's just keep going."

Then again, a moment of wind, closer than before. I still could see and hear nothing in the darkness. My husband was standing stock still, staring. I looked in the same direction and saw it: just above the horizon, backlit by the distant lights of Clonmel, was the black silhouette of a horse. She was throwing her head around, long mane lashing through the air, her mouth open, teeth bared with silent screams.

"Let's turn back," I said. "This field belongs to that horse and she wants us out of it."

"No, it's okay. She's just being territorial."

"What if she runs us down?"

"She won't do that, she's a nice old mare. Her name is Adare."

So we walked on, a little faster now. Suddenly, the horse was confronting us. Again, I hadn't heard her approaching. I stared: I could just make out an inkiness, blacker than the general darkness around us. Even more, I felt a massive presence that didn't seem at all like "a nice old mare." She had a great head with a whipping mane, giant hooves, and strangest of all, two large, baleful, faintly glowing eyes. Not quite like a cat, but from where was the light in them coming?

"HO!" Connor said, raising his hand.

"Connor, let's go!" I started backing away.

"No," Connor said. "You can't show your fear. HO, Adare! HO!" He approached the horse.

A frightful hissing sound came from the creature.

Hissing? Horses don't hiss. I was so scared I almost peed my pants.

"I'm getting out of here." I turned around and began stumbling away.

"Come back! She's just trying to scare us."

"She's succeeding!" I yelled, scrambling now.

Then a faint, whooshing sound again as the horse disappeared again into the night. It passed again, and Connor was on the back of that horse! He was yelling commands for the horse to stop, that the horse wasn't listening to.

Was he nuts? "Connor!" I yelled.

I heard that wind sound, felt it again on my face and through the roots of my hair. Suddenly I fell backwards on my butt. Had they knocked me down, or had I lost my balance in the disorienting darkness? I jumped up and ran, hands held out in front of me, until finally, I bumped against the split rail fence that marked the edge of the field.

I clambered over, breathing hard, my heart beating wildly, trembling all over. I stood there, leaning on the fence until I recovered. I rested there while I waited. I grew colder, straining to hear hooves, or Connor himself, scanning the land, trying to see in that wild blackness all around me. Nothing.

This was the land of fairies and elves, where people fell into other worlds and returned centuries later. Would I ever see my husband again?

Suddenly Connor was there, on the other side of the fence, not more than a few yards away. I heard his labored breath. I hadn't heard him, or the horse, drawing near.

"How did you get here?" I asked. He didn't say anything, just kept staring off into the gloom.

"Connor? What happened?"

Finally he said, "The horse let me go." He sounded strange, somehow. I wondered for a second if he was really my husband, or something had taken his place.

He stood there a long time, while his breath returned to normal, ignoring my questions and begging to get away from there. Finally he climbed over the fence and headed back in the direction of his parents' home. I followed.

"How did you catch the horse?" I asked. "Did you put her in the barn?" But he wouldn't answer. I finally stopped talking, relieved just to be headed back toward light, warmth, and reality.

Once back, I told his parents about the field and the horse, laughing now, believing in the sanity and predictability of light and home. Connor was somber. He didn't add anything to the story.

"What did you say that horse's name was?" I asked him, but he just shrugged. "Adare?"

His mother shook her head. "Couldn't have been Adare," she said. "That horse has been dead for two years."

"Maybe it was a ghost," I said, still joshing. "Or a *night* mare!" But they all just looked at me.

The next day we went to see his grandfather. Over tea and biscuits, I told the story again, funnier than it really had been. I noticed their stony faces and stopped talking. I realized Connor's parents had had pretty much the same lack of reaction.

Finally his grandfather said, "Sounds like ye caught a ride on a *púca*."

"What's a pooka?" I asked.

"A horse-spirit," the old man told me. "Sometimes they mean good luck, sometimes bad. They always have a message for ye." He looked at Connor.

"Really? What was the message?" I asked my husband.

But if he'd gotten one, he wasn't saying.

AFTER WE GOT home to the States, I looked up the pooka and found several folktales about them. She is an Irish nature spirit that most often takes the shape of a horse, is usually benevolent, but can also be an omen of death. Sometimes she will take you for a wild ride. I also read about sightings, people telling about meeting up with pookas.

But what the stories don't mention is how such an encounter changes you. My husband was never the same after that. Always quiet, he became secretive. He focused more on his career, started developing interests that pointedly didn't include me, and most telling, turned away from me in bed at night. He developed severe rashes of unknown origin, pounding headaches, and debilitating back pain. All signs of spiritual unrest, but in spite of the fact that a large part of my education has been in spirituality, he wouldn't talk to me, and rejected my support. I had become part of the problem.

One of the most defining elements of our relationship for me had been the serenity that had allowed me to be profoundly creative as a writer and artist. Apparently his experience of our marriage was completely different, something I only found out when he asked me to move out. A restless spirit sent him on long voyages to exotic lands, moving from job to job, and ultimately out of our marriage.

After seventeen years together, our separation and divorce were devastating for me. I was set adrift in my own life. I found myself unable to write or paint; strangely, I was even unable to conjure fantasies anymore. My creative life pretty much faded, I turned my focus to my spiritual life. I tried meditating and drumming. I attended 12-step program, journaled, and studied my dreams. I began attending a Christian-based church that was inclusive of all people, which was healing of my Catholic upbringing.

At the same time, I became more practical as well. I worked on my house, painting over the dull colors, and pulling up the beige carpet, revealing old oak floors. Not wanting to be a secretary for the rest of my life, I went back to school for another degree and found more fulfilling work.

The relationships I had with men during this time became successively shorter in length. Coupled with my inability to fantasize, I thought it meant my sexual life was over. Then I met and fell in love with a transman.

Prince had transitioned and lived as a man for a few years, but health problems had forced him to de-transition. He still identified as male and trans, and with him, I entered the amazing queer world.

I was crazy about him and became revived in my life. I was thrilled the first time he held my hand, and felt transported just by kissing. I now considered myself queer, and understood now why my het fantasies had dried up. My unconscious was telling me it was time I faced my true sexuality.

Our relationship turned rocky as his health problems interfered with our relationship and left no room for me. I ended it after ten months, but once I'd crossed over, my life changed in a very different way. For one, I began to understand my life more fully. I'd had dreams and secret crushes when I was just beginning to mature that told me I was a lesbian, which never would have been accepted in the shaming, punishing, and violent Catholic environment in which I was raised. I remembered writing a story when I was fourteen about a girl who committed suicide by poison because she was a lesbian. Without realizing it, I was symbolically killing off a vital part of myself.

My love for women came out in many other ways: in becoming a Wiccan, a woman's religion; in a frequent contempt for men; in always seeking out gay people as friends; in my life-long pursuit of women's studies; and of course, in deep friendships with women that I now understand were partly infatuation.

I was in my early fifties, and found I didn't have the fear, self-loathing, or shame that had originally shut me in the closet. I felt so proud and excited to be in the world with women, walking openly, holding hands. It was as if through my studies and friendships, I had been subconsciously working through my internalized homophobia my whole life.

I jumped a fence once in an effort to escape the powerful spirit of change, but she affected my life anyway. I came to be grateful that my husband divorced me. I have lived out and gaily ever since.

Oakland, 2007

Jealousy: a Dark Comedy

WHEN MY FIRST relationship after coming out failed, I spent several months enjoying a lesbian "honeymoon," meeting and dating lots of women, mostly met on Match.com. At first I tried healthy dating, which is avoiding sex until there is a stable relationship; something I used to do when I dated men. After months of that, I got tired of never getting laid, because nothing lasted for more than a few dates. So I wrote an ad and posted it anonymously on Craigslist: "Looking for an older, more experienced butch for romantic and sexual encounters. Please know your way with toys." I wasn't looking for love anymore. I wanted sex.

The responses from that ad were a crash course in dyke drama. One called the silver at my temples "skunk stripes" and suggested I was a liar because I sent a picture that was three years old, along with the explanation saying I'd never dyed my hair (I still haven't). Yet another would search for things in her back seat while driving on the freeway, and crashed her motorcycle one day, and again then very next day, then said it was my fault because she was on her way to my house. Once two butches showed up at my house at the same time, uninvited, and argued about me in the street for an hour—even though I'd already broken it off with both of them. Another thought the photo I sent was so photogenic, it either had to be a fake, or I was a transgender-illusionist, and I never heard from her again.

If not sex, my uproarious romantic connections were providing me and my friends with a great deal of entertainment. I was floundering in the depths of endless processing, finagling my way from one intrigue to the next. I was making up for lost time from having come out so late.

One of the more sober respondents described herself as a "Southern gentle-butch." Her missives were delightful, charming, and eloquent, and she could even spell. She sent me an alluring photo that was mysterious and subtly erotic. She told me she was poly, which I was okay with, figuring she'd know what to do in bed. It would also allow me to try polyamory.

After a few weeks of emails, she suggested we meet, and actually showed up at the small café she had suggested. She had a fresh haircut and wore a dark red suit and striped tie.

"My heart skipped a beat when I saw your photo, but you're even prettier in person," was one of the first things she said to me. She was courtly, solicitous, and very appreciative. I will call her "Rhett" for the romantic Southern association, for her Aries temperament, and her red hair. My erotic adventure had finally begun.

In my first email to her after meeting, I made a request: "Let's not talk about past lovers. I don't care who you've been with, or what you've done. All I want to hear about is what you're going to do for me and to me." Rhett agreed to this.

It was a reasonable enough request; it's rude to be on a date with someone, and have to listen while they process their last relationship—which happened a lot. But the truth is, I am extremely jealous and have an exceptionally visual imagination. Most of the people I've been in relationships with have, over my repeated objections, talked (sometimes endlessly) about former lovers. My first queer partner wouldn't and couldn't keep their mouth shut about extremely intimate sexual details with former lovers—this while I starved for affection and sex for most of the relationship.

Now, for this fantasy connection, I wanted Rhett to be all mine. I wanted to be dined, romanced, and made love to. I wanted someone to flatter me with lines; I didn't care if they were true, and I didn't care if I didn't hear from her afterward. Rhett gallantly agreed to that as well.

"I'll be happy to oblige you, Darling. Over and over again, as many times as you'd like." A response that left me nonplussed. So when she called for a second date, I decided to go with it.

At first, things went according to my hopes. We dated. She gave me flowers, gifts and compliments, took me on wonderful dates. We slow danced to favorite songs in her handsomely appointed "butchelor's pad" ("I decorated it just for you, my dear.") I was getting laid. Best of all, Rhett never talked about past lovers.

I certainly hadn't expected to find an enduring relationship through Craigslist. Everyone said they never had any luck except for connecting with people who were either nuts, or dangerous. Having just come out of a disastrous relationship, I didn't want to get involved right away. Neither did Rhett. But now we found ourselves "partners in crime." At last, I was having fun.

Rhett and I spent more and more time together, talking late into the night, continuing the conversation during long mornings spent over breakfast and tea. We talked about dreams and books and art. We unpacked movies and poetry. She showed me comics she had written and illustrated; I showed her my artwork and told her the stories behind the pieces. The veil of fantasy was wearing thin and the real person was showing through. A fantasy person can't survive in the face of a relationship—which, despite my reluctance, this was turning into.

After we had been going out about six weeks, she told me she had to correct an impression.

"I know I promised not to talk about my past lovers, but we're getting closer, and you might hear about this, then wonder why I didn't tell you. I've told you about my best friend Eve? We were in a long-term relationship. It lasted about ten years, and ended two years ago."

Yes, this was something she had to tell me, because sooner or later I *would* find out, and knowing myself, I'd feel betrayed, even though *I* had asked for the agreement. One of the realities I had to deal with is that in the lesbian world, former lovers often become friends, a function related to the community being so small and romantically incestuous.

I tried not to think about it, but the thoughts came anyway: two years is really not that long for the dissolution of a relationship, especially if you're still hanging out with each other. Was it really completely over, or did they have fuzzy boundaries? Were they friends with benefits? And didn't Rhett say they had gone to the nude hot springs together last year? Did Rhett go nude? *Did her ex?*

But I didn't ask, because I have rules I use to manage jealousy, and one is *don't ask questions I don't want to know the answers to*, especially if I can't trust the person to lie.

"Does my connection with her make you uncomfortable?" Rhett asked. "Because if it does, I'll break it off with her."

But I wouldn't allow that. I had nothing but scorn for jealous lovers and the friends who dropped me for them, so I wasn't about to turn into that jealous girlfriend myself. Even though when I finally met Eve, all I could think about was Rhett's hands on her large, beautiful breasts—which made me hunch my shoulders and cross my arms over my own in mortification.

But even more startling was the fact that Eve wore a small gold pendant, identical to one Rhett wore. I mentioned this.

"Yes, we bought them together when we went to Mexico," she said.

"It's like you're going steady," I said.

"I really love it. It's my name in Mayan glyphs," she said, missing my point.

That ended the conversation, but I grudgingly admired Rhett for not caving to my attempt at manipulation. Which had been to get her to first of all, read my mind, and second of all, to quit wearing the pendant.

Despite our initial agreement, Rhett began asking about my past relationships.

"I'm not triggered hearing about the other people in your past. I'd really like to know about them, if you want to tell me."

I was okay with that, but remained steadfast in not wanting to hear about her own stories. However sometimes after I'd disclosed something, Rhett would start to contribute and stop herself. I knew she had been about to say something about another lover—it was written all over her face. My technique for avoiding jealousy wasn't flawless.

One day in search of floss at Rhett's apartment, I unthinkingly opened a bathroom drawer. Inside were make-up and an eyelash curler. Rhett didn't wear makeup. So here was irrefutable evidence of another woman in Rhett's life.

I had an internal hissy fit. Had it belonged to an ex—to *the* ex? If so, why was it still here? Did this mean they were still enmeshed? Or was Rhett seeing someone *else?* Did it belong to a one-night stand? Did I have a preference? We had made no commitment to each other, we were not exclusive. I didn't care who she fucked—as long as I didn't know about it. But now I knew. Maybe.

Trembling, I picked up the eyelash curler. She had to be a high femme—who other than old ladies and drag queens used those anymore? I hadn't even seen one since I was a child, and my drunk uncle used one upside down and curled his eyelashes into his eyeballs. I had become careless in this still-new relationship by opening that drawer, because another of my rules for managing jealousy is *don't go looking for trouble.* That means I don't nose around in places where I might see things it would be better if I didn't.

So who *was* this high femme? Was she higher than *me?*

What to do? Normally I wouldn't say anything, pretend I hadn't found them, but this involved a transgression—opening a drawer I hadn't been invited to. No matter what I had found, nor how innocently, and no matter what Rhett might be up to, she had a right to her privacy. I called Rhett in.

"I couldn't find the dental floss so I opened this drawer. I'm sorry."

She must have seen something in my expression. She glanced in.

"Oh—that's my stuff. Sometimes I experiment with gender-bending."

I accepted this, because another rule for managing jealousy is that I believe what I am told. And I *wanted* to believe it. But Jealousy had opened her witch-green eyes in my soul.

Nice save, she said.

Was Rhett being gallant, trying to save my feelings? Was she trying to cover her other liaisons? Suddenly everything looked different without rose crystal spectacles. Our romantic hideaway wasn't ours alone, but a love nest where Rhett brought all her women, past and present, including the High Ho who left her eyelash curler *for me to find*—I just knew it. Well, two could play *that* game. I opened my purse and chose between my lipsticks—a fire engine red color named *Hot Lady*—and left it in the same drawer.

I looked around for more evidence. I smelled perfume, but followed the scent to a bar of Chantilly Lace soap Rhett had bought for me. I prowled Rhett's apartment as she made up the futon bed and lit candles for our evening of lovemaking. What among the decorations had been gifts from other loving (conniving) hands (claws)? That would explain the few silly items among the tasteful butch furnishings, like the sequined butterflies on her front door, or the frilly star reaching out, spider-like from beneath a Mexican tin heart. And I didn't even want to think about all her toys, which Rhett was now setting out.

But I did. Who had she used them on before me? And on how many? So that was why she had a box of condoms—a hundred no less. I smirked over how small the toys were. *Is that all you can take? Just how high can you be, Missy?* Suddenly I thought about the times we went to Good Vibrations. Rhett had talked about harnesses.

"I've had lots of them, so I know a lot about them."

Now her words hit me with images of all the fucking she had to do to wear out each one. I was no longer her special, pampered lover; just another notch on one of her dozens of holsters. Did she brag about me to her butch friends?

But what if she *didn't?*

"Would you like something to drink, Sugar?"

I whirled around and only just stopped myself before slapping her.

Don't "sugar" me, you molasses-mouthed, magnolia-sniffing, poly Southern wolf! Is that your M.O., get me drunk so you can take advantage of me like all the rest?

The sex was great. *Fuck me you dog, you gigolo, you pimp! Give it to me, give it all to me. Bring me everything you got from everyone else, kiss me, eat me, love me, only me, forget about them. I'm the smartest, I'm the most beautiful, the sexiest, the only one. I hate you. I hate you!* Later in the dark, I silently wept with rage.

Thoughts continued to slither from my subconscious, horrid deformed slugs that trailed poison over everything we were building. All Rhett's compliments became lies. When she played her guitar and sang to me, I imagined the women she seduced with those same lonesome lyrics and heartbreaking timbre. The blue eyes I had found loving and appreciative, I now saw were calculating—worse, comparing. I left. Not because I was angry at her, but because I couldn't stand another minute of my own obsession.

I knew I wasn't being fair. Like I could get drunk on Martinelli's; Rhett didn't keep alcohol around. And *I* was the one who advertised for a "more experienced older butch." I was the one who had wanted to be chatted up and seduced, and now I was holding it against her. The alternative was an inexperienced or prudish lez for whom Lesbian Bed Death and never-ending hysteria was the definitive happy-ever-after—precisely why I escaped my last relationship. My whimsical, romantic fantasy was transmogrifying into a nightmare.

On top of being sick with jealousy, I was ashamed for *being* jealous: it was so uncool. It didn't fit in with the María Felix persona I had created for myself. I said nothing to Rhett. I didn't want my jealousy to be misinterpreted as caring. It wasn't about caring, and it wasn't even about her. It was about control and power and fear, and I didn't want to reveal the true blackness of my nature.

And what *could* I say? We had no commitment—*I* didn't want one. And Rhett had kept to our agreement not to talk about her lovers. In fact, she was the only one of my girlfriends who had ever followed through. She was blameless; I was creating every bit of my agony.

Because the truth was, Rhett adored me, and thought I was the cat's nose, tail *and* meow. She had told me a few weeks after meeting she had decided she didn't want to be poly—a pronouncement that had felt like a bait-and-switch. But that wasn't enough to convince my suspicious, possessive mind. My obsessions gnawed away at the root of our connection.

Love is a bitch goddess, and Jealousy is her she-demon lover. They claw at each other in a never-ending battle for power and ascendancy until nothing but darkness is left. I ignored Rhett's phone calls and bewildered emails while I tried to figure out what to do. The only solution to this painfully corrosive state was to give up relationships entirely, which I knew would lead to isolation and misery, because "who denies sex, denies life," and there are too many of those lesbians around as it is. I had to find a way of dealing with my jealousy.

But after a lifetime of study and working on this issue, I hadn't gotten very far with it. I'd never been able to heal my jealous nature; was it even possible? All the books and articles I'd read on the subject only talked about management, but there were no solutions.

From working on co-dependent issues, I knew a big part of that disease is the focus on another person instead of my own feelings and behavior. I had been over-focused on Rhett; could I re-route that focus back to myself? How?

I knew from my reading that all our conditions and neuroses serve us in some way. If that was true, then how was jealousy serving me? After thinking about this for a while, I saw how by being jealous, I kept a close watch on those who got close to me. Jealousy kept me ready to end relationships at the first sign of betrayal. I was trying to keep myself from being hurt, trying to protect my heart and my pride. *Jealousy was not my enemy.* Just realizing this relieved a lot of the agony and was probably the first step toward moving back to my center.

The cause: who knew? Was it because my little brother usurped my place in the family as the baby? That didn't seem useful; and yet, the way I had been acting spiritually, was exactly like a screaming, raging little girl who demanded all of Daddy's attention. But maybe the attention that child needed was my own, not Rhett's, nor any of the other many people I had tried to get to take care of me in this way.

So whenever I started to obsess over what Rhett might/might not have done/was doing, I dragged my thinking back to myself. This shift of attention came with a lot of self-reflection and inventory-taking. I prayed, I asked for spiritual guidance. I worked in my journal and did art therapy. I counseled about it with peers. I read books on unresolved grief, and growing up emotionally. I worked out at the gym. I continued to see Rhett, saying nothing about what I was going through. My thoughts were still painful sometimes, but I made myself sit with the feelings. I knew the only way past it, was through it.

Something started to shift. I began to feel that something wasn't right about my refusal to hear about ex-girlfriends. The more we were getting to know each other, the more had to be left out of our conversations. There were big parts of Rhett I didn't know about. Not being able to talk about former relationship experiences wasn't a good way to build a foundation for trust, and it was a set up for resentment. My jealousy threshold was too low; it wasn't just unreasonable, it was draconian. I realized I had wanted the impossible: *I wanted Rhett not to have had a past.* I had gotten her to collude with me in this illusion by not talking about her other experiences, holding her hostage for my own past wounding. But if it was my wound, she couldn't heal me. That was *my* work to do.

"I've been rethinking our agreement not to talk about former relationships," I told Rhett one evening. "It doesn't feel right anymore. I'm thinking that you should just be free to say whatever comes to mind, and I'll find a way to deal with what comes up for me."

I also came clean about all my jealous feelings and thoughts. I wasn't surprised at the compassionate hearing Rhett gave me, but *was* surprised to learn Rhett suffered from the same self-doubt and jealousy over my own past. She too, wondered who else I was seeing, and how she measured up. Our insecurities mirrored each other's.

An odd thing happened: not only was I able to hear about Rhett's romantic history, but I found myself becoming interested about her other women. I asked questions about them, something I'd never before. I learned that part of how we find out about someone, is how they are in connection with others; what they learned, how they grew and changed, even the emotional damage they sustained. My former resistance, no doubt, had added to the pressure and fear of what someone *might* say. Now that was gone, and I found myself free to love.

Something else happened too. When I dealt with the source of the problem, the symptoms—jealousy, obsession, efforts to control—went away. All my past work with jealousy hadn't been effective because I had been addressing the symptoms and not the problem itself. Now I wanted Rhett to be her open, out-going self, and not have to worry if I was being triggered if someone asked her to dance, or if a femme wanted to spend time with her. I decided to trust our connection and Rhett's regard for me, and I was learning I could take care of my own feelings.

One day at a benefit, I saw Rhett with Eve. They are about the same height, and they stood close together, likely to hear each other over the music and ambient noise. I could sense their warmth and conviviality, which they had maintained long after the sexual relationship had died. I was okay with it. I didn't put more on it than was there, I didn't brood on it later, and I didn't try to hide my breasts.

One of my rationalizations for not wanting to know about old lovers was that I couldn't compete with the past. But the reality was *I couldn't compete with my own mind.* Not just in imagining my partner with others, but with my own self-hating, self-comparisons, which the obsession over Rhett hid from me. My jealous behaviors covered a belief in my unworthiness that I thought, deep down, made me profoundly unlovable. This was the real darkness in my soul. These were the issues I needed to heal; baggage that would have sabotaged the relationship, or at least made us both miserable.

Now when I hear something about Rhett's old lovers, I no longer squeeze up inside with fear, become enraged, or depressed with despair. I don't close down. I don't use the information to obsess and torture myself with phantasmagoric comparisons in which I'm homely, unintelligent, and boring. I'm a lot more present for our relationship, and this has led to the deepening of intimacy between us. Best of all, I've been freed of the leprous, powerless scourge of jealousy.

There are many parts to why this process worked. Rhett, by simply honoring my original request and having no judgments about it, gave me the space I needed to see my own unhealthy behavior and patterns. I think maturity had a lot to do with it too. I have reached an age where I can more readily see where I need to change, and have the willingness to try, and have developed tools to do the work. I also understand and appreciate the gift of love, no matter who experiences (or experienced) it. I am at peace in this relationship.

But sometimes I still wonder about that eyelash curler . . .

ESSAY

How I Avoid dyke drama-fraught Relationships

AFTER DIVORCING, COMING out, and dating for a while, I began wondering why most of the people I went out with disappeared after the first date. I started reading self-help books, where I learned about something called *emotional sobriety*. This meant I needed to create healthy boundaries and rules for myself around dating. One way was through *appropriate disclosure*, which means you don't give someone your entire history of sexual and romantic monkeyshines on the first date.

I wondered if maybe some of the subjects I talked about had not been appropriate for a first date. After a lot of soul-searching, I developed a list for myself. On the first date, I will not:

Say I'm in a program for sex and love addicts. I figured that one out from the big, *did-I-ever-luck-out!* smiles that formed on my dates' faces when I made this announcement.

Talk about sex. Being a Scorpio, the sex sign of the zodiac, this is harder than it may appear.

Give an inventory of my sexual acting out. This makes people very insecure.

Recite a litany of my character defects. I don't have to worry about this one: all I have to do is be myself. They'll find out what those are soon enough.

Talk about beating up people. I've trained in martial arts and collegiate wrestling. I also have anger issues, but only at men.

Say that I am a pagan. Most people think this is a synonym for Satanist. It's not, but I won't be able to convince my dates as they're running out the door.

No processing. If something major enough to require processing happens on the first date, that's usually a death knell. And if nothing happened but processing happens anyway, *I* go the other way.

Now, when I'm on a date with someone, I mentally check what I'm going to say against this list, always asking myself, "is this an appropriate subject for someone I'm just getting to know? Is it scary/ off-putting/ too intense or self-denigrating?" If so, I save it for later, when I've gotten to know the person better.

I then made a list of appropriate topics for first dates:

Books and movies (even though my preferred themes are sex, vampires, and serial killers, I make sure to pick inoffensive themes)

Work history (as long as it doesn't involve sex, drugs, or incarceration)

My living space (hopefully I'm not homeless)

Cats (if I don't have more than three)

Cooking (as long as it doesn't involve a sacrifice or cauldron)

New Age subjects: I have a degree in Women's Spirituality and need to know where they stand on these issues. Superficiality tells me as much as depth.

Education. This is important: if the person is threatened by my intelligence, I need to find someone smarter. That can be difficult, but someone more open-minded works too.

I also avoid touchy subjects like politics and religion. My goal is to have a good time and keep it light the first time, check out how we connect, how the energy is; not to interview someone for the position of "girlfriend." On the other hand, it's best I don't wait too long to ask about these subjects.

I now try to use honesty judiciously. Too much can be like a club, as a form of self-abuse, where I give much more information than is needed, wanted, or necessary, and scare people off. Probably because *I'm* scared. I remind myself that tact is about choosing among my truths. This is simple respect, so I extend myself that courtesy as well.

Acknowledgements

Thank you first of all, to Johnny Magnolia, whose real life stories started me on the path that resulted in this collection.

Thank you to my partner, Cheela Romain Smith and my housemate Jean Whittlesea for being a captive audience to my tedious drafts and pestering for feedback.

Thank you to Casey and Claudia at Bedazzled Ink Publishing/ GusGus Press who saw merit in my work and published this book.

Thank you to Linda Zeiser and Carolyn Stull-Zeiser at Works in Progress for providing a venue for nearly two decades, where I presented my work.

Thank you to my sister Lita Zig for her perspective as a straight person with insight and an accepting attitude.

And finally, thank you to Giovanna Capone, Cynthia Wilson, Carole Gifford, and Sandy Morris for their readings, input, and contributions to this book.

Xequina began telling stories in first grade, and writing them as soon as she could put a sentence together. Her greatest dream at the time was to write comics when she grew up. In sixth grade, ignoring the scolding adults and the boys who said only men wrote comics, she combined storytelling with her nascent artistic ability and began her comic strip career. She continued writing and drawing cartoons into high school and beyond. In her teens, with a blue ballpoint pen, she wrote and illustrated *Transpacifichouse Junction* and *You Tannabat*, her first collections of short stories (both unpublished). She earned an Associate degree in Arts and Humanities, then a Bachelor's in English at San Jose State University.

Starting out as a journalist, she found news writing to be the wrong livelihood and began working in the library field. She earned a Master's in Women's Spirituality at California Institute of Integral Studies in San Francisco, later returning to San Jose State for another in Library and Information Studies. During this time she wrote *Santora, the Good Daughter* (a het novel) under the pseudonym Resurrección Cruz, published by Xipactli Publishing/Earthmonster Books. She also authored columns, *La Post Modern Curandera* and *The Coconut Chronicles: essays on bi-culturality* for the *San Francisco New Mission News*. Her second book was for children, *The Mermaid Girl*, published by Dragonfeather Books. After coming out, she created Sapphic art, and performed lesbian-themed skits for the community, before settling down to serious writing. With Giovanna Capone and Cheela Romaine Smith, Xequina co-edited *Dispatches from Lesbian America: 42 Short Stories and Memoir by Lesbian Writers*, published by Bedazzled Ink. In addition to writing and doing art, Xequina is a *curandera*, speaks Spanish fluently, gardens, and loves to cook. She lives in Oakland with her partner, Rome Smith, a.k.a. Johnny Magnolia, who didn't really die after being poisoned by a jilted lover (you have to read the story).

Xequina.net
xequina@yahoo.com

Johnny Magnolia Today

www.ingramcontent.com/pod-product-compliance
Lightning Source LLC
Chambersburg PA
CBHW032006240626
47153CB00003B/1134